D1031944

TRUE CONFESSIONS

TRUE CONFESSIONS

The Novel

MARY BRINGLE

DONALD I. FINE BOOKS
NEW YORK

DONALD I. FINE BOOKS
Published by the Penguin Group
Penguin Books USA Inc., 375 Hudson Street,
New York, New York 10014, U.S.A.
Penguin Books Ltd, 27 Wrights Lane,
London W8 5TZ, England
Penguin Books Australia Ltd, Ringwood,
Victoria, Australia
Penguin Books Canada Ltd, 10 Alcorn Avenue,
Toronto, Ontario, Canada M4V 3B2
Penguin Books (N.Z.) Ltd, 182–190 Wairau Road,
Auckland 10, New Zealand

Penguin Books Ltd, Registered Offices:
Harmondsworth, Middlesex, England

Published in 1996 by Donald I. Fine Books,
an imprint of Penguin Books USA Inc.

1 3 5 7 9 10 8 6 4 2

PUBLISHER'S NOTE

This novel is a work of fiction. Names, characters, places, and incidents are either the product of the author's imagination or are used fictitiously, and any resemblance to actual persons, living or dead, events, or locales is entirely coincidental.

Library of Congress Cataloging-in-Publication Data

Bringle, Mary.
True confessions : the novel / Mary Bringle.
p. cm.
ISBN:1-55611-488-5
1. Divorced women—United States—Psychology—Fiction. I. Title.
PS3552.R485T78 1996
813′.54—dc20 95-46856
CIP

This book is printed on acid-free paper.
∞
Printed in the United States of America

for
Karen Holmes Bringle

I

"Let us suppose," Grace wrote, "that I am about to die and must leave behind a letter for my (imaginary) daughter to read when she is of age. After the usual preamble, this is the advice I would give:

> Do not, my girl, take up with any man named Gregg, Lance, Tony, or Rick. He will be unsavory and faithless and cause you untold misery. Do not name any female child you may bear Fran, Connie, Rose, or Vi. She will inevitably grow up to be a good-natured also-ran, and she will be toyed with by the aforementioned Gregg, Lance, *et al.* She will be one of life's bit players, never finding herself at the heart of the drama. Christen *not* your male children Timmy or Kip—if you do they will sicken and die of obscure diseases, having been too good for this world from the moment they drew breath.
>
> Never, when you are married, look fully into the eyes of men who service your automobile, deliver your babies, or partner your husband in commercial ventures. They are adulterers and you will become one too. Shun envy. The woman whose life seems more adventurous and golden than your own is secretly aching with loneliness and would gladly trade places with you. Do not aspire too high—the rich are not only different, they are immoral. Do not chafe for so-

phisticated pleasures, but draw comfort from the sun's radiance as it glances from the worn linoleum of your decent kitchen floor, the querulous voices of your children as they slander each other at play, from the warm lips and familiar proclivities of your lawful mate. These are far greater in value than all the designer dresses, tropical vacations, or rippling lovers a fevered mind can conjure up.

Above all, do not educate yourself beyond the point of no return —knowledge breeds persistent melancholy. Far better, my daughter, to be possessed of a merry, simple mind that admits to no more truth than can be comfortably discussed over a cup of coffee with your next-door neighbor, Ruth or Helen. You yourself have been named Brittany because—as you know—this name was popular among the right sort of people in the year I bore you. Hoping this letter will not bore you, and conferring a mother's blessing,

I remain,
etc., etc.

Grace reflected that her imaginary daughter would read this letter somewhat impatiently, and then go on to lead whatever life suggested itself to her. The wisdom in her mother's dying words would pass her by, seeming eccentric and arcane. Something was needed to clarify the message, and she turned again to her old electric typewriter and composed an afterthought.

I myself have learned these lessons from confessions magazines with names like *True Romance* and *Real Life Stories,* glorious magazines which may no longer exist when you are old enough to read this. I have read these magazines sporadically for years. In the past year or so I have read nothing else when I could help it . . .

Grace glanced at her watch and saw with some displeasure that she would almost certainly be late for her class. She locked away her papers in the top drawer of her desk and removed her sunglasses. Instantly, the litter on her desk became inoffensive—without her glasses the paper clips and bits of Ko-Rec-Type and household dust seemed merely the detritus any writer might accumulate. She placed one hand on the old IBM and caressed it, already mourning the time when it would break down irretrievably and there would be no more like it to buy anywhere in the city. In the age of computers she had run through three such machines, and soon they would be extinct. Would she stop writing, then, or surrender herself to an officious, twittering computer? Well, there was no time to think about it now.

Grace went to study her reflection in the large mirror at one end of the living room; she was capable of carrying out this activity in any surface that reflected, for she was vain. She was not always pleased with what she saw, but she took great joy in her image when it was behaving well. Tonight it lacked brilliance. She was tired and looked forward to her ordeal at the university with dread. She thought of it as Ordeal by Pathos, or Fatuity. She was afraid Mr. Buonsuccesso would have completed his short story and approach her after class, his face tense with achievement and radiating that creative complicity which only the most lackluster of her aspiring writers seemed to possess. She had not been cut out for the role of mentor and felt sad that her students could not see through her more readily.

The ritual of leaving her apartment calmed her—the self-important symphony of clashing keys and sliding bolts, the long descent in the ancient elevator which sighed intimately in the confines of the prewar shaft, the groaning as the twilit car passed floor after floor, the gentle crepitation as it settled at last on the ground floor, surrendering its cargo to a lobby once splendid and now claiming what the rental agent said was character.

When Grace had first come to the building, she'd been surprised to realize that the other tenants feared her. Fragile old gentlemen in towering Afghan caps shrank back when she held the door for them; women who remembered St. Petersburg before the fall of the Romanovs cried aloud on discovering her in the elevator. Whether it was her relative youth or her sunglasses which linked her to criminality in their minds she never knew, but in time they grew used to her. These days they smiled at her and plucked her sleeve with goodwill, but those initial encounters were set in her mind, indelibly, as the first time she had been seen as socially undesirable. It had been a good lesson.

She passed out of the vaulted doors without incident or encounter. Her neighborhood was one of the last on New York's West Side to remain ungentrified, and the building hunched on a street so strewn with human oddities that to navigate it was to feel forever cut off from the mainstream of American life. An enormous courtyard, into which blew a gay assortment of Blimpie wrappers, *Watchtower* leaflets, empty cough-drop boxes, and the occasional pair of women's underwear, led to the street beyond. In the recesses of this courtyard stood Julio, the melancholy superintendent of Grace's building, scratching his shoulder and surveying the vermilion evening sky so intently she crept past, not wanting to disturb him.

The raffish folks who congregated on her street corner had already assembled for their nocturnal festivities. Two gaunt and towering men, hostlike, swept aside to make room for her to pass. She nodded at them politely. There was about this corner the aura of a party about to begin, with all the usual anxieties—would the ice hold out? Were there enough canapés? Had the guest towels been placed in position? The gaunt men had a constant, worried expression, as if they were pondering these questions. The taller of them wore an immense parka, though it was a warm autumn evening, and a pair of quilted ladies' snowboots.

His companion seemed to be divided in half. Above the neck he was as anxious as any potential host, his eyes blinking rapidly and his mouth set in a grim line, but below there resided a different man, one who was so committed to the good life he couldn't stop capering over the pavement, his legs bending flexibly in all directions until Grace feared he might tie himself into a knot.

From all directions the guests were shambling along, drawn irresistibly to this antic corner of the city, to their standing social engagement in the shadow of Grace's building. Most of them, she imagined, were refusing their medication because it hampered some ability they thought of as indispensable, but some had never seen the inside of a hospital at all. They believed, although these words would never pass their lips, that they had found a superior form of adjustment.

When she returned from the university, they would all be assembled: dogs with their muzzles tied shut with pieces of string, men with trousers that ended comically at midcalf, tall, muscular children who sucked on pastel pacifiers, grandmotherly women with Gristedes bags on their heads, blasted former desk clerks, genial drinkers, witty, libidinous poets from hell.

The tenants in Grace's building held frequent meetings in the hopes of disbanding this group, but nothing was ever accomplished. The building's architect, even in the halcyon days of the Belle Epoque, had foreseen the problem and installed double-thick walls and clever, noise-muffling devices. Noise was not the problem —the tenants slept through the nights undisturbed by the shrieks and explosions of broken glass—nor was it really crime. Most of the revelers were too weak and ill to aspire to felony.

"It doesn't look nice," the old people said, and, "It's so disagreeable." Police officers from the local precinct had been introduced at these meetings. Invariably they wore looks of amusement when they explained that loitering was no longer considered a crime. And—this made the tenants wince—the street people could not be harassed because they, too, had constitutional rights.

"Human refuse," one old lady always muttered. "Living dead."

"Shame, Sophie," someone else would always murmur, and then everyone would take their folding chairs from the lobby and ride the elevator back up to comparative safety.

Grace set off in the direction of the university, ignoring the man who trotted along beside her, singing *"This Bud's for YOU"* in a ruined tenor. She was not threatened by the street people, although she could understand her elderly neighbors' distress, and thought longingly of the story she would read before bedtime some hours from now. Called OFFICE CHEAT—CHET'S KISSES MADE ME

WEAK, EVEN THOUGH HE WAS MY HUSBAND'S BOSS, it promised a classic tale of sin, suffering, and redemption.

She knew such matters were no longer in fashion, but that knowledge only intensified her desire to become Pam, the faithless wife who succumbed to Chet's brand of love. She knew the wife's name was Pam because she'd allowed herself to peek ahead into the text. The husband, of course, was called John.

All of her students were there when she arrived, opening containers of coffee, shuffling papers about in an effort to appear productive, turning eager faces to the door when she entered. They had assumed their customary seating pattern. The two oldest members were sitting as far apart as space would allow, as if to disallow any similarity. Mrs. Klein and Mrs. Dorfman were, in fact, very much alike. Sycophantish Ms. Hatfield was in the chair closest to where Grace would sit. Two very stern young women huddled at the far end, as if to put as much space as possible between themselves and fiery, chauvinistic Mr. Ottway. It was sometimes difficult to remember that Mr. Ottway was only nineteen.

Timid, doleful Mr. García sat midway down the table, and across from him—bathed in the very look of radiant expectation she had feared—was Mr. Buonsuccesso.

Before Grace could even assume her seat, Mrs. Klein had an urgent question. "I don't mean to be troublesome, Miss Peacock, but it's awfully warm in here. Do you think we could ask the custodian to turn down the heat?"

At the word "custodian" Mr. García looked up fearfully, and Mr. Ottway mumbled something about cold-water flats.

"What was that, dear?" asked Mrs. Dorfman. "I didn't catch what you said."

Ottway studied her for some time without replying. His unfashionable Afro seemed to have expanded since the last class. "I said, Mrs. Dorfman, that if you lived where I do you wouldn't complain about too much heat." He looked around the table and

Mr. Buonsuccesso snickered nervously. "Now," he continued, "if Dr. Peacock wants to waste a half-hour or so hunting down the *custodian*"—he pronounced the word so scornfully that Mr. García looked at him in wonder—"that's just fine with me." He turned his militant gaze on Grace, who said:

"First of all, as you very well know, it's not correct to address me as 'doctor.' Second, I'm not at all sure there *is* a custodian. Has anyone ever seen a custodian here?"

"Actually," said Mrs. Dorfman, "I find it rather chilly in here."

"For heaven's sake," Ms. Hatfield weighed in, "couldn't Dorothy just take one of her sweaters off if she's too warm?"

Fingers trembling with rage, Mrs. Klein unbuttoned her cardigan. Grace had a sudden overview of how they would all appear glimpsed from an omnipotent eye: Nine fearful people—well, eight, since Mr. Ottway never seemed fearful—at a shabby table in the basement of a university. Outside the room were long corridors adorned with great outcroppings of pipes and valves, since her classroom was at the heart of what the university called the "physical plant." Cosmic, thrumming noises could be heard if one took the trouble to listen, and only a card taped to the door and reading EXPERIMENTS IN WRITING—PEACOCK—TUES-THURS 6–9:00 P.M. indicated that serious, creative business was going on here.

"Okay," said Grace, "who wants to go first?"

As always, the question threw the class into a panic. Mrs. Klein, who had been burning to read her latest revision of a story, could not bring herself to speak so soon after her humiliation. Mr. García was glancing shyly down at the neat blue folder which contained his novel in progress, *The New World: Pathway to Despair.* Grace was avoiding the ardent eyes of Mr. Buonsuccesso, who held a bulging manila envelope on his lap, like a literary flasher.

"Shall we begin," said Grace, "with Mr. Ottway?"

Ottway chuckled as if they were sharing a rich joke, as if, in fact, they had been in bed together not an hour earlier, discussing the merits of his poetry. He withdrew a folded sheet of paper from his breast pocket and began to read without preamble.

"The subway sways and lurches,
On its way to Harlem,
Funky A train—awash with human misery—
What tales you could tell.

Tales of old men who feel their
Organs palpitating
As they survey Ms. Subway—Polish-Irish cunt,
Moron of the streets . . .

Better to die in cradle,
Victim of Lead Poisoning,
Than live for this—this void, this dumb abyss
Where Nothingness is King:

Young dudes have not the answers,
They falter, too, and fail,
But grant them this—for all their swagger and false
Cool—
They yearn not for white tail!"

There was a deep silence when he had finished, the silence of white folk too uneasy to say what they thought. At last Mrs. Dorfman cleared her throat and said, "It has great . . . *anger,* Gilbert," she said. "Anger can be powerful."

"I found it extremely insulting," said stern Miss LoCasso.

Grace allowed Mr. Ottway to lecture them on the futility of judging his poem from a white perspective. She was aware that she was abdicating her position as their leader, but sometimes she was at a loss for words. Sometimes, in fact, she had to ask herself what she was doing here at all.

"You won't be a real instructor," the man who had found her this job had admitted. "You'll be an adjunct. Your students will be fringe people." Fringe people. It seemed a cruel designation for her little band of hopefuls, and she tried to treat them like real students in a real university. It was one of the reasons she addressed them formally, refusing to use their first names.

Ottway was beaming now, becoming more genial by the minute as he noted his fellow students' upset over his poem. He was a small boy whose deep blackness and enormous Afro made him seem larger than life. Grace often fancied that Mr. Ottway's hair could, if tended and watered regularly, bear pine cones or hazelnuts. She could imagine him talking to his hair in a gentle, coaxing manner, urging it to grow more lushly, more magically. For all his mannerisms, Mr. Ottway had about him the air of a shaman. When he turned to her for the ultimate comment on his work she smiled.

"I liked the last line."

"And the rest?"

"You were putting us on," she said.

His dark eyes narrowed in an expression of menace. Mrs. Dorfman began to bite her knuckles. Ottway maintained his pose for a moment and then began to croon with laughter, shaking his head. "She sees where I'm coming from," he gasped. "Dr. Peacock, you're all right."

"You were pulling our chain?" Mr. Buonsuccesso asked.

"What a waste of time," breathed Ms. Hatfield in Grace's ear.

"Let's hear from Mrs. Klein," said Grace.

For the next twenty minutes the class sat, stupefied, while Mrs. Klein read haltingly from her revised story, "The City Mouse." It was all about how she could not sleep at night when she visited her cousin in Great Barrington, and Mrs. Klein was determined to polish it to perfection and publish it in the *New Yorker.*

"It may seem odd," she read, "but the sounds of the city, with all their violence and clashing turbulence, form a soothing lullabye for me which rocks me to forgetfulness. Sirens, garbage trucks, strange shrieks in the night—these are old friends for the true city dweller. Without them I lie awake, wondering, wondering . . ."

Grace bent her head to conceal her rage. Why did they want to commit their thoughts to paper? The creative urge, as Mrs. Klein would undoubtedly call it, seemed to Grace the most malicious of impulses. It seduced these nice people in the nastiest sort of way, tempting them to corral their commonplace thoughts and then present them to an audience that fairly cried for blood.

Mrs. Dorfman, for example, was even now thinking of slighting things to say about "The City Mouse," yet when it was her turn to read she would hear her own brave words fall into a hostile or uncomprehending silence. Grace, herself the author of one forgotten novel, knew better than anyone how futile the whole process was, and she felt slain with pity.

If she allowed her eyes to rest upon *The New World: Pathway to Despair,* she would weep; if Mr. Ottway had not treated them to what was, mercifully, a joke, she might have wailed out loud. But was it a joke, or had Gilbert transformed himself into that kneeslapping god of mirth to save face? She would not think about it. She would make a few remarks on Mrs. Klein's improving mastery of language and hope the *New Yorker* would not creep into the conversation.

As the class crept into its last half-hour she forced herself to say: "And now it's time to hear from Mr. Buonsuccesso."

It was necessary to exercise both tact and deceit to get away from the university unaccompanied. If she ducked into the ladies' room on the plaza floor, Ms. Hatfield was sure to follow. Mrs. Dorfman also haunted the lavatory after class, washing her hands, her face wearing a spent expression, as if the creative forces called into play during the seminar had depleted her. Once she had turned directly to Grace and said, "Whew! It really takes it out of you."

The younger women, Womrath and LoCasso, walked in the same direction as Grace and had proposed a cup of coffee more than once. Only Ottway and García refrained from the impulse to associate with authority—even an authority as dubious as Grace's—and departed directly. Mr. García seemed literally to vanish, passing through the portals of the university and melting into the night. Ottway strode up the hall, Afro vibrating, and head held high, as if in anticipation of a brilliant soiree that would follow "Experiments in Writing."

It was Buonsuccesso she found hardest to avoid. He was always waiting at the main door, smiling, even courtly, attaching himself to her like a mastiff, an animal he somewhat resembled. He was eager for literary talk, trotting out statements for her approval, whisking them away if they didn't meet with an immediate response. Didn't she think that the mysticism of Graham Greene was essentially secular? Would she allow Stephen King a measure of respect for his ability to reach millions of readers? He would plod along beside her, swinging an enormous briefcase, and wait for her replies. "That's a thought," she might say, or "I believe this is your subway stop."

Only a week ago she had hit on the perfect way to elude them. She had invented an office on the twelfth floor to which she must repair to do some work and they, of course, had accepted it. Now she was able to bid them farewell at the bank of elevators and embark on a journey to nowhere, since she had no office on the twelfth or any other floor. She encountered few people at this hour, since enrollment was down and it was past nine, and she simply wandered around on the English Department floor until she was sure her students had left the premises.

Tonight she slipped into the ladies' lounge. An exhausted young woman lay stretched out on a leatherette couch. Her face was bleached of color in the ghastly, fluorescent light; her eyes behind the tightly shut lids seemed to leap and jerk as if she were in the grip of a nightmare. But for this she might be dead, a book cracked open on her chest. Grace drew near to see what the book might be, but the woman moaned and thrashed her legs in subconscious alarm.

Grace slipped away and pretended to study the notices on the bulletin board in the hall. Mentally, she disposed of her students. Surely Mr. Ottway was swaying in the aisles of a subway train by now, haughty and graceful as ever. Mrs. Klein would be preparing to relish a long night rent by sirens. She pictured Alonzo García on the first leg of an unbearably long journey involving trains, tubes, buses, perhaps even a ferry, while Mr. Buonsuccesso would be taking up two spaces on the D train, his enormous briefcase in pride of place.

And Grace Peacock, that fraudulent teacher of creative writing who was nearly, admit it, destitute? That freelance editor who had accepted a cheesy job at the university to augment her income—how would she get home?

She would walk the ten short blocks, of course, and at the end of her walk she would find solace in OFFICE CHEAT. It would give her what Mr. García and Mrs. Klein could never do with their heartfelt accounts of the disparity between what life ought to be and was. OFFICE CHEAT would point the way to the place where she ought to be in a more perfect world.

Cygnet Cottage,
13, The High Street,
Barstone,
Near Thorpe,
Wiltshire, England

Dear Mother,

Autumn here in Wiltshire is unlike anything I have ever experienced. The days are cool but a fine, bright sun beats through the clouds until by midday it feels like high summer. There are still dozens of flowers in our garden—dahlias and late roses and something called Michaelmas daisies, I believe. One night last week I was driving back from Upply Heath to the village, and breasted a hill only to find myself in the center of a huge conflagration. All around, as far as the eye could see, there was nothing but masses of flame. A dense cloud of smoke hung over the fields. I was afraid there had been a calamity, but when I returned to the cottage Fiona told me it was merely the wheat fields being "burnt off." Seems they do it every September for some agrarian purpose I can't quite grasp. It was, as the mistress of our local pub would say, "a fair treat."

I am well and happy and getting lots of work done. I have written three short stories and am presently at work on a volume of poetry. Fiona is extremely taken up with her painting—she did a nifty oil the other day of Old Reg, the retired eel catcher. She sends her love, as do I.

Grace

Dear Fiona,

Enclosed is Mother's biweekly letter. You can mail it the day it arrives if convenient. Everything here about the same. I'm teaching a course in "creative writing" which is truly terrifying, if you think about it. I confine my own reading to those magazines which so appall you. It's doing me, as the mistress of the local pub would say, "a world of good." Thanks for helping out. Cheeriby!

Grace

PS What *is* the name of the local pub? I need some authentic detail for these letters. Write and tell me, or I shall refer to it as the Cheese & Biscuit—G.

The letters had been written the night before, directly after her return from the university. They lay on a small table near her bed; since Grace liked to reappraise things in the morning she had not sealed the pale blue airmail envelope. Yes, the one to her mother would do very well. It captured the air of self-consciousness characteristic of all her dealings with Mrs. Peacock. All in all, she had done a good job. The letter to her cousin, Fiona, was less masterful. Fiona would not be taken in by the breezy nature of the note; Fiona disapproved of Grace and only carried out the letter hoax because she felt sorry for Grace's mother.

Grace conjured up Fiona now, wanting to both defend and explain her motives for the elaborate ruse they helped to perpetrate on Mrs. Peacock. First it was necessary to picture Fiona in the proper setting. This was not so difficult; Grace had visited her cousin two years ago, had even spent several nights in the spare bedroom of the tiny cottage Fiona owned in rural Wiltshire. She pictured herself in this loftlike room, perhaps combing her hair and preparing to descend, by ladder, to the second floor. The ladder was a precarious affair which hooked to the wall and could be pulled up by Grace, if she so desired, when she had arrived at her destination. The chamber had once been a hayloft, or a drying cupboard, or a niche for a storage heater, depending upon whom one chose to believe in the village. Very well. Grace located herself in memory and summoned up her cousin . . .

Grace has just laid her comb down when she feels the room shake slightly. It is a tremor of very small consequence, but it alerts her to the fact that someone is on her ladder, is even now preparing to invade her privacy. The intruder is, of course, Fiona.

"Are you awake, Grace? It's almost noon."

"I was on my way down."

"I've made you a cup of tea—I'll just pop up with it."

The tremors grow larger. The crown of Fiona's fair, round head appears in the well at the ladder's top. It is rather like witnessing the birth of an enormous baby. Fiona advances slowly, hampered by the cup and saucer which she balances on one palm. Her large, pink face comes floating up into the gloom of Grace's chamber, then her shoulders. She grasps the top of the ladder in one capable hand and proffers the teacup in the other. She has not spilled a drop.

"Thanks," says Grace.

Fiona's torso becomes visible. She waits for Grace to sip at the tea, standing alertly, like a soldier in the trenches, on the top rung of the ladder. Then the room quakes alarmingly as she heaves over, fishlike, into the chamber itself.

"Whew," says Fiona, getting up from the floor, "such a lot of cigarette smoke, Grace."

She advances straight to the small dormer window and flings it open, then she flops girlishly on Grace's bed. There is barely room for both of them in the room. "To tell you the truth, Grace," she says somewhat sternly, "I'm worried about you."

Grace regards her cousin, child of her father's sister, Anglo-American flesh of Peacock flesh, eight months older than herself. Fiona's small, intensely blue eyes stare back at her in cousinly distress; her mouth elongates, then purses slightly, preparatory to forming words. Grace thinks of her cousin as a genetic centaur; from the neck up Fiona is all English—her milky skin and blooming russet cheeks, her abundant fair hair and slightly ovine jaw are to be seen in the National Portrait Gallery in earlier models. She might be minted and struck off as coin of the realm. From the neck down, however, she is of the New World. Her long, fine legs, always carelessly disported—through naïveté, not art—are definitely, quintessentially, American. Ten years of jolly play on the hockey fields of a girls' school in Cumberland have not been able to diminish their glory. They are, in fact, like Grace's own legs. And more—Fiona's hands chop about as she talks in a manner that sometimes causes the villagers to inquire if she is not, possibly, Italian? Fiona's voice, though, is purely English. Like her father, who had been a career officer in the Royal Navy, Fiona speaks in a sort of outdated, military slang. She seems always to be weighing her words, as if a slip of the tongue might result in intelligence leaks. Now she furrows pale brows and says firmly:

"It's just not on, Grace. You must know that?"

"Know what, Fiona? What's 'on' mean? Please let's don't be oblique."

"You know quite well what I'm talking about." Fiona sits a bit straighter, mindful, for once, that her position on the bed might seem to the untutored mind to hint at recklessness.

"What?" Grace, of course, knows.

"Aunt Winnie."

This designation of her mother makes Grace feel quite hilarious, but she subdues herself and asks, "What about her?"

"Well, you know—" Fiona makes chopping gestures, rolls her

eyes—"It's quite ridiculous for you to pretend to live here at Cygnet Cottage. It's all so unnecessary."

"If you find it morally repugnant to forward letters from me to Mother, you've only to say so."

"Oh, crumbs," wails Fiona in anguish, "it's not the ethics of the thing that bothers me. It's so *unnatural,* Grace. Why can't you be like other people? Why this subterfuge?" Fiona's voice becomes deep, thrilling: "She *is* your mother."

Grace permits a small silence to emphasize the idiocy of this last remark. Then she says pleasantly: "It suits me to have her think I'm four thousand miles away. I don't want to have to speak to her. Is that so difficult to understand? It's not as if you had to *do* anything, Fiona—I write the letters, I even provide the stamps. Mother's perfectly happy. Nobody suffers. You see?"

"No. I don't see at all. What's so dreadful about speaking to Aunt Winnie? I mean to say, she always struck me as quite a good hat."

Grace considers. Fiona's face is becoming pinker by the minute. "It's not that she's dreadful, dear. I just don't want to answer my phone and find her at the other end."

"Well, we can't have everything we want, Grace. Life isn't a lark—it's not just one enormous round of fun, is it? I'm sure Aunt Winnie didn't want to be widowed, did she? I can't believe Daddy wanted to die in Burma, for that matter, or that Mummy was ecstatic about emigrating to Canada; I don't suppose for a minute that you wanted to have your second marriage go and end in divorce . . ."

Fiona bites her lip. She has, she thinks, gone too far.

"Yes I did. That's exactly what I wanted."

"Well, it just cheeses me off," says Fiona daringly. "It makes me livid that a perfectly nice woman like Aunt Winnie should be the victim of a confidence game."

"Fiona, darling, it's not a confidence game. I don't expect to gain by it—I'm not screwing Mother out of money. I simply think it's better, happier, for her to believe I'm in England. I write such lovely letters—you should see the latest. It's all about the burning of the fields, written in very simple, declarative sentences. She'll adore it."

Fiona seems almost on the brink of tears. "What if she comes to New York to shop, or something? What if she *saw* you?" Grace laughs this off. New York is, after all, very large. Nevertheless, her voice has lost its note of authority. The vision of running into Mrs. Peacock on Fifth Avenue has more than once plagued her; mentally, she gives her cousin credit for summoning up so astutely the material of nightmare. Fiona, no fool, pursues her advantage.

"What if she rings me up again, as she did at Christmas? I had to say you were in London, at a party. It must have cost the earth for her to phone."

"If that ever happens again," says Grace in a calm, instructive voice, "you must call me at once, collect, in New York. I'll take care of it."

Fiona looks openly scornful, but Grace is quick-witted. She has thought it all out before.

"I'll turn on my hair dryer," she begins thoughtfully. "Then I'll place it near the phone, so it makes a confusing, humming noise, and I'll dial Mother. I'll do a pretty good imitation of the International Operator, hoot out 'Ready on your call to the States!' and then I'll come on and say 'Hello, Mother' and everything will be just fine. When I don't want to talk any longer I'll move the dryer right up to the mouthpiece and shout 'I'm losing the connection—better hang up now!' and Mother will feel she's part of something very cosmopolitan and thrilling, and that will be that . . ."

Grace spreads her hands soothingly and looks at her cousin, but it is too late. At the first mention of the hair dryer, Fiona has fainted. She has never encountered such an unwholesome outlook in all her thirty-one years. Grace looks out the window and notices the sun is almost directly overhead. The pubs are open! Nimbly, she skirts Fiona's prostrate body and climbs down the ladder. She hopes her cousin won't be too cheesed off when she regains consciousness . . .

This, thought Grace, huddling beneath her quilt at high noon, was essentially what might happen if she were to confront Fiona in the flesh. Except that she, Grace, would not be nearly so lucid and firm. Her wit was keen enough, but pity did her in every time. Pity for Fiona, who in every respect led a life more pleasant than Grace's own, lay at the heart of their relationship. Fiona, who had a pleasant cottage in a green county, a small fixed income, two affectionate brindle bitches and a budgie, and a deep conviction that her paintings would one day bring her fame, was a tragic case straight from the pages of a confessions magazine.

Fiona, although she did not admit it, was in love with the rich farmer whose fields Grace had so fecklessly burned off for the amusement of Mrs. Peacock. The farmer was a decent chap—a bit too stocky and windburned for Grace's taste—whose wife was "difficult." Fiona had painted portraits of the entire family and claimed Mrs. Bowstitch had once gone off into an alcoholic stupor in the midst of a sitting, pitching forward with a loud snore and knocking over a vase of peonies. She drank so heavily—and Grace had seen the lady in her cups; it was not a vice dreamed up by a jealous Fiona to excuse her yearnings for another woman's mate—that more than once she had been forbidden to drive the family car. "Poor, dear Richard," Fiona would sigh, "he's too honorable to abandon her and too loyal to complain. If only he had someone to talk to, it wouldn't be so hard for him." The three Bowstitch children were now of an age to see through Mummy's headaches, and the eldest boy openly made fun of her, imitating her boozy walk for the village children with savage virtuosity.

Fiona invented little excuses for visiting Richard. Once she had contrived to run into him in Salisbury, on market day, and they had taken high tea together in a shop. So far as Grace knew, it was the only time they had ever been alone together. Ah, but what opportunities, as yet unexplored, might lie in wait for her cousin. Grace could see it all. Mrs. Bowstitch would inevitably have to be sent to a posh retreat to dry out, wouldn't she? Fiona might encounter Richard, strolling alone, at evening, near the churchyard, and offer him her large and freckled hand in a gesture of innocent condolence, only to have him fall on her there in the mossy dell with great countryish gasps of lust. No, that wouldn't do. There would be too many others around, perhaps even the eldest Bowstitch boy smirking about in the foliage with his transistor radio. Fiona would have to go to the farmhouse. It was very grand, and quite old, a perfect setting for the sort of seduction required to coax a thirtyish virgin into adulterous activity . . . Grace was becoming quite animated, imagining the scenario. The principal players possessed the necessary innocence; they would feel acutely the sense of sin which it was all but impossible for Grace or any of her acquaintances to even imagine. They would, she realized with a thrill of envy, feel momentous in their small moment of passion.

She pushed the quilt back, no longer cold although her chill apartment had not altered in any particular, and pictured the title: I STOLE MY NEIGHBOR'S HUSBAND, and after it the cunning, trailing blurb: OUR MOMENTS OF BLISS LED TO A LIFETIME OF TRAGEDY! Of course, it was a bit tame for the American trade. Her favorite magazines were embracing the new sexual freedom with a will, scorning the old line for zesty tales about addicted babies and multiracial orgies, but—like princesses of the blood dressed in rags—they could never hide the excellent structure. Fiona, if she had only properly realized it before, was a natural heroine, and it was all, alas, a matter of genes. The father who had died in Burma had endowed Fiona with an endearing capacity for heroism simply by being so insufferably stupid that his daughter, who in the natural course of things would have been stupid also, had gently warped herself so that the minutest grain of eccentricity might enter in. Fiona's mother had helped things along by being the willing butt of anti-American humor in her life as a colonial. Fiona herself had developed without any outstanding merit and knew only that she must style herself along different lines. And thus—from a barely perceptible desire to better herself—had sprung the flaw in Fiona's character which could make her a Leading Player: Fiona was romantic. That Grace had never before perceived her in the proper light was appalling enough; that she was now able to weave about her cousin a tale of cosmic sin and redemption was catastrophic. She lay back on her pillows and pursued the story line.

Her interest was far from prurient. It mattered not a whit if Farmer Bowstitch and Fiona came to simultaneous orgasm in this, their first encounter. The manner of their coupling was unimportant; in fact, Grace mentally abandoned them after the first swooning kiss, envisioning a long trail of dots as bridge from sexual passion to earnest narrative. No. What concerned her were the alternatives. Should Fiona and her swain meet often after this initial plunge from grace? Should they deceive poor, staggering Mrs. Bowstitch in her own drawing room? Would Fiona, alone in her cottage after these delirious sessions, weep bitterly on her narrow bed? A natural, cousinly delicacy prevented Grace from examining too closely the first symptoms which heralded Fiona's unwelcome pregnancy. Suffice that she must grow pale over her morning tea and all but faint in the village shop. It would be necessary for her to go away—perhaps to London—and have her baby secretly. And then? Could she return to the village, where even the dimmest persons could snicker and cast knowing looks as she pushed her infant up the High Street in its pram? Should Mrs. Bowstitch commit suicide, or should the eldest boy, emboldened by a victory at cricket, insult her openly in front of the vicar of Barstone? This last, Grace knew, was more Thomas Hardy than *True Confessions.* She must expunge any details that marked Fiona's saga as English. She closed her eyes, and composed:

> It was growing dark. Johnny had been bathed and fed. He lay in his crib, rosy mouth slightly open, breathing evenly. I bent down, brushing my lips over his satiny cheek, and thought of all that I had to do before I could seek oblivion in sleep. Two of Johnny's tiny coveralls needed mending, and I hadn't even washed the supper dishes yet. They stood on the drainboard. My single cup and plate reminded me of how lonely life would be from now on . . . No more suppers with Richard, our heads bent close over the scrubbed

wood table . . . No more rambles through the sunny meadow on warm spring afternoons . . . No more the thrill of expectation when I knew that soon, soon, the world would recede and only Richard's warm lips and strong arms would exist for me . . . I had done wrong, even though love such as ours had felt so unutterably right, and Johnny had come into the world under a shadow of guilt.

I felt tears pricking at my eyes and forced them back. I would need all my strength to do what I had to do. I could not afford the luxury of tears. I had to go away before it was too late—too late for Richard, for Edith, for all of us . . . 'Oh, my darling,' I whispered to the night, 'forgive me for loving you.' Somewhere, my child and I would start afresh. It wouldn't be easy, and I prayed that God would grant me the courage to begin a new life . . .

*I*t had definite possibilities and Grace cursed herself for inventing it. Now she would be unable to think of Fiona as she really was—too sensible to become pregnant, for one thing—and would suffer pangs of jealousy at her unworthy cousin's elevation to the rank of literary heroine. Any afterthoughts on the subject could not comfort her. Ordeal by Envy, and only herself to blame.

Grace's desire to inquire after Richard Bowstitch in a postscript was almost overwhelming. She sealed the envelope in desperate haste and flung it halfway across the room. She would not become malicious, indulging in sins of manipulation; far better to leave meddling to those who had no sense of evil—they were inevitably better at it.

If she remained in bed much longer her mind would turn to Mr. Buonsuccesso's *oeuvre,* and more particularly to that portion he had read last night in class. She almost imagined that Mr. Buonsuccesso himself might come plodding into her bedroom, attaché case swinging in a way that meant business, and sit heavily by her side amongst the rumpled bedclothes. "You do see," he might say, "what I'm getting at here? The Faust legend has never been more relevant . . . I'm not saying I'm the one to retell it, but I'm sure going to give it a try!" Stop, stop!

She could sense that even now people were preparing to contact her. Fingers were poised over dials; they would pluck out her number. Letters waited in the mailbox six floors below. All over Greater New York her students, released from their jobs for the lunch break, were plotting new and heartbreaking works of fiction to bring to class next week. Perhaps her mother was even now poring over a British Airways brochure, dreaming of a surprise raid on Wiltshire. Grace compiled a list of awful certitudes: the phone would ring and each time she answered the voice at the other end would be that of someone she did not wish to speak to. There would be no stamps in her desk and she would have to make an exhausting trip to the chaotic local post office. The dinner party she could not avoid that evening would pivot, conversationally, around the recent achievements of the host, a man she despised. If there were surprises in store, they would be unwelcome.

"Grace, my love," cried Jenny Briscoe, "we have such a surprise for you!"

These words came to Grace from a great darkness, not a metaphysical but a real darkness—the Briscoes' foyer was always in deep gloom, the better to accentuate the hectic radiance of the living room. Jenny groped expertly for Grace's coat. If it had been any other guest, Sam Briscoe would be here, hostish, in her place, but he did not like to perform even the smallest courtesy for Jenny's friend of twelve years. He and Grace were old enemies. From the living room Grace could hear his voice, raucous with glee; just beneath it came the merest suggestion of other voices murmuring appreciation. One of them put Grace on alert.

"Do you like my hair?" Jenny was saying.

"I can't see it. What surprise?"

"Come along and find out," said Jenny. Did Grace imagine it, or was there a shade of anticipatory malice in her friend's inflection? Jenny was walking briskly up the long hall toward the voices. She appeared to be wearing something voluminous and violently patterned which rustled officiously as she went. If, thought Grace, Jenny had come to the door, she herself must be the last to arrive. She braced herself for the moment when she would stand, temporarily blinded, at the threshold of the alarmingly illuminated chocolate-colored room. It was exactly like walking on to a proscenium stage—one passed through a high arch and found oneself on the boards, seen but not seeing. Even the halt in conversation was theatrical. A few polite coughs, an uneasy shifting of feet, faces—barely distinguishable at first—turning toward the performer. There was, of course, no applause.

Blinking, smiling, Grace entered on cue.

"Grace!" shouted Sam, all but smacking his forehead in a false gesture of regret. "I didn't hear the bell."

Jenny's fingers clasped Grace's elbow, propelling her forward into the room. Grace had a sudden feeling of vertigo, a fear of falling into the orchestra pit if she took too many steps. "You know the Weinstocks, Joe and Naomi," Jenny said, and at that moment Grace's vision returned with a vengeance. There, sitting not three feet from her on a sand velvet love seat, was Edward, smiling villainously.

"Hello, Amazing Grace," he said.

"Hello," said Grace. "Jenny mentioned a surprise."

"I'm it."

A blonde woman who looked both fierce and prim, if such a combination could be credited, leaned forward. Primly, she extended a hand. Fiercely, she said: "I'm Christine."

"This is Christine," said Edward.

"Jenny, get a drink for Grace," said Sam.

Grace sat on a needlepoint hassock, considering her feelings. She was really rather glad to see Edward; he cheered her, as always, with his air of arcane hopelessness. It was like running across the Unicorn Tapestry tacked up in the ladies room of the university, or finding a cashew nestling in a jar of peanuts. On the other hand, Sam—and to a lesser degree Jenny—had anticipated her reaction as acute discomfort, perhaps even rage. Their intent had been bad and this never failed to anger her.

"It's nice to see you," she said to Edward with such unmistakably genuine warmth that Sam could not hope to feel victorious. She had forgotten Christine, whose eyes registered wonder at Grace's effusion.

"Are you and Edward married?" Grace said, hoping it were so.

This had been a mistake—Edward, who was normally a perfect social animal, cried out a negative with such fervor that the entire room was obliged to hurl itself into conversation in the vain hope Christine would overlook his gaffe.

"Where did you two meet?" inquired Naomi Weinstock.

"Haven't you been in Alaska, Edward?" asked Joe.

Sam Briscoe hugged himself, smiling beneath his moustache. Jenny brought Grace's drink, exaggerating her movements like a super at the opera, clicking the fine, fat ice cubes together and creating drafts with her caftan as she advanced.

"Let's catch up," she said brightly, sinking at her husband's feet as if after a dreadful exertion. Grace thought she looked like an emormous, handsome disciple, clasping her chin in her hands and directing hyperthyroid eyes in Edward's vicinity. "Edward has been away for two years," began Jenny. "In all that time he never wrote a single letter. I don't say this in anger—after all, some people find it a strain to keep up a correspondence—but with affection. Well. Just this afternoon he called! I was giving this little dinner and naturally I told him to come along. As you can see, he did. I don't know any more about what's happening in Edward's life than anyone else in the room." She spread her hands and gazed at Edward; this was her way of tossing the conversational ball. Edward smiled uneasily.

Christine said, "We met at the airport. JFK."

"Today?" asked Joe Weinstock.

"Oh, no," said Edward. "I've been back for a month."

"Had you been in Alaska, too, Christine?"

"B-r-r-r, no," said Christine. "I was seeing a friend off to San

Francisco. Edward and I met when he asked me a question about some missing baggage. He mistook me for airline personnel!"

Christine laughed merrily, but no one joined her, except for kind Naomi Weinstock. There was something about Christine that made it quite natural for her to be mistaken in this fashion. She possessed a brisk, official quality encountered in UN guides and elementary school teachers. She was, Grace thought, completely *adult.* Grace contrasted her with Jenny, whose large, fussy prettiness perfectly advertised the infantile mind within, with Naomi, whose bitten fingernails attested to certain creative and appealing disorders, and to herself, who was taken for a Puerto Rican student at the university where she taught. All three of them were of an age; Christine, who was no doubt five years their junior, reminded Grace of Winifred Peacock, her mother.

"However you met, I think it was a fortunate thing," said Sam unctuously. He underscored his point by looking from Grace to Christine, and back. Good Angel versus Bad. He might have said: "Good for you, Edward. Enough of these neurotic bitches."

"Alaska," said Edward, "wasn't half bad. I liked the cold and the long, dark nights, and when it got to be summer I liked that, too. The only trouble with Alaska is that it reminds you of a fraternity party."

Eyebrows raised encouragingly. Lips quirked, ready to smile. Grace thought she'd help out. "You mean everybody drinks beer and says things like 'what a blast'? That sort of thing? Lots of camaraderie?"

"Exactly! That's it, Grace!" Edward looked so pleased that Grace was forced to withdraw. Sam, she could see, could hardly control his irritation.

"What's wrong with camaraderie?" he said. "You pronounce it as if you were talking about the fucking plague, Grace. You're always so damn clever—always leaping in with these terribly witty, deprecatory comments. How should people be—I mean, how should they *be* to please you? God forbid I should offend you with too much—what was it?—camaraderie." He maintained an artificial twinkle during this speech, implied a taken-for-granted affection which was, in fact, not there.

For a long time Grace had been civil to Sam for the sake of her friend, Jenny. She often felt like a very large cannon withholding its shot in the face of a little BB gun's fusillade of pellets. She realized it would be impossible to withold her fire after this new treachery had been perpetrated on her, this producing of Edward without warning, this—call it by its right name—bullying.

"I think," she said, "you're making your guests uncomfortable, Sam. If I want to quarrel with you, I'll let you know, but don't let's make a meal of it."

Naomi squeezed Grace's ankle in a small, covert gesture of approval. Jenny bit her lip. Sam chuckled paternally and said: "What makes you so sure I want to quarrel?" but this crafty retort went unmarked because Christine rounded on Grace and asked:

"How long were you and Edward married?"

"It was—two years, wasn't it?"

"Slightly under," said Edward. "More like a year and eight months."

"There's something about people who've been married," said Christine. "They can finish each other's sentences, complete each other's thoughts. The way you did."

"Maybe," said Sam, "they got married because they thought the same about everything."

"Oh, no," said Edward with a peculiar intensity, "that wasn't it, was it, Grace?"

"Let's eat," said Jenny, "I'm starving."

There was to be no spirited discussion of Sam's new government grant this evening. Petulantly, he refused to talk about it when Joe Weinstock expressed interest. Jenny, who always took too much wine at her own table, ignored the danger signals and took up the topic with great vivacity.

"It's just extraordinary—Sam's too modest to tell you about it—he's been picked over hundreds of candidates to head a study on anomie in the urban ghetto areas!"

Christine looked at sea.

"He's a sociologist," Jenny explained, helping herself to another glass, "and—oh, I see, it's 'anomie' you're wondering about. Anomie is when structures collapse and people feel alienated and become antisocial in their behavior—" She looked to her husband, who was carving seconds from the rare roast. Sam grinned slightly, and in that smile, and the flash of the carving knife as it refracted candlelight, was something to silence her.

Grace was the first to depart. Unexpectedly, Sam came with her down the long, tenebrous hallway. When she was buttoned into her coat, he swept her into his arms, hugging her with all his strength and rocking her back and forth. "Oh, Grace," he said loudly, lovingly, "what are we going to do with you?"

Then he brought his moustache close to her ear. Softly, venomously, he whispered: "Cunt!"

Dearest Grace,

I only heard about Jules today. We've been in Pittsburgh visiting Sam's parents. Oh, Grace, what can I say? You have always been braver and better than I in almost every way. I know you'll get over it eventually, but in the meantime *please* don't be stern with yourself. You have every right to grieve, and should, in fact ***must***. If I can do anything let me know, day or night. I'm here. I'll wait to hear from you. I love you.

Jenny

Grace:

I am writing to you because I couldn't bring myself to say these things in person, or on the phone. Sam is aware of my feelings and approves of this letter. Because we have always been such good friends, Grace, I'll come to the point without further ado. I'm worried about you. I think you're in danger of becoming totally alienated from your friends, and when that happens you will be entirely on your own. The men who are eager to step in and take care of you whenever anything goes wrong DO NOT have your best interests at heart. I don't need to tell you that! You're more "sophisticated" than I am—you can run rings around me conversationally and make me look like a fool, but you aren't happy anymore. Without happiness, Grace, nothing matters—*don't laugh* . . . I've been willing to overlook a lot of crappy behavior on your part because in some sense you're a special person and demand and *get* special treatment. BUT —I will not put up with your cavalier treatment of Sam, who only wants to help. When he suggested therapy the other evening he wasn't trying to be smug or insulting. He and I both feel you would benefit immensely from really digging into yourself and setting your emotional house in order. The way you behaved to L. at our last party only went to prove how much you need help. Please come to your senses soon. Don't be too proud to take advice from people who *care*. After all, Grace, you're not THAT special.

Lovingly,
Jenny

Grace occasionally unearthed these documents. The first had been written after the death of her long-ago husband, Jules, nearly seven years ago. It served to remind her of why she had been so fond of Jenny, and counterbalanced the second letter, which Jenny had jotted off in a white heat some six months past. The occasion for her wrath had been a party to celebrate the sale of a sexual self-help book, written by one of the Briscoes' newsier friends. The author, who wore a shirt split to the belt, under which gleamed many chains of vaguely zodiacal nature, had proposed bed; Grace declined politely. He launched then on a long and ponderous discussion of his slim and barely literate book, and Grace—bored beyond endurance—had run off to another group the moment he turned his back to grab a canapé. Sam had been furious, Jenny mystified.

Grace could imagine how Sam had stoked Jenny's bewilderment with barbed comments. "She thinks she's too good for people who work in the real world," he might have said, thus including himself in Grace's all-encompassing sphere of censure. Or, "Your friend Grace fears successful men—that's why she tries to make me look small in your eyes." Under such pablumlike pronouncements did Jenny's anger burgeon. Nothing, of course, could have been less fair. Grace recognized the justice of Sam's hatred—he was able to sniff out her true feelings by that mysterious radar unlovable people invariably possess; but that she had tried to impress Jenny with her dislike of Sam was quite untrue. From the first she had excused Sam his bullying, laughed at his jokes, endured his fatuous insights, all for the sake of Jenny, whose illusions of happiness were essential to her very survival.

Long ago, when they were very young, Jenny had kept a diary. Sometimes she read from this journal to Grace, ostensibly to ask for advice. The entries had nothing to do with the substance of Jenny's life. Setbacks became triumphs, hurtful episodes with men metamorphosed, as if by magic, into glowing hymns to Jenny's earthy sexuality. Once Jenny had been mugged. A knife had been held to her throat and her shoulder bag had been ripped so violently from her arm she had been injured. Afterwards the mugger turned back quite intentionally and spat in her face. On that day she read to Grace: "I can't be sorry that it happened. Violence is a part of life, and as such it is beautiful, too. Standing in that dim hallway, I realized we were both only human beings, and that nothing too terrible could possibly happen." Three days later she had tried to kill herself. Ah, well, she had been a dear girl in her way.

Grace had just finished the last paragraph of a disappointing confessions story when the bell rang. Useless to inquire over the intercom, which was always broken. She knew who it would be, had been expecting him, although she'd hoped he'd have more sense. She padded down the hall and waited resignedly at the door. The elevator sighed open, light footsteps approached. "It's me," he called softly through the door.

And once again she was truly glad to see him. She thought

perhaps he had aged a bit; it had been impossible to tell in the strobelike ambience of the Briscoes' stage set—everyone there looked ageless.

He was a rather delicate man, thin and finely boned. His colorless hair and pale eyes gave him a monkish air, but he was too well-cared-for to maintain the illusion of asceticism. He had a polite, vaguely aristocratic beauty which pleased, rather than stirred. He had brought her a bottle of Cinzano. "Sorry," he said, "it was all I could lay hands on in the dark."

"You left her at your place?"

"She sleeps very soundly," Edward said. "I waited until I was sure she was off. Then I just popped into these clothes, grabbed a bottle, and cabbed over."

"Edward, I will not have enemies."

"Honestly, Grace, she won't know. If she should wake up—but she never does—she'll think I'm reading in the living room."

"Won't she get up and come looking for you?"

There was a silence. They both knew Christine would not. They were sitting on the quilt on Grace's bed. Here, close to him, she could see fine lines radiating from the corners of his eyes; she imagined they had come about from staring into the Arctic glare. They suited him.

"I really liked it up there, you know. I only went north to put some distance between us, but I ended up quite fond of Alaska."

"Why did you leave?"

"Oh"—Edward shrugged—"my uncle died and I had to come back to see to the will."

Edward had always had money. Some said it had been his undoing, but Grace knew better. Without it, he would have become a blue-eyed Bowery bum who swiped at one's windshield with filthy newspaper, or, summoning up the reserves of energy he only displayed on rare occasions, a petty criminal. Edward's money, never enough for grand living but sufficient to keep him from desperation if he lived to be one hundred, was what made him nice. Now, apparently, there would be more.

"Which uncle was that?" said Grace. "Did you like him?"

"It was Theo. He was OK."

"Will you be rich now?"

"Well, almost."

"Will you marry Christine?"

"I wish you'd stop that. I don't want to marry Christine. I thought she'd make me feel more real, that's all. She's very here and now."

"Does she know she functions as a yardstick?"

Edward looked surprised. "That's not like you, Grace."

"You're right. I don't really care about her, of course, but I do try to preserve nice instincts, even when they're not deeply felt."

Edward laughed. He picked up *True Story* and leafed through its pages. "I'm glad you still read these. I always thought they were nice. This model—this one here, in MY HUSBAND FORCED ME TO POSE NUDE—looks like someone I knew in Alaska. She was a teacher at the university, in Fairbanks. Pleasant woman."

"What did you do up there for two years?"

"I read a lot of books about Eskimos, got quite involved in them. Maybe one day I'll open an art gallery."

"Soapstone walruses?"

"There's something quite awe-inspiring about Eskimos. The way they used to live, I mean. Did you know that for years Europeans—that's us, a euphemism for whites—believed that Eskimo women were fiercer than the men? All because the recorded instances of cannibalism had to do with females. You know, when search parties found the remains of people who'd starved to death, only the women had resorted to eating human flesh. The men might eat their clothes, their sleds, even the dogs, but not other men."

"Men are such sissies," said Grace.

"Only recently somebody figured out why. It's just that the women weren't taught how to hunt, except for a few forays on little birds, so they came to a state of despair more easily. The men believed, right up to the last, that they'd be able to bag a bear or something." Edward took a long swallow of Cinzano, shook his head wonderingly. "I wonder," he said, "what Sam Briscoe would make of that?"

"He called me a cunt tonight when I was leaving."

"Did he? What a little moron he is. I wonder what keeps him going."

"Bullying Jenny, I suppose. That and studying anomie."

"Jenny used to be sweet. She was always silly, but she really cared about you; I liked her for it."

"It isn't," Grace said, "that I'm so hard to care about."

Edward crossed himself quickly, did a comic turn ceilingward and murmured: "Hit me not."

It was an old and much-used expression between them. Edward, who felt himself incapable of passion, had always been embarrassed by Grace's ability to call up powerful waves of feeling in him. These he labeled "sentimentality;" they had moved him, in their past life, to extremes of joy and sorrow.

"Sam would say," Grace said, hugging herself and assuming a Briscotic expression, " 'You need therapy, Edward . . . You must set your emotional house in order.' "

"Up his," said Edward, smiling. "Don't they have any kids?"

"Sam feels Jenny's too immature at present. They're waiting. She told me once he said: 'But, darling, if it's taken us all this time to know each other, how can we expect to open our lives to a child?' "

"They'd better make haste. We're all getting old, Grace-o. You don't look older, though. Why is that?"

"Good genes. Winnie's still presentable, I think."

"You think?"

Grace explained the Fiona subterfuge, which Edward liked enormously. "You do have nice instincts," he said, stroking her foot. "I wonder, if my mother were still alive, if I'd want to talk to her? I don't think so, really, though she couldn't have been nicer. I always regretted that I had so little family to bring to you, did you know that? I felt genetically . . . impoverished, I suppose. And then—what good would it have done? You'd only have got sort of attached, and then—pouf! That wouldn't have been good for you at all, Amazing Grace."

"It wasn't exactly heaven for you, was it?"

"Oh, well," said Edward, "these things happen."

Edward's family had been obscurely aristocratic Midwesterners. He had always told her that they were the nicest imaginable people. His younger sister, Martha, was able to do wonderful imitations of the governor, who often came to dinner. His father had possessed a wry and self-deprecating wit that had convulsed the young Edward to the point of tears; he had admired and loved his father almost slavishly. The only person he loved more was beautiful Mama, who scared him silly with tales of Cape buffalo hiding in the nursery, then kissed away his childish frowns of terror and invented friendly forest animals who graced his nights with nibbling lips and fluttering eyelids. Even Frieda, the housekeeper, was a jolly sort. She allowed the little Edward to nip at her heels in the kitchen, screaming with feigned horror and turning from the stove to cry: "Who's that? Who's biting at my heels?" Things began to turn sour when it was noted that the family house, set high above Lake Michigan, was in danger. Erosion had eaten away at the lofting cliff and it was rumored that the house might one day collapse into the water, scattering its inhabitants to the four winds. This so unstrung Martha that she began to turn "strange;" upon returning from her boarding school one spring she set fire to her room, causing no end of publicity in the local papers. The family, which had never possessed what one might call a strong hold on life, dissolved in discord. Should Martha be punished? Should it be put down to adolescent jitters? Edward's father resolved the whole puzzling problem one day, when Edward was in his freshman year at Princeton, by shooting them all—even Frieda—and then himself.

Edward swore the entire affair had no other effect than to sadden him permanently. "Who am I," he used to say in the days when they were first married, "to claim catastrophe? All I know is, it makes me feel lonesome." The sole discernible scar he bore was this: occasionally, when he was overtired, he dreamed of the house on the eroding cliff. Always in this dream he was approaching the kitchen in search of something good to eat. Before he could actually enter the kitchen, he heard a voice, vast and unreal, saying: *"Who's that? Who's biting at my heels?"*

"Edward," Grace said, "please have that gallery with Uncle Theo's money, I really think you should."

Edward remained silent. She knew why. Edward feared that even she would be easy on him, forgive him his sins of omission through mere compassion. He did not like to be either censured or forgiven; he believed in some austere chamber of his sensibility that he was beyond judgment, and this not, as one might have supposed, because he had been so injured, but because he suspected he did not exist.

"Edward," Grace said, "you're such a fool."

He looked relieved. "You know," he said, "I've been thinking we ought to get married again."

"You choose Christine because she's very 'here-and-now' and yet you harbor thoughts of me? I can't believe you've forgotten how unhappy we were, Edward. I'm the very last person to make you feel real." She felt close to tears; quite suddenly the course of the conversation had been charted in a disastrous direction. This was one of Edward's specialties. "Don't you remember?"

"Sure I do. But it's better to be unhappy with someone you like than pretend to be happy with someone you wouldn't remember two weeks from today. If she disappeared, that is."

"Well, just chuck it then! Forget about women! There's no law that says we have to be endlessly diddling around with members of the opposite sex. Just forget the whole, boring business."

"Don't you have any lovers, then?" asked Edward with a sly air. "Are you celibate?"

"Yes. No," said Grace. "I have a lover and now you'll be sorry you asked."

"Where is he? Why didn't he come with you to the Briscoes' tonight?"

"One of my conditions for appearing at Sam and Jenny's is that I will not bring any man with me. Sensible, isn't it? I don't go there often anymore."

"Will he—your lover—be looking in later?"

"He's away."

"Oh. Good. The thing is, Grace, I can't give up women just because the only one I care about is you. That would be absurd. Why shouldn't you come to live with me—we wouldn't have to do it officially, although I'd rather—and we could have other people around for the times when we couldn't bear each other."

"Other mates?"

"Why not? Christine, for example, could function as a sort of carpenter's level. You could have a man who made you feel grown-up and important, too. For the really serious, emotional stuff, we'd have each other."

"I'd be number one wife?"

"Don't make fun. It's a good idea. The sex, well, sex is easily arranged. Christine would do for that if you weren't around, although I'd almost always rather fuck you, and I wouldn't mind if you sacked in with the other guy now and then."

"How *noblesse oblige* of you. What would the second-stringers get out of it?"

"The same as they get now, I imagine. Look. I like Christine, I do. If there were something I could do to please her and it didn't cost me great effort, I'd do it. Just like that! I'd go to some lengths to rescue her if she were about to be devoured by wild tigers, but if it happened anyway and she vanished forever, I wouldn't be able to cry salty tears." Edward paused, looked at her craftily.

"But if the tigers got me?"

"I'd give my fucking life for you, Grace. You move me, always did."

"That's precisely the kind of thing I don't want to hear from you, Edward. It doesn't do me any good, baby, none at all. It makes me want to cry and it's ridiculous and not even true."

"Well, think about it," urged Edward. "Think about our being together. Don't say 'no' before you've considered all the possibilities."

"Right," said Grace, lying. "I'll consider it. Would you like me to read to you now?" She picked up *True Story* and waved it invitingly over the bed. "I could read MY HUSBAND FORCED ME TO POSE NUDE."

"What if it makes me rage with lust for you?"

"Tough."

"I don't seem to have as keen a sex drive lately. I didn't have all that much even then, did I? Still, it was nice. We weren't trying for the Guinness book. It was nice, wasn't it?"

"Lovely," said Grace briskly.

"I'd like to take a bath with you," said Edward. "Shall we, for friendship's sake?"

"No."

Edward glanced at the small clock near the bedside. It was 3:15. "I should get home in about three hours. Why don't we set the alarm, in case we fall asleep?" It had grown very cold in the room, and Grace drew the quilt over both of them. Edward's neat and fragrant head leaned against her own, his knee snaked up to lodge at her thigh, one of his hands cupped the back of her neck where it touched the pile of pillows; he made another pillow for her of his hand.

He had always understood her addiction to confessions stories. They had never discussed it. To say that Grace liked them because the lives of the heroines seemed more real to her than her own would merely have been stating the obvious.

"My husband forced me to pose nude," Grace began. "He never guessed my secret shame . . . how much I enjoyed it . . ."

"Ginny, we've got to do something," Bob exclaimed. "We're up to our ears in debt."

We were staring at our monthly balance, trying desperately to make the terrible columns of figures add up the right way. It was no use. "What's this for?" Bob stared at me accusingly. He was looking at the large bill from Crane's Department Store. His smoky gray eyes held mine steadily. "Twenty-five dollars for a kid's dress! Honey, Kim is only eight years old! What do you think we are, the Rockefellers?"

"Bob," I replied, my voice shaking, "it was her first school assembly. Things like that are important to a girl." I knew. All my life, my Mom and Dad had had to scrimp and save and count their pennies. I had wanted things to be different for Bob and me. I had hoped we could give Kim and Terri all the things I'd never had. And now I knew it would never work . . . Bob's job at the hardware store just didn't net us enough money.

I guess if we'd talked it out that night things would have turned out differently. As it was, one harsh word led to another. "You think it's easy working ten hours a day just to keep my head above water?" Bob shouted. "You've got a nerve complaining—try working a job *and* keeping house like Marge Blake—maybe then we could afford all those fancy extras." Bob stormed out to Greeley's Tavern and I cried myself to sleep, wondering what had happened to the gentle, understanding man I had married. "I don't want you working, Ginny," he'd always said. "I want you home with me and the girls, where you belong . . ."

That was why I could hardly believe it when Bob encouraged me to answer an ad in the local paper. I thought he was joking! *'IF YOU are attractive, between the ages of 18 and 30, have a good figure, and want to earn fantastic money as a figure model, apply IN PERSON, Monday nights, at 7:30 . . .'* The address was on a shabby street near the Hi-Hat Lounge, the wildest place in town.

"Honey, there can't be anything wrong with it," scoffed Bob when I blushed. "Nobody thinks anything's wrong with the human body anymore—why be so old-fashioned?"

I wanted to burst into tears then and there, but I maintained my calm as I asked: "But the girls? What about Terri and Kim?" What I meant was, how would our daughters feel about a mother who posed nude for a living? Bob took me into his arms then, pressing my body to his and caressing me with an ardor that reminded me of the days when we had parked out in back of the school . . . days when his eager lips and warm, urgent hands had swept me into a daze of ecstatic delirium. "Oh, honey," he moaned, "you're as beautiful as ever. Terri and Kim haven't changed your figure one little bit . . . it's as good as it ever was . . ." I should have known then, but with a groan of bliss I surrendered myself to Bob's impetuous lovemaking. Somewhere, a tiny voice warned me that trouble was ahead . . .

Edward fell asleep before the heroine was forced to strip for Nick Vico. Grace read on for a column or two; then she stuffed *True Story* under her pillow, turned off the light, and arranged Edward's free arm around herself. He was a very pleasant man to sleep with; she had always appreciated this aspect of their relationship. He slept quietly and wholeheartedly, breathing with a sweet regularity and cradling her against him with exactly the right amount of pressure —no more, no less, than she would have desired. He seemed happiest this way, unless he dreamed, and used often to remark that life wouldn't be half bad if waking up weren't a part of it. She kissed his shoulder softly. Courteous even in sleep, he murmured a goodnight.

When she wakened he was gone and it was midmorning. Beside her bed, under the empty bottle of Cinzano, was a slip of paper. On it was written: "A much belated birthday gift from Uncle Theo." Beneath it lay a large and orderly pile of hundred dollar bills. Well, that was nice. Her freelance editing came less frequently these days, and she couldn't pay the bills with what the university paid her for conducting "Experiments in Writing." Grace thought briefly of Edward, slipping like a thief into his bed beside Christine; then she turned and slept again.

Later that same day, a calamity occurred. The elevator in Grace's building broke down. It had always been temperamental—frequently it wheezed to brief standstills between floors, and more than once it had progressed directly to the basement, where nobody at all wanted to go. At one time it had been rumored that a cable was fraying. The tenants had talked of demanding repairs of the landlord, but before any concrete steps could be taken, Julio performed a mysterious rite in the shaft and declared it safe again. Most of the tenants were fond of the elevator—like them, it was both old and distinguished—and liked to discuss its odd quirks among themselves. They chuckled as they told anecdotes, tales of things that had happened before Grace had been born, about the time Mr. Belinski had fitted his key into the wrong lock, unaware that he was standing five stories above his own door, or the way a certain marriage, foundering at the time, had been patched when the warring couple found themselves stranded for twenty minutes in the basement with no one to talk to but each other. The elevator, in fact, had been an icebreaker for Grace in the days when the old parties were still afraid of her. A few tentative elevator remarks, several mock despairing gestures at the panel, and she was accepted as one of them. Now it was broken utterly. At first Grace, waiting on the sixth floor, had been unaware of the disaster. It seemed to her something was amiss, but the feeling was vague and had to do with a sound—tantalizing but vague—which floated up from an unknown source. The moment she opened the door to the stairwell, prepared to walk down, it became clear. The sounds of human suffering had penetrated so dimly through the closed and heavy door they had been more felt than heard, but now they combined to form one long sigh of anguish. Above and below her, the tenants toiled along the narrow staircase, gasping with effort. Even as she watched, ancient Mrs. Belinski came hobbling down around the corner from the flight above, placing each small foot deliberately before the other and cursing under her breath in Russian; from below the frail skull of another old tenant came into view as he labored upward.

"What has happened?" said Grace, but her neighbors seemed not to see her. The physical effort required of them was so great she felt she must not force them to talk. Nevertheless, Mrs. Belinski paused on the landing and gazed at her.

"The elevator has broken," she announced when her breathing

had quieted. "It has been broken since ten this morning. No one was in it, fortunately." She regarded Grace enviously. "If only," she said, "I had your legs."

"Where is Julio?"

"Who can tell?" said Mr. Lubovitz, who had crept up to the landing and half slumped against the banister, gasping. "When there's trouble he disappears."

"Sonia," said Mrs. Belinski, "has been trying to get down since noon." It was now half-past one.

"Where is she now?" asked Mr. Lubovitz.

"I passed her on the ninth."

In a moment, Grace thought, her neighbors would turn into a vaudeville team, trading one-liners. "What time is it?" Mrs. Belinski might ask Mr. Interlocutor. "I have to be downstairs by midnight."

"Why does she have to go out?" asked Grace. "Couldn't she wait until they fix the elevator?"

"There's a concert at Lincoln Center at 2:00," said Mrs. Belinski. "Sonia doesn't like to miss out."

"How about the freight elevator?"

"Only Julio has the key," said Mr. Lubovitz.

"You run along, dear," said Mrs. Belinski, "no need to hold you up."

Mr. Lubovitz tipped his hat and there seemed nothing more to say. Grace began the descent, walking slowly so as not to arouse too much envy. Far above she could hear occasional groans and ominous, panting sounds. She felt she might be in the midst of a wartime operating theatre, just after a bloody attack. The cries of the wounded and dying pierced her with guilt for being whole. She progressed cautiously, but even so she nearly stepped on the body of a tenant at the third-floor landing. The old woman was a stranger to Grace; she seemed infinitely tinier and more frail than any of the others. Her birdlike legs protruded from beneath a voluminous fur coat, reminding Grace of a turkey she had made in the second grade whose sturdy potato body balanced on toothpicks. The woman's eyes were closed and her head lolled back alarmingly. A large fur cap had fallen from it and lay, unregarded, on the step above her. Grace knelt down. "Are you all right?" she asked, dreading that there would be no answer. "Do you need help?"

The eyelids fluttered, drooped again, at last opened. She seemed bewildered, unfocused. "Dorothy?" she asked timidly. "Is it Dorothy?"

"No—I'm on the sixth floor, a neighbor. Are you ill?"

The woman righted herself slowly, gathering her coat in all its great folds around her body. "I thought you were my daughter," she said irritably. "It's so dim here, I can't see well. I'm on my way to my daughter. I'll stay with her until they fix the elevator."

"Yes, good idea. I only thought you might have fallen, injured yourself."

"Fallen? Oh, goodness, no. I was just having a little rest. I've come all the way from the twelfth floor, you know. I'm Mrs. Kriapine, 12D." Her elbows began a slight pumping motion and the tiny feet pawed the step beneath them. Was she trying to get up? Grace slipped an arm under Mrs. Kriapine's and hoisted gently. The effort was no greater than that of deposing a cat from a kitchen counter.

Mrs. Kriapine disengaged herself with a show of vigor. "I'll be fine now. Don't wait for me or you'll be late for wherever you're going."

"Isn't there something I can do?"

Mrs. Kriapine considered. "Do you know, there is something, now you mention it. You see, when I left the apartment I didn't know about the elevator. I expected to be back in half an hour. I'm sure I've left my windows open. I think, too, that my percolator is plugged in. Not that it matters, but with electric bills so high . . . And I wouldn't be surprised if the radio wasn't playing in the bedroom. Now it might be better to leave it on, in case of burglars, that and the light in the hall—it shines under the door—but the windows and the coffeepot, well, I'd appreciate it."

"Of course."

Mrs. Kriapine plucked away at her key chain for some time before she succeeded in dislodging the appropriate key. "When you finish," she said, "just drop this in my mailbox." She stared into Grace's face, as if trying to determine the true identity of her benefactress. "It's very kind," she said at last. "It's good to meet a young person who doesn't think only of herself."

Grace was almost at the foot of the staircase when she heard Mrs. Kriapine calling to her from above: "If you think of it, you might just water the plants."

The lobby was a scene of infernal pandemonium. Tenants milled about, complaining loudly. One very old man lay, exhausted, on the bench in front of the elevator doors. "He needs his medicine!" exclaimed someone. "Maurice must have his medicine." Grace offered to run up for it and almost collided with Mrs. Kriapine, who had at last emerged from the mouth of the stairwell. A small round of applause greeted her as she staggered out, announcing, "I'm going to my daughter." Grace passed Mr. Lubovitz and the concert-bound Sonia somewhere in the middle reaches of her journey; Mrs. Belinski had apparently reached the haven of her apartment and was nowhere in sight.

For a very long time—it might have been all that afternoon—Grace went up and down the stairs on errands for the old people. She appreciated the simplicity of the situation, unclouded as it was by problems of ethics and spiritual self-sacrifice. She could not ignore the pressing needs of her neighbors which were—unlike those of her students or of Edward—undeniably real. Maurice's need for his medicine was indisputably urgent; without it he might fall ill there in the lobby, even die. Mr. Buonsuccesso would not die for lack of literary conversation, nor would the others perish because she denied them her presence in the tricky moments of release, after class. Even Edward's claims upon her, weighty as they might be in the balance of her life, were not wholly real. The suffering of the spirit was as nothing compared to the possible sufferings of the body—this was something one knew deeply and seldom thought of. So she told herself as she rummaged through Maurice's bathroom cabinet for the medicine, as she sped down the stairs, holding it to her breast; she repeated it as she knelt to retrieve arthritic Mrs. Bardoff's carpet slippers from under the old lady's bed in 5B. Her thighs began to ache from the unaccustomed exercise, and there were weak, fluttering sensations in her upper arms. She had forgotten what it was she had set out to do that afternoon. She knew only that she was, as usual, needed, and that for once there was no possible way to avoid the needy.

It was toward the end of the ordeal that the curious thing happened. Perhaps it was her physical tiredness, or the fact that she had eaten nothing since the night before, at Jenny's table. Her body, which had functioned fairly smoothly throughout the errands of mercy, betrayed her in the strangest possible manner. Somewhere on the interminable flight of stairs it informed her, imperiously and without doubt, that she was in a state of acute sexual desire. How it came about or why she could not say. Surely poking around in the possessions of these old people, her neighbors, could not have summoned such arousal! The countless shawls, slippers, syrups, and pills—reeking with their intimations of infirmity and death—were not the props of erotica, nor was her mission the stuff of fantasy. Why, then, did she feel her body growing heavier by the moment, more liquid with every step she took? Scenes from her past sexual life flickered before her in the stairwell like reels from a stag film; occasionally these were intercut with other images of men and women unknown to her. The woman, Ginny, whose husband had forced her to pose nude, was one of them. It was not the model in the magazine, the one who had reminded Edward of his friend in Fairbanks, but a woman of vastly more lewd propensities. She stood naked and immense, voluptuous and smiling, pressing the head of Nick Vico between her thighs while a third man photographed the proceedings. Grace supposed they were at the Hi-Hat Lounge. She vanished to be replaced by Grace herself—Grace and Jules humping away on the terrace of a hotel in Italy. She had a moment of terrible self-consciousness when she arrived at the lobby, heroine of the moment, bearing Mrs. Bardoff's carpet slippers in trembling hands. Would they be able to tell? "Stone her!" they might cry, shuffling toward her in communal outrage. "Kill the harlot!" But they applauded her brightly and thanked her yet again.

Maurice, strong enough now to sit up on his bench, motioned for her to rest beside him for a moment. "Sit, young lady," he said, moving aside in a courtly gesture. "You've earned a rest."

He was a handsome old gent, this Maurice, with sharp cheekbones not unlike Edward's and immaculate, swansdown hair. He patted her hand, and even this innocent contact made her sigh, perhaps swoon was the word, with erotic feeling. She had recently been in his medicine cabinet, seen the numerous preparations and emollients which proclaimed him a vain and well-kept old man. Was he still capable of making love? She wondered about his sexual parts, mused on the nether hair, thought it might glow as whitely as that upon his head. The autonomous inner eye zeroed in on a vision of his octogenarian—but nonetheless appetizing—member. It sprang, slight but nimble, from its nest of snowy seltzer, the prettier for the contrast. Then it vanished as swiftly as it had come to reveal Mrs. Kriapine, wishbone shanks spread upon the stairs, guiding Mr. Lubovitz to her body with practiced hands . . .

"You know," Maurice murmured, "we'll never forget you for this."

"Nor I you," said Grace.

"Sometimes I think it's a sin to be old."

"I look forward to it."

"Do you?" said Maurice doubtfully. "Take my word for it, my dear, young is better. I've been both; I can testify."

"I'm not young. I had my thirty-first birthday last spring."

"Thirty-one," said Maurice judiciously, "is young to me. Still, I see what you mean. There are certain *obligations*. I would prefer to be either younger or older than thirty-one, if I had a choice. Seventeen, perhaps, or forty-eight. Fifty, even. Yes, fifty would be good."

"You liked fifty? That was a good year?"

Maurice laughed. "The year I turned fifty, you were being born, weren't you? Yes, yes, that would be so . . . you were entering the world." This seemed to amuse him vastly. He shook his head and chuckled, casting appraising looks at her the while. She felt confused. He expected her to reply to this observation, perhaps to laugh with him, but she could not understand what lay at the heart of his mirth.

"And here we both are," she said lamely, smiling.

But he continued to shake with laughter, withholding his vital information, his old man's joke, from her.

IV

Dear [imaginary] daughter,

Today I would like to discuss Your Most Embarassing Moment. This is a very tricky subject, the more so because I have no way of knowing which way you will go as you mature. If you take my earlier instructions to heart and grow up according to the wise guidelines set forth in confessions magazines, you will not need this lesson. Indeed, you may not understand what I am about to say. If, on the other hand, you find the call of heredity inescapable and become a woman such as I am, you will understand all too well, even at your tender age.

There was once (perhaps still is; I don't know) a column in the *Daily News* called "Five Dollars for Your Most Embarrassing Moment." People wrote to tell of the time they spilled a glass of apple juice on the PTA president's blouse, or confused the neighbor's newborn son with a stuffed animal, or told the boss off, thinking he was the elevator boy. There was a comforting, ritualistic format to these little tales. Almost always the words "Picture my embarrassment" appeared at the denouement, or, alternately, "Was my face red!" I think you have the idea.

Now, if you will, please listen to an anecdote of my own. It concerns an incident that occurred in boarding school, when I was sixteen. Three senior girls entered my room for what was termed a "spot check" one afternoon. As it happened, I had concealed a fifth of gin in my shoe bag. This was a crime of such awful proportions that the punishment would be instant expulsion if I were caught. I had not drunk any of the gin—I did not, then, drink—and the seal on the bottle was unbroken. Nevertheless, if it were discovered, I would have been packed off home in disgrace. While the seniors poked around in my closet and drawers I held my breath, sure that at any moment the snick of the shoe bag's zipper would sound my knell. Several abrasive comments were made about the state of my hairbrush and the condition of my tennis shoes, but the girls were ready to leave, to plod out as grimly as they had come, when I forced myself to say: "How about the, ha-ha, gin in my shoe bag?" The leader looked at me and said: "Very funny, Peacock," and left without further comment . . .

I learned early on that the easiest way to avoid punishment is to confess quite readily to heinous crimes. Nobody will believe you, and you may even acquire a modest reputation for wit. You may: tell your husband you were detained at an orgy, explain to the oculist you don't want a new prescription because to see perfectly is to know horror, pencil in on your gas bill that the balance is high because you spent all Wednesday night with your head in the oven. You will go free of censure and know the pleasure of being scrupulously honest.

Do not expect, however, to get $5.00 from the *Daily News* for your Most Embarrassing Moment, because you won't have any. Do you understand? That emotion is reserved for the pure of heart, of whom there are thousands even now blushing, or preparing to blush, as the baby toddles into the room with a fistful of Tampax.

Your loving mother,
etc., etc., etc.

Grace was reflecting on terror. She drew up a mental list of her friends' terrors so that she might contrast them with her own.

Jenny was afraid of not being happy, or rather, of being considered unhappy. Edward was afraid of losing the sole surviving member of his family, herself. Naomi Weinstock was, she had told Grace, afraid of being unjustly accused of some crime. Not because she feared punishment, but because her own rage would pervert her spirit forever after. Joe, Naomi's husband, was afraid of drowning; so much did he abhor water that the Weinstocks had never set foot in the Hamptons or on Fire Island or in those stretches of Central Park near the reservoir. Jules, Grace's first husband, had been afraid of odd things, like the gigantic Mr. Peanut who roved Broadway in his shell and top hat, or the mechanical Santa Clauses in liquor stores whose arms jerked about bearing quarts of whiskey at Christmas time. Her current lover feared growing old without having a child, but knew only boredom in the company of others' children, which terrified him even more. Her students—she could only think of them as a unit—chiefly feared that they were not, after all, special. Fiona, like Mrs. Peacock, feared being thought unkind; the man who had unearthed Grace's job for her was the opposite—he would go to great lengths to avoid a consoling remark.

On Grace's desk stood a large and handsome floral offering. It was composed of bright yellow and copper mums. Affixed to one stem was a card which read: WITH ALL OUR GRATITUDE—YOUR FELLOW TENANTS. It had prompted Grace's ruminations on terrors because the last of her chores in the old peoples' service had, improbably, brought her face to face with one of her own.

It had been dark when Julio entered the building, holding the key to the service elevator before him like a chalice. He had been anticipating a tidal wave of rage ever since word of the calamity had reached him. He said he had passed the afternoon at Roosevelt Hospital, where his nephew lay fighting off a near-fatal attack of asthma. The landlord had granted him permission to be at Luis's bedside—how was he to know the elevator would break down? Repeating these words like a litany, he ferried the tenants up on the freight car. They crowded in with loud sighs of gratitude. The adventure was over—at their age one did not want adventures. Few of them believed Julio's story—Maurice winked at Grace and whispered that Julio had been at a cockfight—but it was not satisfying to argue with him. He merely withdrew, looking doleful. They would express their wrath in scornful letters to the landlord, threatening to withhold rent checks if the incident occurred again.

Grace asked Julio to take her to the twelfth floor. It was the first chance she had had all afternoon to honor Mrs. Kriapine's modest request. Presumably that lady would remain with her daughter now that dark had fallen; all the same Grace felt like an intruder as she entered the closed foyer of 12D. It was, like all the apartments in its line, enormous. Rooms blossomed off fitfully from the central hallway in all directions. Grace entered one at random, switching on a lamp, and sat abruptly on a faded green sofa. Gone were the sexual impulses—they had begun to seem impossibly grotesque from the moment Julio appeared in the lobby. Her legs had begun to ache in earnest now and she felt almost desperately tired. The room that now assaulted her—for it was oppressive—seemed to be a dining room. A large walnut table stood in its center; around the table eight chairs were drawn. Close around this central fixture were crowded armchairs, occasional tables, two desks, and the couch she sat on. One would have to thread through all this excess furniture to approach the dining table, and even then the act of scraping back a chair would surely result in collision. Grace guessed the dining room had not been used, except as a depository for Mrs. Kriapine's overflow of furniture, in many years. Grace sat idly for some time gathering strength, and then found her way to the kitchen.

Here, illuminated only by the glow of the percolator's light, was the center of Mrs. Kriapine's solitary meals—a card table covered in oilcloth which simulated lace. In the middle of the table stood a bowl of fruit; on the counter beyond the remains of a tunafish sandwich invited roaches. Grace dropped the crusts in a bin, feeling squeamish. There were two framed programs from a music festival in Munich on the wall over the sink. They were dated August 11 and August 13, but the year was omitted. Grace pulled the percolator's plug and returned to the dining room. She could see the corner of a grand piano through an archway; from another direction came the sound of music, spectrally cheerful. She followed the sound, passing two small rooms which seemed abandoned by everything but the steam heat, which was beginning to hiss and sizzle in the pipes. The music came, as Mrs. Kriapine had said it would, from the radio in the bedroom, which blandly dispensed soothing strains even in the absence of its mistress. "Love Is Blue" greeted Grace as she stepped over the threshold of what might have been, except for the many framed photographs of children on the bureau, a courtesan's boudoir. Mrs. Kriapine's satin comforter was apricot and lemon yellow. A gaudy Chinese robe lay across the arm of a velvet chaise; beneath it tiny mules trimmed in maribou frisked, toe to toe. Grace closed the windows, remembered that she was to leave the radio on, and lingered at the bureau, smitten by curiosity. She wanted a closer look at the framed photos.

Here was Mrs. Kriapine as a bride, fresh and fleshy, looking up with a mixture of gravity and coyness at a man with a face like a comely meat cleaver. Mr. Kriapine's face had been all angles and sharp edges; you might have cut cheese with his bladelike jaw. His eyes were dark and fine, glinting even in matte sepia. His hair was luxuriant and beautifully groomed, folding back in supple, winging crests from his temples. Another picture showed them both on what appeared to be a picnic. Mrs. Kriapine crouched in her sailor suit, poking a long stick into a small fire and smiling while her husband stood like a guardian above her. Babies began to appear, three of them, two boys and a girl, distinguishable as such in a family portrait. One of the boys looked like his papa. The other sported his father's razor-edged features but had sparse hair, which gave his skull a fierce, pointed look. The daughter seemed an amalgamation of both. She was about seven in the photograph.

Grace found herself scanning the bureau for further evidence of the daughter, about whom there was something familiar. Yes. Here was the daughter, graduating from high school, hair elaborately arranged beneath the mortarboard, squinting into what must have been a formidable sun. And here another, with a baby of her own on her lap. Grace's breath began to come faster, she was acutely aware now of the cramping in her legs. There was something to fear, but she could not tell what. *Dorothy* Mrs. Kriapine had called her when she had wakened from her catnap on the stairs. *I'm going to my daughter,* she had said. Now Grace was almost sure. She forced herself to seek out the most current photograph, and yes—of course—there, wearing a blue suit Grace had seen several times in the seminar room, was Mrs. Dorfman. *The world,* thought Grace, *is joined at the hip.* She no longer felt alone in the apartment. She fled through the long halls, turning lights out and resisting the impulse to look back. What she felt was terror.

This, then, was Grace's own fear, to be added to the list: the certain knowledge that faces will turn up at inappropriate times, that moments of seeming solitude are sure to disgorge unwelcome presences. Beware, beware! Grace would never again look into the innocent plate-glass windows of neighborhood banks, for fear that the guard, gun on hip, would be Mr. García.

"Nice flowers," said Deveraux, when they had returned to her apartment. "Who from?" He talked in shorthand whenever he was uneasy. Grace had learned to anticipate trouble when Deveraux's normal articulacy descended to sulky monsyllables.

"From the old people." She had told him about the elevator breakdown at dinner. They had eaten at a favorite restaurant, sedate and Italian. He had listened to her story with seeming interest, yet now he looked bewildered.

"What old people?"

"My neighbors, the ones I helped."

"Oh. Those old people."

Deveraux sat at Grace's desk, swiveling in the chair. He was frowning now, pouting, even, although he would have denied it. At last he said: "You don't seem glad. To see me."

"I'm glad enough, Dev. I'm just a little tired."

"Tired? What do you have to be tired about?"

Deveraux had returned from Guatemala only that morning, where he had spent three weeks with a documentary film crew. He had been at great pains to inform Grace that he had slept only five hours before rushing to be at her side.

"You never wrote me. A letter. Not once."

"Oh, Dev, I was so busy."

"You're supposed to be a writer."

"I'm not! Not at all! I only teach at the university to pay the rent, that's all. I didn't know how much postage to put on a card to Guatemala."

"Postage. That's just like you." He said this without affection.

"I'm sorry," Grace repeated, "I should have written."

"A couple of times I wondered. Said to myself, 'What would Grace be doing now?' And do you know? What I came up with?"

Grace did not reply.

"A picture of you reading. Not reading anything good. Nothing constructive. Just reading *True Life Fucks.* Whatever it's called."

"You make it sound erotic, Dev. They're not, you know. Confessions stories aren't very prurient at all. That's missing the point. Anyway—I told you about them because I thought I could trust you. I didn't have to tell you. You would never have known, never have guessed. Don't betray confidences."

"And then," said Deveraux, "I got another picture. You. At that school, university, whatever it is. With all those lowlifes. I figured sooner or later you'd wake up to their potential."

"Potential?"

"As lovers." Deveraux regarded the tip of his shoe. He was about to turn really argumentative, to speak fluently. Grace welcomed the change in diction but dreaded the direction of his thoughts. "Lovers! If you could see them you'd know how ridiculous the very thought is. The male students are all little kids, except for Mr. García, and he's hardly lover material. I can't understand you, Dev. Where do you find such unwholesome thoughts?"

"Hah! Talk about unwholesome! Unwholesome is your middle name."

"Oh? And what was your very first thought when I told you I still had Mrs. Kriapine's key? What did you want to do?"

"Perfectly natural reaction," said Deveraux, "nothing wrong with that."

"Nothing wrong with wanting to go screw in some old lady's apartment?" Actually, Grace had not found this suggestion particularly disturbing, but she needed ammunition for the coming quarrel. "Ghoulish," she said, shaking her head.

"Now if you want to talk about ghoulish, Grace, I'll be happy to oblige. Ghoulish . . ." Deveraux examined the ceiling, as if gathering data there among the cracking plaster. Several times he nodded to himself, smiling secretively. He was very effective at this sort of playacting. "Right, ghoulish," he said at length. "Let's just refresh our memories a little. Let's go back to the time when we were barely acquainted. We'd met once or twice, and you were unimaginative enough to remark—just like everyone else—on my first name. I explained it was really my last name, but that I preferred it to my first."

"Get to the point, Armand."

"That led to my explaining I was French-Canadian. You elicited from me a good deal of information about myself." Deveraux chalked up points in midair. "That I came from a small town in Vermont, close to the Canadian border, that my father was a tavern keeper, that my mother had, on occasion, taken in laundry, that I had six brothers and sisters, that I was, in short, your classical, blue-collar person. You should have seen your eyes light up, baby! I mean, I couldn't get the time of day from you when you thought I was this fashionable film-maker type, but as soon as you realized I was just a slob you were amenable, Grace, oh yes you were."

"*Díos míos,*" said Grace to her elbow, "he's getting all worked up over nothing."

"I'm not through here. Do you remember the first time we went to bed? Do you remember what we'd been talking about when you decided to open up the gates of Paradise for sweaty old Dev?"

"We were talking about the time you killed your cousin by mistake."

"You're direct, honey. Direct and ghoulish."

"Don't tell me you've never told that little story before."

"Rarely. Rarely! I've certainly never used it as an aphrodisiac. You may not realize it, Grace, but you're probably the only woman in the world who finds it a turn-on."

"May I suggest that it made me feel sorry for you, in the nicest sort of way?"

"May I suggest you're full of shit? I'll tell you exactly what you thought. You thought: 'Here's a living, breathing, authentic character straight from those magazines I like so much. He's riddled with guilt. Good gracious—he's handsome and presentable, too, not like some smelly old welfare creep. Better grab him quick.' "

"You can't possibly imagine how silly you sound. What happened with you and your cousin isn't confessions material at all. If you were to write it up and send it in, they'd reject your manuscript."

"Because I'm a man."

"Well, yes, the protagonists are always women, but not only that."

"Not enough sex?"

"It would be rejected," said Grace patiently, "because you didn't commit any sin. You didn't mean to harm Leonie. It was just an accident. Freakish."

"So," said Deveraux, "I'm to be robbed even of *True Story* level dignity. I'm just a joke."

"You brought it up. The whole stupid idea was yours, not mine. How can you be a joke when nobody knows about you? I didn't, once and for all, go to bed with you because you dared your cousin to dive off a bridge and she broke her neck. I didn't go to bed with you for any reason except that I wanted to."

"And you didn't marry that bloodless weirdo because his daddy wiped the whole family out?"

"That," said Grace, "is not your affair. I told you that, also, in confidence. I married Edward because I loved him."

"Love! His tragedy was better than mine, that's all."

"If that were true I'd sit home reading Sophocles instead of *True Story.*"

"You told me confessions were like Greek tragedy."

"Maybe and maybe not."

Deveraux sprang from the swivel chair and paced the room. He was at his best in a state of agitation. His dark handsomeness was of the sort that was dull to behold; he did not photograph well. In motion, however, he was beautiful. Grace did not wish to be beguiled. She rose and went to the kitchen, where she poured herself an enormous drink. When she returned, holding the bottle as a sort of peace offering, Deveraux waved it away and perched on the edge of the desk, warlike.

"What do you want from me, Grace? You don't want to get married, as far as I can tell. You don't want to live with me. You aren't my sex slave, God knows. You won't take me to meet your friends, the Briscoes . . ."

"That's because Sam is a pig. It's nothing to do with you. He called me a cunt the other night, when I was leaving."

"I might get along fine with him."

Grace deliberated. She had been formulating a plan, ever since Edward had left the money on her bedside table, under the Cinzano bottle. "Ask me again what I want from you," she said.

"What do you want from me?"

"I want to have an adventure with you."

"I'm listening."

Grace was overcome by shyness. This seemed to have a softening effect on Deveraux, who came to her directly. He knelt before her, clasping her knee lightly and encouraging her to speak. He was really, she decided, very nice.

"I want to go on a trip, to the Midwest. I want to take my time, drive from town to town, be leisurely."

For the first time, Deveraux smiled. "That's a pretty dull adventure, baby. Why the Midwest? Do you want to see your mother?"

"No, no. Not that Midwest—not where I grew up, what I grew up in. The little towns, the places that have bars called the Hi-Hat."

"We had one in Vermont called the Hi-Hat. The mens' and ladies' rooms were called 'pointers' and 'setters.' We could go there —you could visit my cousin's grave and get all sexy." This he said kindly, but Grace could not afford to be charmed.

"That's not what I have in mind. New England isn't it. I want to go to—you won't like this, Dev—True Story Country."

Deveraux's hand fell from her knee, his eyes flattened. "Maybe you should just check in to Bellevue. It's much closer. Save you lots of traveling time."

"I will ignore that."

"Why do you want me along on your nutty pilgrimage? I'm not even a believer."

"I can't drive," said Grace. "I never learned how."

This appeared to stun Deveraux, who rocked back on his heels away from her. "You must be the only woman in America who can't drive," he said at last.

"I know how," said Grace, "but I don't have a license. I'm sure I couldn't get one. It's not the sort of thing I do well."

"So. You want me to come along as a chauffeur? Will I have to wear a peaked cap?"

"I want your company, too. I don't need you only to drive. You understand, don't you?"

"No, Grace, no. I don't know what you expect to find out there and I don't think you know either."

"I can't talk about it, but I know what I'm looking for."

"Love in a cornfield?"

"Not that."

"You want to hear America singing?"

"Definitely not."

"You think people are any different there than here? Do you imagine human beings are more wise and decent once you cross the Hudson?"

Grace sighed. "I'm not naïve, Dev. Please remember you're not talking to a total idiot."

"You're only crazy, honey. Why do I always pair up with the nuts? There's a whole world of sane women and all I ever meet are the whackos."

Deveraux had been involved with a rope freak before meeting Grace. Often he recounted for her the practices in which his deceptively bland lover had reveled. "I only got involved with her because she looked like a Sunday School teacher," he said plaintively. "I needed someone bland after Marika. You only had to look at Marika to know she was off the wall. Those big, gleaming eyes—did I ever tell you they turned almost purple at times? Especially when she'd wake me in the middle of the night with her fingers on my throat. But this other one! She was almost boring to look at—so pretty and broad-faced and countrified—and I guess I mistook her for a tonic. The first time she ever asked me to tie her up, well, I've told you all this, but I couldn't believe it! You know what she liked best?"

"To have the rope passed between her little and second to last toe," said Grace.

"Yeah. I've told you, I know. What makes a woman want to have a rope between her toes for Crissake?"

"Got me," said Grace. "I don't like to have my toes touched at all. Maybe she just fell into it by mistake. Maybe when she was young she was fooling around with a rope and had an involuntary orgasm. Didn't you ever ask her?"

Deveraux ignored this. "Marika had some excuse. She'd had a really totally rotten childhood in Yugoslavia. When she tried to throttle me she wasn't herself. The rope freak, though, was only herself when she was getting trussed. That's the impression I got . . . Here's something I never told you. The first girl I ever loved, back in high school, married a cripple. He was much older than she was; he'd been injured in a farming accident, and he clumped around with two metal canes. Christ. Probably turned her on. Maybe all women are crazy."

"Deveraux, I don't want to kill you or make you tie me up. I don't want to see you crippled. I don't even want to make love on Mrs. Kriapine's bedspread. I just want to drive around the Midwest for a while."

"Yes," said Deveraux, "that's it. All women are crazy. It's the result of centuries of oppression, I guess. Or maybe it's just you live longer now that you don't die in childbirth so much. Maybe women were never intended to live beyond twenty-six or so. It's like cancer. There's no more cancer around now than there was in the time of the Greeks. We just live long enough to get it, that's all."

"That's a very interesting theory, Dev. It's a good thing you killed off your cousin when she was ten. That way you didn't have to see her turn into a maniac."

For a moment she thought he would strike her. She did not relish the idea and poised, tightly coiled in all parts, on the edge of her chair. His nostrils blanched in anger but he was, after all, a fair-minded man. He laughed a trifle weakly, hugging his knees, and said: "You're a tough one, Grace. Maybe you're not even human at all."

"Tosh," said Grace. "That's a lot of tosh, as my cousin Fiona would say."

"Is she crazy too?"

"Oh, goodness no. She's as sane as they come. You'd like her, I think, but you wouldn't want to sleep with her."

Deveraux reached for the whiskey bottle and poured himself a drink. "Does she want to have children?"

Grace considered. "Probably. She may still think they grow in the garden, under the stinging nettles."

"Yum. That's for me. Lead me to her."

It was late when they stumbled drunkenly into Grace's bedroom.

Deveraux began to remove his clothes at the threshold. He tripped on a trouser leg and hopped about beside the bed, swearing.

"You have a lot of bites," observed Grace.

"Mosquitoes," said Deveraux, "in Guatemala."

"Do they itch?"

"Now that you mention it." He dived into the bed beside her, hooking his ankle over hers and drawing her legs apart. He lowered his head so that he could sing against her clavicle:

"I've been truuuuue . . . Have Youuuuuu?"

"Except for some fantasies about an eighty-year-old man."

"Don't stroke me like that, it makes the bites itch."

"Never mind, my darling. Soon we will be one, swimming in a sea of blissful ecstasy."

"Is that how they talk in those magazines?"

"More or less."

"I wish you'd take it more seriously."

"I do, Dev, I do." Grace thought of the rope freak and of Marika, whose eyes turned purple when her murderous passion was upon her, and opened her legs: a straightforward gesture of affection. Tonight they would not prolong their activities, would not perform for unseen audiences or even for each other. They would, she realized happily, join at the middle and work briskly, almost breezily, toward a joyful end. A good connection.

"I'm glad to see you, Dev," she said. "I'm sorry I never wrote."

She sat bolt upright, nerves quivering. Adrenalin pumped into the uttermost reaches of her body; she had never been so awake. Beside her, Deveraux slept, not stirring. There it was again, the ringing of the phone. She pounced across the floor and through the connecting closet into the dim living room. She grasped the receiver and said, furiously, "Hello? Who is it?"

There was a hesitating, indrawn breath, the sounds of music at the other end. Then the voice, polite, apologetic.

"Dr. Peacock? I woke you up?"

"Mr. *Ottway?*"

"Well, yes, I'm sorry. It's only a little after one."

"I went to bed early." Then, angry for apologizing, "How did you get my number? I'm not in the book."

"I thought you might like to come to this party, I thought you might enjoy it."

"Whatever gave you that idea? You haven't answered my question."

There was a delicate silence. He was giving her time to repent. Through it she could hear a voice singing "I'm Just a Love Machine." At last he said, "There's friends of yours here. They found out I knew you. Actually, you know, it was their idea."

"What friends?"

"Well, dude name of Briscoe and his old lady. We got to talking about the university . . ." Mr. Ottway's voice trailed off, unsure. "Look, go back to sleep. It was a bad idea."

Grace lit a cigarette, coughing slightly as she inhaled. It was one of Deveraux's—a harsh, Guatemalan, no-nonsense smoke. The giant digital clock on Broadway, which she could see from her window, told her it was 2:15. Mr. Ottway had lied, but she was rarely asleep at this hour and had to count this fact in his favor.

"Let me guess," she said indolently. "You're talking about urban anomie. Alienation in the ghetto. Maybe you're even reciting your poem about the funky A train?"

"Shit," said Mr. Ottway, "no need to turn mean. As a matter of fact, we're at Central Park South."

"You travel in funny circles, Mr. Ottway."

"Briscoe isn't so bad. He don't like you much, though. That's the impression I get."

"I hope you're right in there defending me."

"I am, and that's the truth. Jane looks like she's gonna pop her skull any time now."

"Jenny, her name is Jenny. You be nice to her."

"Right. She's one fucked-up lady, Jenny is. She keeps smiling and smiling and nodding like a wind-up toy. Also, she keeps touching me. She pats at my arm every time I say something, or she'll go slapping at my wrist when I hand her a drink."

"It doesn't mean anything."

"Shame on you, Dr. Peacock. Course it means something. It means she's twitchy around black people, that's what it means."

"Is it all black people there, except for Sam and Jenny?"

"Well, there's about four other honkies here, but I would say we overwhelmingly a party of people of color." Mr. Ottway laughed, repeating the last words delightedly. "People of color."

"What do you want with me?"

"I'll tell you, and then you just forget I said it. I have this feeling about you, Dr. Peacock. I've had it right from the beginning. You're just one of those people—you meet them once in a while, not often—who just doesn't belong anyplace at all. You're a genuine Citizen of Nowhere, that's the feeling I get. And I'm one, too. We recognize each other."

"That's very romantic, Mr. Ottway. A true Citizen of Nowhere doesn't have such thoughts."

"The thing is, I'm young yet."

This time the pause lengthened. Grace could hear the music distinctly now. She guessed that Mr. Ottway was several rooms from its source. She pictured him, crouching lightly on his heels, talking into a bedroom Princess phone near a large pile of coats. "Will you do me a favor?" she asked now, trying to restrain her impulse and knowing she would fail. "Would you recite your poem to Sam Briscoe?"

Ottway laughed. "You really don't like him, huh?"

"I'd appreciate it."

"You're a real mystery, Dr. Peacock," he said approvingly. "Any messages for your friends?"

"No," said Grace, "no messages."

She knew she should hang up, but there was great enjoyment in this furtive morning phone call, a refreshing sense of innocent complicity that cheered her.

"Tell me," she said, "do you know how to drive a car?"

"Sure I do. You want me to pick you up?"

"No, no. I just wondered. Got to go now."

After she had hung up she sat at the darkened desk for a long time, giggling. At length she crossed through into the bedroom and bent over the sleeping form of Deveraux. The sheet was drawn up, messily, between his legs. One arm lay flung out across the place where she, Grace, had been; the other curved up over his chest, where the fingers arched delicately. He looked as if he were about to play a sonata on his breastbone. She pulled the quilt up over him and went into the bathroom. Here she drew a tub full of hot water and, selecting a copy of *True Story* from her linen closet, slipped into the tub for a good read.

V

"Drina, you're breaking our hearts," Mom said with a sob. "We've tried to raise you to be decent and good, and now, now . . ." She broke down, hiding her face in her hands and crying helplessly. Dad came to her, kneeling beside her chair and putting an arm around her shaking shoulders. "Now, Nella," he said gruffly, trying to conceal his emotion, "let Drina have her say."

"Have I ever refused to listen to her?" Mom asked accusingly. "Have I ever denied her anything?" She regarded me with tear-stained eyes.

"Mom, it isn't as if I wanted to hurt you and Dad. I'm not asking for your permission to commit a crime—I just want to marry Carl. Is that so terrible?"

"He has a criminal record, Drina. There's no way to get around it. Carl Peters has been in prison. He's not the sort of man I want for a son-in-law."

"Honey," Dad put in, "Carl seems like a good man. I like what I know of him. But you can't deny he's been behind bars."

"An ex-convict," Mom said bitterly. "My daughter wants to marry an ex-convict."

I wanted to scream at them, to let loose a flood of reproach. How could they condemn a man like Carl? Hadn't he paid his debt to society? Wasn't he just as good as the rest of us now? The Lord teaches us to forgive our enemies, to welcome them back into the fold, but my parents had evidently forgotten that . . .

Later, when Carl came to pick me up, Mom stared at him with a cold hatred, and then rose and marched from the room. "My wife has a bit of a headache," Dad said, which fooled nobody.

"Have you told them?" Carl asked me, when we'd parked at our favorite spot, near Hayley's Dam. "Sure," I said tonelessly. "I've told them we're in love and plan to be married. They were real enthusiastic. You'd think I'd announced I was about to die."

"Drina!" Carl sounded shocked. I looked up at his blue eyes, crinkled around the edges from working out-of-doors, and wondered how anyone could fail to love him. I smoothed his blond hair back in a tender gesture, and then I pressed my body to his with all my strength. Nothing would separate us . . . Nothing! "Oh, honey," I gasped, "take me away. I can't fight them. All I know is that I love you. I want to be completely yours."

I knew, somehow, that we'd make love that night. For weeks now we had been stopping at the crucial moment, even though it was agony to tear ourselves away. It was mostly Carl. He'd clutch me to his chest and moan: "No, Drina, we've got to stop. Soon we'll be married and then I can show you how much I love you . . ."

"But I want you now," I would sob, bewildered and tormented by the wild surge of desire that could not be put down. Then Carl would kiss the tip of my nose and rumple my hair. "Just a little longer, Drina," he would murmur. "Just wait. It will be that much more beautiful. When I make love to you for the first time, I want it to be perfect."

And that was the man my mother thought wasn't good enough! All because he had spent three years at the State penitentiary. Three long years, in which he'd learned to prize honesty and decency more than any other man I'd ever met . . .

"Did I ever tell you what my mother said to me the day of my wedding?" Naomi asked Grace the next day.

"Let me guess. She told you never to refuse Joe. To do it even if you had a headache. Something like that?"

"Much more unusual, something really odd."

"I give up."

"She said: 'You know, dear, men like women to be a little earthy sometimes; we've never talked about this, but I'd like you to remember that cleanliness can be carried too far.' I was appalled! Imagine my mother thinking about things like that. It made me feel I never really knew her at all."

"How do you suppose she meant it?" said Grace. "Were you one of those girls who spent all her time locked in the bathroom? Maybe she thought you were actually bathing."

"I was," said Naomi, "that's exactly what I was doing. Bathing and washing my hair. Sometimes three times a day. Once my cousin sneezed on me and I rushed straight in and took a shampoo."

"Well, there you have it. She was afraid sex might unhinge you when you discovered it was messy."

"But I already knew that! Joe and I had been living together for a year. No. What puzzles me is: what made my mother come out after twenty years of meaningless chitchat and say I mustn't wash all the time? I thought it was perfectly extraordinary, like an old whore indoctrinating the new girl."

They were in Central Park, pacing the perimeter of a large playground. Inside the tall fence, Naomi's children played; the older child, a girl, stood in a treehouse engaged in shrill conversation. The small boy circled the playground tirelessly, riding a plastic car which emitted loud, offensive growls whenever a small lever was turned. The noise level was, on the whole, quite awesome. Grace understood why Naomi refused to actually enter the playground and preferred to stalk around it, ever alert, on the other side of the fence. Other mothers lined the benches, seemed almost to be a part of the playground's architecture, but Naomi insisted that to enter and take a seat was to become a different sort of woman. "Call me an elitist," she would say, "but the day I sit on one of those benches watching the kids play is the day they'll cart me away."

Grace felt always grateful to Naomi for refusing to submit to the role which it would have been so natural for her to assume. Privately, she wondered if Naomi loved her children. Naomi seemed to love them, indeed Grace hoped that her friend did love the children, but Naomi was a pragmatist and the children were not, so to speak, outstanding.

"I think," said Naomi, returning to the subject of her mother, "she was simply bewildered by me. My brother she could cope with, but I wasn't what she'd been led to expect in the way of a daughter."

"Better than she deserved?"

"Oh, Grace. Better, better. That doesn't mean anything. Just . . . puzzling. Poor woman, she should have had a daughter with big boobs and a bouffant hairdo. A nice sort of girl who ran to fat and named her children Scott and Stacey."

Grace laughed. "Your children. Do they puzzle you?"

"Alice does. Robert's too young to be puzzling; he's just a happy little idiot. But Alice, well, she doesn't really seem to live with us. Sometimes I think we have her on loan, like a library book." Naomi lit a cigarette, waved to one of the women on the benches, and turned away. "Sometimes," she said in a lower voice, "it's not even a book I want to finish."

Grace was at a loss. She wanted to defend the girl, for Naomi's sake, but did not know how. She scanned the treehouse. Alice was standing, back to the green clapboard, demonstrating something to her friends. Her mouth and hands moved extravagantly; she seemed to be delivering a lecture. Now her hands plumped down on her sturdy hips in an exaggerated gesture of chagrin. She tossed her hair, pursed her lips. Yes, to look at Alice was to feel irritation. One of the captive children seemed intimidated, the other bored.

"At this moment," said Naomi, "she's probably telling those little girls the entire plot of an Andy Griffith rerun. She loves to recapitulate, synopsize. The trouble is, she's so inept at it. It takes

Alice absolutely forever to get anything said. She can be excruciatingly boring." Naomi studied Grace's face. "Don't take it so hard," she said. "It's OK. I can find Alice boring—it's allowed. I'm not even complaining."

"I didn't know whether to laugh or offer my sympathy," said Grace. "It's all a mystery to me."

"Children," said Naomi. "Look at them. It might be a scene from Hell. Look at that baby there, the one with the load in his pants. Doesn't he look tormented? And that black boy—the enormous one who seems about fifty years old? I see him here all the time. He's always hoping to cadge a ride on some little kid's tricycle. He stands around for hours sometimes with this sad, hungry look on his face, very alert. When he does get to ride he's much too big for the bike and they all laugh at him. Pretty soon there'll be a fight of some sort. You know what they scream at each other? Black, white, Puerto Rican, doesn't matter what they are, they yell: Faggot! Faggot and motherfucker. When Alice tries to talk black it's so tragic, you should hear. She can't quite master it, bi-dialecticalism, and she sounds like Tonto . . . I don't know, I don't know. The discouraging thing about children is, they're all such sheep."

"That can't be a popular viewpoint," said Grace. "Isn't one supposed to think of children as terribly inventive? Little minds, unsullied by adult preconceptions, arriving at breathtaking solutions?"

"That's a lot of crap. Not one kid in a hundred has anything in his head that wasn't put there by television."

"Do you have to let them watch?"

Naomi considered, as if to be fair. "You can fight it for a while," she said. "You can hide the set, or turn it on late at night when the kids are in bed, but it doesn't work in the long run. All their friends watch it incessantly—unless you want them to be social pariahs they'll be contaminated sooner or later. Anyway, when they get to school the bloody *teachers* talk about television. My neighbor's son writes illiterate themes about the relative merits of some horrendous program, actual *themes,* in the seventh grade."

Grace looked at the playground enclosure with new vision. Before she had been neutrally aware of children playing; she had felt neither joy nor animosity in their presence. Now she saw them, as in a trick postcard which changes images when it is examined from different angles, as apish and warlike. Even the babies among them appeared to her ill-favored. A certain slackness of feature, a loose-lipped, sluggish look, transformed them into a brigade of lurching, drooling imbeciles. She had never liked the park, avoided it as much as possible, especially in sunny weather. There had always seemed to her something pathetic about the antics of New Yorkers in the park, a spirit of forced recreational enjoyment which so far exceeded the pleasures at hand that it was painful to watch. These same frolicsome people, set down free in a pastoral meadow, could not possibly summon up such rictuses of ecstasy as they did here in the presence of a few blades of worn grass beneath an oily and malevolent sun. She thought of the people in the park uncharitably, and aware of her lack of charity, as being struck dumb in the presence of anything that was not ugly.

"I shouldn't have come with you," she said to Naomi. "You're only thinking these things because I'm here."

But Naomi was not listening. "Probably," she was saying, "we should have sent Alice to public school. Now it's too late. I thought I couldn't bear it if she came home all bloody from lavatory muggings, but I wonder, which is worse? Maybe if she had to use her wits, merely to survive, she wouldn't be such a complacent little twit? Here we are, Joe and me, forking over three thousand a year to keep her safe, and all her teacher can talk about is 'enrichment.' "

"What's that supposed to mean?"

"Who knows? This woman gets a coy, twinkly look and says that the school feels proud of providing enrichment. My trouble is, I can't even talk to such people. For my daughter's sake I ought to put up a fight, but I can't lower myself, do you see? It's like refusing to sign a complaint when you've been raped because you don't want to tell the cop the details, you feel so superior to him you can't imagine he'd be able to get the facts down straight . . ."

"You're in the wrong tax bracket, Naomi. You should have been very rich or very poor."

"Democracy stinks," said Naomi. "It punishes everybody. Nobody gets away free."

"What kind of Jewish mother are you? Letting a babbling moron rape your daughter's mind because you don't want to interfere?"

"Sometimes," said Naomi glumly, "I don't feel Jewish at all. Sometimes I think my mother had an affair with a played-out, effete WASP graduate student and passed me off as a genuine article. Oh, I'm sorry, Grace, but you know what I mean. It's alright for people like you and Edward to be melancholy and inbred—it's your birthright—but look at me. I'm supposed to be vigorous, committed, humanistically inclined. Smart and scrappy. Instead I sit around nursing spiteful thoughts about everybody. I was actually happy when it rained on our block party."

Grace began to laugh and found she could not stop. Several mothers turned from their bench seats, frowning slightly. A small child whose hand had been buried deep in the soiled cleft of its cotton pants stared openly, jaw hanging. Grace grasped the bars of the fence and steadied herself.

"They think you're crazy," said Naomi practically.

Alice had lumbered down from her treetop perch and was striding importantly toward them. Beneath her T-shirt, which was emblazoned with the legend FOXY LADY, puffy new breasts were visible. The young matured earlier these days, Grace had read, but surely eight was altogether too early?

"What's so funny, Auntie Grace?" said Alice, thrusting her face close through the bars.

"Don't call her Auntie Grace," said Naomi.

"Jennifer calls her mother's friends Auntie," said Alice reasonably, and then, with the tenacity of a mongoose, "What's so funny?"

"Just something your mother said."

Alice's eyes dilated suspiciously. "Something about me?"

"Extended frame of self-reference," muttered Naomi.

"Of course not about you," said Grace, feeling sorry for the girl. "Your mother said she was glad when it rained on the block party."

Alice unwrapped a roll of breath mints dextrously, offering them around and popping several into her mouth. "Can Jennifer come over and watch TV?" she said, addressing her mother for the first time.

"Not today."

"Shee-it," said Alice. "You no fun at all." Before turning away she subjected Grace to a close scrutiny. "My friend thinks you look a little like Mary Tyler Moore," she said grudgingly. "Me—I don't see it."

They walked home toward Naomi's through a press of maddened Frisbee players. Robert preceded them on his noisy machine; Alice sauntered along well ahead of the adults.

"I was wondering," said Naomi, "if there had ever been a Jewish mass murderer? I can't seem to think of any, unless you count Hitler."

"I think they're mainly Midwesterners," said Grace, "and not Jewish. Edward's father, now, you couldn't really call him a mass murderer. He only killed his family because he felt they belonged to him."

"What about the housekeeper?"

"She was family, Edward says. Then there's the sort of mass murderer, like Starkweather or Speck, or the boys in the Capote book, or the kid in the Texas tower—who aren't motivated by anything in particular. With them, it's not personal."

"What does it matter?" said Naomi. "Dead is dead."

"Lunacy is quite impartial. Warps in the genes, screwy endocrines—they don't count. Either does rampaging when you're drunk, and slicing up your wife and mother-in-law. The other sort of killer, the one like Edward's daddy, is just someone with no respect for human life. It's a personality trait, like preferring sweet tastes to sour, or hating cats. It's also quite civilized. I'm sure Edward's father never did anything cruel or spiteful, never bullied anyone. He wouldn't have cheated on his business associates, or tormented his wife, or overworked poor Frieda—what would be the point? A person like Edward's father doesn't hope to gain anything; he just doesn't see why things shouldn't run smoothly so long as he lives. If there's a hitch in the machinery, why not pack it all in? Repairs are so boring. Better say bye-bye."

"You're right about one thing," said Naomi, "it's not very Jewish. All the same, it sounds rather attractive."

"Naomi," said Grace, "what would you say to a trip to the Midwest?"

Grace curled her toes against the porcelain, forcing herself to stand beneath the cold spray of water for as long as possible. The showerhead compounded the ordeal by releasing the water in uneven spurts, dwindling to a mere drizzle every so often before returning to full force. Grace felt her hair being beaten about her cheeks and down her back, but she did not move to avoid it. She wanted to wash the filth of the park from her and forget she had been there, not an hour ago, with her friend Naomi Weinstock. To take her mind from the physical discomfort she was enduring, she tried to picture those few times when she had experienced pleasure in the park. Perhaps once, in her early days in New York, with Jules? But no, he had been no keener on weekend rambles than she, and to really find a joyful, park-centered memory she had to think back to solitary winter visits, to those rare days when the snow had fallen and still lay, plastic, mauve, and undisturbed, about the pedestal of the statue of King Casimir of Poland. Here she had come several times, booted and gloved, with a distinct sense of pleasure, feeling utterly alone. The day immediately following the snowfall she would stay away, knowing that hordes of children would invade with sleds and round plastic discs; she did not begrudge them their hilarity but neither did she want to watch others acknowledging it. People became unhinged in the presence of children. Their eyes crinkled with goodwill in the aisles of supermarkets at sight of a baby in a cart; sometimes they reached out and tousled the hair of a passing child, smiling foolishly as if in the toils of some unbearably tender emotion. This seemed, to Grace, akin to rubbing the backs of the deformed for luck, or jumping up three times and whistling when an albino passed. Talismanic ritual. No wonder children feared and distrusted adults. They sensed the hatred which lay behind such acts, propelling the caressing, groping hands toward their persons, without understanding its meaning. She herself felt about children exactly as she did about grownups. She liked a few of them and felt no interest in the rest. A small number she actively despised. Yet if she thought of the plight of children, actually dwelt upon it, she found herself pitying them with an intensity she could scarcely credit. It was not unlike the feeling she had for her students. Take Naomi's daughter, Alice: a graceless and unexceptional child whose only method of calling up strong emotion in her mother was to emphasize the very qualities of gracelessness which made her so unappealing. She hulked through her mother's life like a pesky but unfatal disease, something destined to disappear in a decade or so and linger on at the borders of the landscape, intruding occasionally to call forth fretful memories. Naomi herself was not to blame because she could not manufacture fierce love for Alice or for Robert; fierce love was not in the cards for Naomi and never had been. Of all the women Grace knew, saving only the earlier Jenny, Naomi was the woman she liked most. Morose Naomi who lamented daily the lack of grandeur in her world, who had once told Grace that she could have multiple orgasms whenever she liked if she thought of herself on a seesaw with her bladder full. "It almost makes me long to be frigid," she had said. "At least I'd feel more dignified."

Grace stepped from the shower, shivering but cleansed, and wrapped a towel around her body. She walked through her apartment, visiting the bare kitchen and then patrolling both bed and living room, letting the air currents dry her. Her hair hung straight as licorice whips. When the phone rang she picked it up immediately, switching on a small tape recorder at the same time. "This is Grace Peacock," the announcement she had taped began. "I am either not at home or do not wish to talk. Please leave your name and a message. Thank you." There was the sound of an indrawn breath, and then a male voice: "Grace, you raging phony, you don't have one of those machines. This is just a tape recorder and you're right there, at the other end. Fuck you!" The receiver crashed down and Grace smiled. She thought the voice was that of a man she had known briefly a few months back. It would be like him to take the recording as a personal offense, hanging up before she had time to cut in on his indignation. Good then. He wouldn't call back today.

She put on a pair of jeans and an old shirt of Edward's, selected a copy of *My Intimate Confession,* and left the apartment, locking her door carefully behind her. Her hair was still wet and, not wanting to alarm any of the old people, she took the stairwell to the roof. Here was a large and unattractive space, tar-floored and windswept, flat and colorless between its four small parapets, which filled her with peace. Nobody came here. In a building inhabited by younger people, the roof would be cluttered with sunbathers from May to September. Even this late in the autumn there would surely be a gaggle of sociable tenants milling about, perhaps even setting up bazaars on the weekends to collect money for the block. Here there was no one. Grace climbed up on one of the parapets and lay, belly-downward, surveying embattled Broadway twelve stories below. She thought she could detect the crown of the stately pimp's hat, loitering its way along beside the Blimpie Base, but she was not sure. The sound of the traffic was nearly as loud as it would be at street level, the barking of dogs even louder. Sound traveled up. But they were far below and that in itself made the sound bearable. She did not like the West Side, felt contempt for those who enthused about the wonderful sense of community, the civic-minded diehards who refused to acknowledge what was happening all around them. They capered through the decay, casting a cold eye on renegades who pulled up stakes and decamped for the East Side or the suburbs. They felt superior for no comprehensible reason; they often said they were the only "real" people left in New York. Naomi knew a few people of this sort, but she was far too realistic for their taste and existed with them in a state of truce. In Naomi's vast co-op on Central Park West it was possible to feel quite private for hours on end, but the children who lived above the Weinstocks played touch football in their bedrooms and the sound of falling bodies was ominous and horrible to Grace when it occurred. The muted thudding punctuated evening conversations with Naomi and Joe; Grace pictured the children as enormous caterpillars falling from a tree and splitting as they hit the earth. There were no children living in the Briscoes' building, which sat prettily in the middle of a block in the East Eighties, but inside the flat the steady drone of a neighbor's television could be heard through the thin walls, and over their heads heels clicked endlessly across varnished, uncarpeted floors in the apartment above. A large and hideous dog, a creature from a child's nightmare, lived in the courtyard below Deveraux's Greenwich Village walkup; a single bark from its deep, reverberant throat could waken five dozen people from their sleep. A neighbor of Deveraux's devised many plans for disposing of the dog, most of them involving poison which would be lowered by means of a pulley to the courtyard, but he never put these plans into action. Grace had read once of a woman who, dying and alone in a clamorous slum apartment on Columbus Avenue, had pierced her eardrums with knitting needles so that her last days should be less terrible . . . Here, in her great fortress of a building with its double walls and recessed courtyards, Grace had quiet, and having had it could not imagine surrendering it. Let the streets become as murderous as the back alleys of Naples, and she knew she would not stir. Better to die of knife wounds, gasping on the threshold of a reeking souvlaki stand, bleeding over Broadway, object of curiosity, event of the week, than to dream of throttling children, shooting dogs. Only the sounds of sirens pierced the quiet in Grace's bed, and these she did not mind. Now, facedown on the parapet, she gave herself up to the rising tide of noise, safe in the knowledge she could make it disappear. She opened her magazine to a bonus-length fiction piece called, intriguingly, THE SPIRIT VOICE REVEALED: YOUR HUSBAND HAS THREE WIVES. The photo layout showed a care-worn young woman, hands clasped in her lap, leaning forward anxiously. Across from her, a Gypsy in heavy eyeliner consulted a crystal ball. The blurb read: "If what Madame Olga said was true, I was married to a bigamist!" The Gypsy looked rather like Naomi, or like the version of Naomi her mother would have preferred.

Naomi would not be the one to accompany her on her journey. She had known Naomi would have to refuse, to plead the children and Joe as excuse. Grace suspected that her friend would be uncomfortable in the Midwest, anyway. She would bristle at the sight of blonde waitresses who brought ice water without being asked, sure that they had grown to maturity believing Jews had horns. Deveraux would go with her only under duress, and she could not imagine taxing him so heavily. Edward was the most logical possibility, but there were the twin ethical problems of Christine and of Edward's possible chagrin at visiting, so to speak, the scene of the crime. Mr. Ottway would surely be either lynched or made mayor of the first town he visited, and she could not seriously contemplate taking a student with her on her odyssey. Briefly, she considered asking old Maurice. She envisioned them stopping at motels on the edges of cornfields, having long, scholarly talks over shrimp cocktails at a succession of Holiday Inns. His aristocratic demeanor would allay suspicion wherever they went and she, Grace, would wear dowdy shirtwaist dresses and barrettes in her hair so no one could mistake her for an old man's *houri*. She would give him his medicine each night; perhaps they would watch the late news on television before retiring. She would introduce him to Squirt, and buy him a leisure suit. But no, it was almost certain that Maurice had never learned to drive, either.

For the first time in many years, she missed Jules.

I'll never forget the moment they told me. You don't forget such things, not if you live to be a hundred. The whole scene is etched in my mind so clearly it could have happened yesterday.

I was in the kitchen, grating carrots for little Kevin's supper. I'd done my hair a new way, and I was wearing Keith's favorite perfume. "You look pretty, Mama," said Becki, my daughter, casting an appraising eye in my direction. "You bet I do, honey!" I had resolved to turn over a new leaf, to be the woman my husband had fallen in love with. Who could blame a man for turning cold when his wife dragged to the door each evening in runover bedroom slippers and curlers in her hair? How could I have turned away from Keith, night after night, mumbling about how tired I was, how early I had to get up in the morning? What had I expected?

"Mommy, there's two men at the door," called Trisha, my oldest.

Kevin banged his spoon on the high-chair tray, delightedly trying to imitate his sister.

I didn't know. Not then. It wasn't until I saw their faces that my blood ran cold. A tingling began at the base of my spine and traveled all the way up to the roots of my hair. Belatedly, I wished I had taken my apron off. I knew the men, although I couldn't tell you their names. I'd seen them at company picnics and Christmas parties at the plant. They were coworkers of Keith's, and there was only **one** reason why they **would** be here, at my door, on a Tuesday evening at supper time. They were looking at me, but not meeting my eyes, the way a jury does when the verdict is guilty . . .

I held onto the doorframe with all my strength. "It's Keith, isn't it?" My voice emerged in a hoarse whisper.

The taller of the two men met my gaze then. "I'm sorry, Mrs. Jensen. It was an accident . . . a freak accident . . ."

Then the other man was explaining. A piece of machinery at the plant . . . nobody could have foreseen . . . Keith didn't suffer . . .

I must have been half-crazy, because I invited them in for coffee, as cool as you please. It wasn't until they stepped inside that the voice began to scream. It just went on and on, that disembodied voice. Little Kevin began to shriek from his high chair, and Trisha and Becki came running, and still the scream went on and on. When I realized the voice was mine, everything went black and I whirled round and round into a tunnel of merciful oblivion . . .

The real pain began when I regained consciousness. I was lying on our old couch, and my first feeling was one of embarrassment because the slipcovers were old and yellowed and there were strangers in the house. Then I remembered. I would live the rest of my life without seeing Keith smile, without feeling his touch. Keith was dead. I wanted to ask God to help me, but the prayer turned to ashes on my lips. What kind of God would take a man like Keith? I turned my head and began to weep soundlessly.

"Hush, Mrs. Jensen . . . Everything's going to be alright . . ."

He was wrong, I knew. Nothing would ever be alright again . . .

Dear [imaginary] daughter,

You have probably wondered what your father was like. It's customary. You have seen several photographs, but they in no way convey the sense of the man, or rather boy, since he was not fortunate enough to live beyond the age of twenty-six.

Jules Meisel was a nicely put together man of medium height, rather more dark than otherwise. His hair was particularly lustrous, like mine, but unlike mine it had a good deal of body. I used to envy him the body in his hair. His eyebrows were, perhaps, his most interesting feature, being of a particularly silky texture, and framing his eyes in such a way as to make him resemble a Saracen. What's that? You say you're interested in his soul, not his eyebrows? You have much to learn.

Your father's soul was of the standard variety for intelligent males who had been raised by ruthless mothers, but with a difference: he seemed to have escaped his harrowing upbringing without being unduly harmed. In other words—he had no unseemly interest in his mother. He neither loved nor hated her. She was a mild irritation, no more. He felt, as did so many people in those days, that much of what went on in the world had nothing to do with him. Now people seem to believe that everything has a meaning, that a vast importance attaches to one's every movement, but Jules died long before this Nosy Parker concept of human relations became the fashion. I often think he would have taken to it with some relief.

In many ways he was a difficult man. He was jealous of his time, resented those who wanted to take it up, abhorred waste. He was neither sentimental nor—in current terms—"highly motivated." He was never sure what he wanted to be when he grew up, and this state of mind was with him to the day of his death. He was quick to find fault. He did not like most people, but he didn't take pains to let them know. He was not fatuous. He was good in bed. He liked, for a joke, to pose impossible ethical questions: "Would you eat your tennis sweater for world peace?"

He was a fairly well educated man, having taken degrees in literature and political science at Columbia University. Nevertheless, at the time of his death he was working as an editor at a lowbrow men's magazine. When he died I neither screamed nor fainted, unlike the heroine of GODLESS WIDOW: I TRIED TO BURY MY GRIEF IN EVERY BED IN TOWN, nor did I experience agonizing grief. I was merely very sad, and felt sorry it should have happened to him. This is precisely what he would have wished me to feel. I know, because we discussed it many times, never dreaming, of course, it would be put to the test so soon.

(In case you are worried about hereditary defects, rest your mind. Jules died because he was foolish enough to ride a bicycle on the West Side Drive when he was drunk.) His mother, Mrs. Florence Meisel, is still alive. You may apply to her for additional information.

Your loving mother,
etc., etc., etc.

It was her habit, after she and Deveraux had made love, to think of Edward, just as, in the days when she was married to Edward, she thought of Jules. This was not even a technical infidelity, since she did not think of either of them with longing. It was simply that the act of making love reminded Grace of previous acts, and she assumed one day she would lie wide-eyed beside another sleeping man and think of Deveraux. Occasionally, other lovers crept into the ritual, but these she was able to dismiss since she had not known them for a sufficient length of time to make reminiscence and comparison enjoyable. The professor who had suggested her job at the university, for example, she had been to bed with ten times at most. The man whose voice had sworn at her earlier in the afternoon had entered her body precisely twice, and neither time had been memorable. She dwelt only on the men she had known for a long time, because here she was able to recapture some sense of her past life. If she thought of the time Edward had playfully tied a silk scarf around his penis—an uncharacteristic action—she would be able to remember where she had purchased the scarf (Bloomingdale's), what the weather had been like (sultry) and where she and Edward had been earlier in the evening (a play about the antics of a madcap girl). Tonight she abandoned her usual routine. Separating herself gently from Deveraux's embrace, cupping his still warm genitals in a soothing manner, bypassing Edward—she set her mind on Jules. She **chose** to see him cinematically . . .

Jules Meisel walks toward the camera, impeccable in a cheap but becoming black trench coat. It doesn't matter that the day is fine and cloudless; the raincoat is Jules's favorite garment and the first shot should definitely reveal him as he would like to have been seen. He is wearing the sort of smile invariably described as "wry"; beneath it lurks outright distaste. Of course—he does not like to be photographed. He walks gracefully, lightly. He looks the sort of man who could get away quickly if the occasion demanded. Correction: he looks the sort of man who spends most of his time getting away quickly from unpleasant situations. He is not the sort of man you would ask for the time, or a match, unless—of course—you wanted to attract his attention. You would select, for the match or the time, someone who looked less forbidding. If you were a person of fine instincts you would automatically understand that Jules doesn't like to be bothered. As he comes closer to the camera he looks away—an exquisite gesture with much artifice to it—and manages to ruin the opening scene of the vehicle Grace is manufacturing for him. She tries again.

Jules and she are sitting in a booth at Reuben's Restaurant. Across from them are seated Winifred Peacock and Florence Meisel, both widows. Mrs. Meisel is the older woman, and looks it. Her face is tanned to a leathery finish; her body is large and comfortable, having borne four children, the youngest of whom is Jules. Winifred Peacock, who has borne only Grace, has flown to New York that same day for this meeting. Althought the flight lasted only two and a half hours, she tells the group she is suffering from jet lag. Nevertheless, she looks fresh and endearingly foolish in her seersucker suit from Marshall Field. She is ordering another screwdriver and a white-meat turkey sandwich, giggling over the bewildering variety of exotic foodstuffs on the menu. A Big *Shiksa*.

Mrs. Meisel says she'll have a Reuben and a glass of celery tonic. "How wise of you, Florence, in all this heat," says Winifred Peacock. It is her third non sequitur. Mrs. Meisel darts a look at Jules. "You see?" she might have said out loud. "She's got her head in the clouds, same as her daughter."

Grace and Jules have only just told their respective mothers that they have contrived to get married without anyone's knowledge.

Mrs. Meisel is furious, but if Grace is the wife of Julie's heart she is prepared to pretend to accept her. Winifred Peacock, who was given the news via long-distance telephone the night before, is bewildered. Why would Grace want to marry Jules? He appears nice enough in a swarthy way, but—good gracious—isn't it silly to tie oneself down at the age of twenty-two? She has tried to broach this topic, but a hasty computation of Jules's age, together with the knowledge that he is the youngest of Florence's children, instructs her that Mrs. Meisel was yet a younger bride. She turns her attention, publically, to Jules's appearance. "I've been admiring your tan," she says rather flirtatiously, nibbling at her swizzle stick. Jules gives Grace a friendly horsebite under the table and says, quite seriously, "That's just my natural color, Mrs. Peacock." Not for nothing does Grace pinch Jules's subterranean hand. She has seen her mother blanch before and guesses what effect this will have on her new mother-in-law. Also, she is afraid she will laugh. Defiantly, she orders a third Bloody Mary, capriciously changes the order to vermouth cassis. "Don't get tight," says Winifred Peacock in a silvery, admonitory voice, and this time she really has gone too far. Florence Meisel's worst fears are confirmed. She has always suspected that drinking is a *shiksa* vice, acquired from years of hanging around restricted country clubs, flirting with trashy golf pros and ordering oddly colored drinks as soon as they're big enough to look over the bar. Jules clears his throat: a warning. "We hope you don't object to the rather furtive way in which we married," he says in his stilted way. Furtive. He's laid it right on the line, right out on the table for them. Once he's said it, nobody else can. He understands, does Jules, the efficacy of free confession. Winifred Peacock laughs outright. "I might have wished for it to happen differently," she says, taking her cue, "but Grace's life is her own, surely. I feel I have no real right to object—don't you feel that way, Florence?"

Clearly, Mrs. Meisel does not agree. She sighs, picking at her Reuben sandwich in a cold fury. "Would it matter," she says gloomily, "if I did?"

"Nope," says Jules, placing Grace's hand on his private parts beneath the table. "Grace and I can't convince ourselves it's anyone's business but our own."

Grace gives him a resounding slap of approval, forgetting where her hand is resting. Jules winces. Mrs. Meisel narrows her eyes shrewdly. She knows exactly what they are doing, and Grace feels a new respect for her mother-in-law. Winifred Peacock is smiling brightly around the room, like royalty. It is she who is getting tight . . .

CUT TO: the interior of the Perry Street flat where Grace and Jules lived all the days of their marriage. Jules is wearing jockey shorts and a pajama top which has three buttons missing. Grace is attired in a long blue nightgown which Winifred Peacock has sent to her. "But, Jules," she is saying for the second time, "I don't want to write a novel." They have been quarreling sporadically ever since they came back from the Mexican restaurant where they dine at least three times a week. It will be years before Grace understands that many of their quarrels stem from the preponderance of Mexican food which enters their systems. When they do not eat Mexican food, they eat Chinese food. Grace cannot cook, and Jules will not press her. He understands that if he complains about the dearth of wholesome, home-cooked meals he will be acting predictably, just as Grace understands that any whining on her part about money or status—the lack of it—would be predictable. If there is anything that Grace and Jules feel they are not, it is common.

"What do you want to do?" Jules asks witheringly. "Sleep late every day until you're eighty?" He has been trying to explain to her that her lack of ambition will be a source of pain to her on that far-off day when she hits thirty. Grace has acted in some plays, and she writes rather well. Why, then, doesn't she set out to be an actress? A writer? Jules has chosen the latter profession for her because it requires less actual effort. Grace is very good, very energetic and attractive as an actress, but she will not rise early enough to make the rounds. Neither will she push herself on agents. "Just because one is good at something doesn't mean one has to milk it for all it's worth," she says spitefully. Now she has managed to make Jules feel vulgar, and he is enraged. "That nightgown is hideous," he says softly. "It looks like something an exchange student from Pakistan would wear." This makes Grace almost dizzy with anger, because she cannot bear to have her appearance criticized, and because Winifred Peacock does indeed choose ugly garments to send to her daughter. Grace rises from the bed and goes to the only other room large enough to retreat to: the bathroom. She calls back over her shoulder: "At least my mother doesn't call a couch a *davenport.*" Now she has Jules where she wants him. He must get to bed in order to be able to get up and go to work at the magazine tomorrow. If she runs a bath and sits in it, reading, he will have to tap at the door eventually. The sight of Grace, rosy in her tub, never fails to move him. This way they'll be able to make love without either of them having to apologize . . .

Rather than dwell on the manner of their lovemaking that long-ago night on Perry Street, Grace instructs the camera to PAN IN on an aerial view of a town in Tuscany. She wants an atmospheric montage of slate rooftops and green Mediterranean shutters, a quick view of the Duomo and teeming town square, and then a direct descent to the balcony outside the best room in a five-star Italian hotel. The balcony is circumscribed by fat, sugary balustrades. Its floor is made of tiles, alternating in white and lapis lazuli. In the exact center of the balcony, lying naked on the tiles and oblivious to the discomfort, are two figures fucking. They are Grace and Jules.

Night has fallen; there is scant danger that they will be seen and ordered out of Italy by Papal Bull. Jules is on top, his knees rubbed raw. He is tanned darkly—everybody in Italy believes he is an Italian-American making a sentimental return to the Old Country. If Winifred Peacock could see him now she would drink six screwdrivers to absorb the shock. Grace has emerged the color of a lightly done brown n' serve roll; she is sure she is taken for a glamorous Eurasian. She is absorbed in the lovemaking, but beyond the absorption is the knowledge that the bathroom that goes with their room is fashioned entirely of dove-gray marble, that the linens on the bed are finer even than the linens of her youth, and this—together with her physical well-being—urges her to a spontaneous eroticism she has never before felt in her twenty-four years.

She has liked screwing well enough; in fact, if she and Jules do not make love each night she feels something is amiss—but she has never really understood the principle of ecstasy. Pleasure in sex has always been achieved through grinding contact, or from the rear in undignified doggie position, and even then it is fleeting and not commensurate to the effort involved. For the first time, she understands that it is possible to slyly wait for pleasure, to let one's feet aim high without getting a cramp in the toes, to sling toward it with a lazy ardor that is all the better for not being strenuous. She loves it. She says "Whooooo-eeee," surprising herself and Jules, who is not aware that this time is different for her. She does not want to mar his pleasure, or hers, by explaining. He would want to know what she felt in all the times before, and from this day forth he would be sure to ask if each bout measured up to the Italian Breakthrough. She keeps her pleasure to herself, but this does not mean she loves him the less.

It is the only major trip they are ever to take together . . .

Deveraux stirred fitfully, emitting a low moan which sounded a trifle too theatrical to be real. Perhaps, thought Grace, he was equipped with extrasensory radar which operated on a special band for the sexually jealous. She pictured sonar bleepings piercing to the peaceful shoals of his unconsciousness, warning him of her betrayal. She gentled him, stroking his naked chest gently, murmuring conventional reassurances: "Hush, baby. Are you having a bad dream? Sleep . . . sleep . . . sleep . . ."

Deveraux sat up stiffly, corpselike, the sheet falling away from his torso. "Don't. Do that," he said.

"Do what?"

"Say 'sleep . . . sleep' in that spooky voice. It sounds like you're urging me to die."

That was a new one. "I thought you were having a bad dream," said Grace.

"I was," said Deveraux, fumbling for a cigarette on the cluttered bedside table. "That's it. I was having a horrible dream and then I woke to find you acting like a witch doctor." He lit his cigarette, cupping the match in his hand as if he were standing on a windy bluff. Grace thought of war correspondents scanning the skies above Normandy. "Wide-eyed in the dark, willing me back to unconsciousness like a goddam witch," he continued, sounding more wounded than angry.

"I believe it's a conventional way of soothing troubled sleepers," said Grace. "Mothers do it regularly to children."

"What would you know about mothers?"

Grace declined to rise to the bait. In truth, she didn't mind quarreling with Deveraux, who had no real venom in his veins, but her sense of order was disturbed. She had been quietly weaving a scenario about Jules, minding her own business, keeping to her own side of the bed, when Deveraux had come snorting and groaning out of the depths of a bad dream to reproach her. For what?

"I had a bad dream in Guatemala," said Deveraux, trying to make amends. "Tonight I had it again, with a few variations." He slipped an arm beneath her shoulders, drawing her to him in a companionable and conciliatory way. "In this dream you kept urging me to go to the Mato Grosso. You were as real as you are now. You, Grace, except you were sitting cross-legged in my tent, coaxing me to go. I kept trying to explain about how dangerous it was in the Mato Grosso, and you just laughed. '*I'm* not going,' you said, very patiently, as if you were addressing a kid. '*You're* the one who's going.' Then the dream cut to a big encyclopedia, open to the 'M' pages. Right at the top was 'Mato Grosso' and underneath it said: *Mato Grosso: A euphemism for death, as in: 'going to the Mato Grosso.'* "

"Like Crossing the Bar," said Grace, "or Meeting Your Pilot."

"Worse."

Grace sighed. She considered several possibilities. It was possible that Deveraux had contracted a fatal undulant fever in Guatemala—the sort of illness that rendered him fairly sane one moment and mad as a hatter the next. It was not possible that her mordant scenario—mordant because it would lead irrevocably to Jules's demise—had entered Deveraux's unconscious mind, crossing psychic wires and making him dream of death. Hadn't he said *cut to* the encyclopedia? But then, he was a documentary film maker and thought in such terms. She found other people's dreams supremely boring as a topic of conversation, but this one had dramatic possibilities. "Going to the Mato Grosso," she murmured, causing Deveraux to stiffen.

"The trouble with you, Dev, is that you're a very melodramatic person. I don't want you to go off anywhere. Listen. It's quiet here, isn't it? No dog in the courtyard; phone's off the hook. You're tired, baby, that's all. Try to sleep. If you can't, we'll get up and go for a walk." This, as they both knew, was impossible. The utter absurdity of the suggestion—going for a walk on Broadway at 3:00 in the morning—made Deveraux laugh softly into Grace's upper arm, which was crushed beneath his shoulder. Tenderly, he rolled her to the other side of the bed, arranging himself so that his left small toe touched her right big one; he was still uneasy about his Guatemalan nightmare, but Grace knew he would sleep now, immobile as a Roman bust, until morning.

As soon as she felt sure that he was, indeed, asleep, she tried to return to her scenario. A passing siren helped. It was an appropriate sound, a sound designed to hover over the final frames of Jules's life as a warning of approaching tragedy. She did not intend to reconstruct the actual moment of death. Let it occur offstage in classical style. Perhaps she would not even bring on the messenger but would content herself with a faithful reconstruction of their last minutes together . . .

CUT TO: Perry Street. Jules is sitting at his desk in the cluttered work-corner of their miniscule apartment. Tonight they have dined at a Spanish restaurant on Horatio Street. There is a party Grace would like to go to, but Jules is adamant. He must finish the outline for one of his freelance articles at the magazine. Grace, he says, is welcome to go to the party alone. He will join her when he can. Grace doesn't want to go alone. Sam and Jenny will be there, and Sam is already showing those signs of loathsomeness which will totally eclipse the worthier aspects of his character in a year or two. Grace wants to go with Jules. She is wearing a long workshirt of Jules's and nothing else. This in itself is not unusual, except that she is sitting on the fire-escape balcony, feeling like a character from *Street Scene*. If the neighborhood teenagers wish to view her snatch from below, they are welcome. She does not care. She is also drinking Scotch, a bad brand Jules insists is indistinguishable from Johnnie Walker Black once it has been placed in a crystal decanter. He is wrong about this, but Grace admires his guile. Jules, too, is drinking the Scotch, and at a much greater rate than Grace. He is cursing softly in the corner, banging his glass against the typewriter and balling sheets of paper viciously in his fist. He must come up with a plausible outline for his article—"Showbusiness Con Men" —in time to make his monthly bonus at the magazine. All the men who work for Jules's company contribute two-fisted stories; their salaries are not high enough to make the job worthwhile unless they do. Last month Jules wrote a fraudulent account of a bullet-eating paratrooper who single-handedly wiped out a village of Gooks in a mythical Asian hamlet. The week before he did an extra, unsolicited piece on suburban wife-swapping. In the offing is an article on a man who survived an hour of hand-to-hand combat with a kodiak bear. He is stockpiling these ludicrous pieces of writing so that he and Grace can go on another long trip; perhaps he is more aware of the red-letter quality of their Tuscan intercourse than she thinks. But for now he must compile a sufficient number of lurid producers and casting agents to make the con-men article work. Grace has told him, from her own experience, more than he ever wanted to know about such things. She likes to help him with his articles; in fact, she thinks his job is an enormous lark and dearly loves to show friends the masthead which proclaims JULES MEISEL as managing editor of *Male Tales*. (She is even more enamored of the office down the hall from Jules's quarters, where confessions books are edited, but her true fascination for these unsung works of literature will not surface until later.)

Grace calls to him from the fire escape: "Be sure to put in that man who wanted me to stand naked in a plastic bag!" Jules grinds his teeth. "That didn't have anything to do with show business," he calls back. "What about the guys who put fake ads in trade papers?" she counters. (Once Grace answered just such an ad. She found herself in an office with a man who said: "You're too young for the part, but how about giving me some head?") Jules refills his glass. "Too general," he mutters. His voice is beginning to slur. The story won't come clear, and he is feeling sorry for himself, and for Grace, who has the ill fortune to be married to him. When he considers the things he might be doing, he is full of self-loathing. He especially dislikes the part of him which must admit that—normally—he is quite pleased with his life. It is only when he is stalled at the typewriter, drinking too much, that he suspects he is a fool. He stands up, switching off the desk light with a certain finality. "This is no job for a grown-up," he says.

Before Grace realizes it, he is unlocking the door of their apartment and running down the stairs. The camera moves in for a CLOSE UP of Grace's face. She is bewildered, slightly annoyed. She peers down, seeing him between the slats in the fire escape as he emerges at street level. He has taken her bicycle. "Where are you going?" she calls softly. "Just to clear my head," he replies. "I'll be back in half an hour." He blows her a kiss and mounts, throwing his leg up and over, even though it is a girl's bike and there is no need. Weaving a bit, he pedals up Perry Street, turns on Bleecker, and passes from her vision forever . . .

The bell, coarse as a grackle's caw, did not waken Deveraux when it rang, just before dawn. Grace, who had fallen asleep soon after the close of her scenario, sat up with dread on the second ring. She felt she was still in the grip of a dream, or, worse, caught up in her scenario. Perhaps Florence Meisel, slumbering in her New Jersey retirement village, had divined that her son's widow was using Jules's death to put herself to sleep. Now, after all these years, she would hurl herself at Grace and hiss recriminations. What had Jules been riding when the Chrysler ran him off the drive near the Italian Line docks? Grace's bicycle! What had he been drinking? Scotch! Had it gone to his head because Grace never gave him a decent meal? And how had she contrived to drive him from his home and up the Henry Hudson Parkway at midnight?

Naked, shivering, Grace clambered over Deveraux's body and stood beside the bed. Could it be Edward, come to reiterate his proposals of communal marriage, with Grace as Queen Bee? She crept up the long hall. At the intercom, which worked sporadically, she hesitated. No doubt it was a hard-working junkie, trying desperately to meet his quota, hoping that one of the old people might be expecting an ambulance and let him in. As she stood before the intercom, the bell rang again with such a jaunty persistency that she took down the receiver and called sternly: "Who is it?"

There was a long period of crackling, and then a voice stated distinctly: "I tried to phone, but your line was engaged."

"Who *is* it?" shrieked Grace.

This time the voice was unmistakable. "Fiona!" it said. "Let me in!"

The day I found Mother and Todd together, I thought my life had ended. I'll never forget the look on Mom's face when she saw me standing at the door to her bedroom. Her blue eyes opened wide and she made a little motion with her hands as if she could push me away, push me away forever . . . "Tammi, it's not what you think!" she whispered. "Oh, Todd, tell her. Tell her!" But Todd merely looked as if he wanted to sink through the floor and disappear. Mom prodded him, pleading with him to say something, but I turned on my heel and walked straight out of the house.

Later, when I came back to pack my things, Mom was sitting at the kitchen table. She'd been crying, but otherwise she looked as gorgeous as ever. With her china doll face and shoulder-length red hair, she didn't seem much older than I did. I tossed her a look of contempt, then marched up to my room, hauled my suitcase down, and began to pack as fast as I could.

"Tammi, honey," Mom muttered brokenly when I brushed past her to the door, "I want you to know that Todd and I are deeply in love. We plan to be married next month. I would have told you, but I couldn't stand to hurt you."

I laughed harshly. "Hurt me, Mother? What would make you think I've been hurt? Just because you've stolen my fiancé?"

Beneath her makeup, Mom's face went white as paper. It was as if I'd slapped her. "Don't hate me, baby," she begged. "You're young —you'll find plenty of men to fall in love with."

"Sure," I said flippantly. "The more the better. That way I can get to be just as big a tramp as you!"

The last I saw of Mom, she was crumpled against the door, sobbing as if her heart would break. I didn't even turn back. She'd taken the only man I'd ever loved, just as she'd taken everything from me from the time I was a baby . . . I guess I should explain that my mother was sixteen, little more than a child herself, when I was born. My father was killed in Vietnam before he ever saw me, and I grew up in the shadow of my mother's beauty and self-centered charm. "You don't look old enough to be that child's mother," people would say to her, or, "Tammi, your mama looks more like your sister!" When I was twelve, we moved to another town and Mom cautioned me not to let on that she was my mother. I had to call her Tina. "See, honey," she'd say, "isn't it more fun like this?" At other times she'd get glum and tell me that no man wanted a woman with a ready-made family. Oh, she had plenty of boyfriends alright. They swarmed around her thick as flies, but none of them ever seemed to mention marriage. And then came Todd. Todd, who fell in love with Tammi, the dull, responsible sister. "Tina's gorgeous," he'd say to me, "but it's you I want." I believed him, too. Believed him and trusted him, until the day I found him in bed with my mother. I never wanted to see her again . . . never, as long as I lived!

Grace, Fiona, and Deveraux sat in the room which, in Grace's apartment, passed for a kitchen. It was late in the afternoon; they had slept most of the day. Fiona looked bright and perky. She had caught a few winks on her flight and slept with perfect comfort on Grace's living-room sofa. Grace and Deveraux, in the comfort of the big bed, had slept less well for knowing she was there. Her arrival had badly shaken Deveraux, who sleepily asked, "But why didn't you know she was coming? How could you not know?" He had wanted to taxi home immediately, but Fiona, averting her eyes politely from the rumpled bed, would not hear of such a thing. Her flight had been delayed; she'd tried to call but Grace's line was continually engaged. Fiona pretended not to notice that the phone was stuffed into a drawer of Grace's desk. "I did write," she said almost plaintively, and "it's only for a few days."

Now, dressed in an alarmingly crisp blue skirt and flowered blouse, she was making an inventory of Grace's refrigerator. "Actually," she said, "there's nothing here." Deveraux laughed snidely. "There never is," he said. "The milk hasn't gone sour," Fiona continued, "but the only other thing is this." She pulled a glass jar from the depths of the refrigerator and held it at arm's length, as if it might be dangerous. The jar contained an unclear liquid in which swam several olives past their prime.

"I suppose," said Grace, "it's a fetus."

"I'll just chuck it out," said Fiona.

"Why are you going through the refrigerator?" asked Grace. "There's coffee brewing and some tea bags in the cupboard. What more do we need?"

"I like a proper breakfast," said Fiona, addressing herself to Deveraux. "I feel awfully peckish in the morning."

"It's four-thirty in the afternoon," said Grace.

Deveraux smiled at Fiona. "When I was little," he said, "my mother always made farina and bacon."

Grace excused herself and left the room. If Deveraux and Fiona wanted to carry on like a couple of housewives she preferred to be out of earshot. While her bath was running she scanned the final columns of LOVE THIEF—MY MOTHER STOLE MY MAN, but the ending didn't please her as the opening had. She was preoccupied, perplexed. Why had she never received Fiona's letter? It was easy to lose those blue onionskin envelopes, or to throw them away, sandwiched between free coupons addressed to "Occupant," but it terrified Grace to think that Fiona's modest request for accommodation had never been seen by her. Her cousin's mere presence in

New York was jarring. Regularly, Fiona flew to Toronto to visit her mother, but she had never before felt the need to cross the border into the United States. There was something ominous in her arrival. From the kitchen, Grace could hear the sounds of companionable chatting; it irritated her unreasonably and she wanted to shout "Quiet back there!" like an irate moviegoer in a noisy theatre. Instead, she lay in the tub whistling under her breath. Presently there came a tapping at the door.

"Grace?" It was Deveraux. "I'm going down to the supermarket to get some groceries," he called. "Do you want anything?"

"Just cigarettes," she said, feeling unwholesome. She tried not to sound as churlish as she felt. She did not want to face Fiona without Deveraux as a buffer, so she lolled in the tub until he returned. The matey dialogue resumed, and with it the sound of Grace's few pots and pans, unused for years, being resurrected from banishment. When she stepped into the kitchen, faint from her long exile in the tub, Fiona had assembled a breakfast so vast in scope that Grace could only gape. There were eggs and bacon and sausage, muffins and butter and marmalade, a large dish of mandarin oranges, and even what proved to be, on close inspection, grilled tomatoes.

"Grub's on," cried Fiona cheerfully. Deveraux perched on the counter, smiling fatuously as if all his fears of going to the Mato Grosso had been miraculously dispelled by the sight of so much food in Grace's kitchen. Perhaps, thought Grace, he regarded it as a primitive ritual, something appropriate and seemly to witness in his capacity as documentary film maker. "This Englishwoman," his sound track might say, "is adhering to the ancient Druid custom of *lennistaan,* which means, literally, the overwhelming of one's host by domestic activity. The dish of mandarin oranges symbolizes the rebirth of kinship through the seeding of goodwill and friendship. Note the look of displeasure on the North American woman's face. It is customary for the recipient to feign anger in the face of such largesse."

Grace, remembering that Edward had, only a few nights ago, accused her of having nice instincts, smiled and said: "This is marvelous, Fiona. How did you manage?"

"It was jolly hard. You've only got two pans. Here—pass your plate." Fiona heaped food on their plates and then fell to with relish. "As I was telling Deveraux," she said between courses, "I had an absolutely super time with Mummy in Toronto. And then I thought, as I was so close, I might just as well run down to see you."

"You didn't tell your mother about our arrangement, did you?" Grace asked with obvious alarm. "Didn't she want to know why you were coming to New York?"

"I said I was going to do the galleries." Fiona turned to Deveraux. "Can't you convince Grace to stop this senseless subterfuge? Aunt Winnie's bound to find out one day."

Deveraux, who did not know of the senseless subterfuge, looked bewildered.

"Fiona," said Grace, "we'll talk about this later. I've got my seminar tonight. When we come back we'll have a nice, long chat."

"Hey," said Deveraux. "I've got a good idea. Why don't I show Fiona around a bit while you're at school?" He jumped boyishly from the counter, looking eager and trustworthy.

Fiona helped herself to grilled tomato. "If Grace wouldn't mind," she said almost coquettishly.

"No, of course not. You two go off and have a fine time while I laugh it up with my group of tragically deluded, heartbreakingly untalented immigrants and widows." She laughed, to show it was a joke.

"Fine, then," said Fiona.

"Super," said Deveraux.

At Grace's place on the long seminar table reposed a box of chocolates, carefully centered and topped with a small white card. "For being so sweet to my mother," read the neat script. "Thanks!—Dorothy Dorfman." Grace had forgotten the coincidence which had so jarred her earlier; indeed she had forgotten the old people's plight altogether.

"You didn't have to do this," said Grace. They were the only people to have arrived, although it was nearly six-fifteen.

"Oh, but I wanted to," said Mrs. Dorfman. "You were so good to Mother, and I'm sure you didn't even realize she was *mine.*"

"No, I didn't," said Grace, "but then I saw your picture in her bedroom." Hastily, lest Mrs. Dorfman think she had been snooping, she explained: "I went in there to turn the radio off."

"Do you know how I knew it was you?" asked Mrs. Dorfman rather coyly. Slowly, she dipped into her large handbag and extracted a pale blue airmail envelope. "This was put in Mother's mailbox the day before—she was going to pop it in your box, but the excitement over the elevator made her forget all about it. I can't see how the mailman could confuse 'Peacock' and 'Kriapine,' can you?"

Grace took Fiona's letter and smiled weakly.

"Poor Mother," sighed Mrs. Dorfman, obviously encouraged by the brace of coincidences to confide in Grace, "she's getting so difficult. She's bright as a button, but her poor mind gets things confused. Just the other day she asked me if I'd had a good time in Florida. I said: 'Mother, that was three years ago I went to Florida,' but she just shook her head and said: 'No, dear, you just got back home, don't you remember?' And sometimes she'll call and tell me she's seen me on television." Mrs. Dorfman lowered her voice. "She must have been watching one of those National Geographic shows, you know, with all the naked colored women, because she said: 'Dorothy, you shouldn't dance around like that without your brassiere on. It doesn't look good at your age." Mrs. Dorfman regarded Grace reproachfully. "I suppose your own mother isn't old enough to be senile yet?"

Grace shook her head.

"It's no picnic, I can tell you."

Heavy footfalls could be heard in the hallway. "Good evening, ladies," said Mr. Buonsuccesso, lowering his briefcase to half-mast and settling in with a groan of well-being. "I read in the papers where Saul Bellow is getting another prize." He was followed almost immediately by Alicia LoCasso, who explained that her friend O'Toole was having a pregnancy terminated and would not be with them tonight, causing Mrs. Dorfman to tighten her lips fastidiously. The incident went no further, because Mrs. Klein and Alonzo García arrived together, although surely not by design, and Grace decided to begin without the others.

"Mr. García, what have you brought for us tonight?" she asked, trying to make her voice less overtly kind when addressing him. It would not do to let him know that he reduced her almost to tears each time he opened his mouth.

He flushed and withdrew a sheaf of papers from his bulging folder. "I think," he said in his apologetic voice, "that I will read the latest chapter?" They were in for more of *The New World: Pathway to Despair,* and the two older women sighed ever so slightly.

"It was very hot in the apartment on 116th Street," began Mr. García:

> Wherever I would go the heat persisted. It was not like the heat in Puerto Rico, where all of life is geared to hotness. It was the heat of New York, where the sun's rays sink into the old stone of the tenements and keep everything hot even after the sun have gone down. I was told it was also very humid in New York City, and boy, was that true! All ready my clean shirt was soaked with sweat and I felt dirty. That was another thing about life in New York. You always felt dirty, even after you just took a bath . . .

Mrs. Klein leaned forward and made a notation on the clean page of her composition book. This made Mr. García stop dead, as if someone had rung a bell.

"Go on," said Grace.

> . . . even after you just took a bath. There were many questions I wanted to ask of myself, but the noise of my neighbor's radio was blaring so loud from the fire escape I couldn't hear myself think. They say Puerto Ricans are naturally loud people, I thought to myself, but I, for one, would appreciate some quiet! Yes. Quiet! Did that make me some sort of crazy person? I work hard all day and wanted to come home and relax. You tell people Puerto Ricans like noise, and pretty soon they will begin to believe it . . .

His voice, soft and less timid now that he had begun to hit his stride, pleased Grace. Mr. García's syntax did not detract from the soothing effect his epic novel always had on her. She would give him a grammar book, marking certain passages, and commend him on his efforts. He would get an A. This was not, strictly speaking, fair, but how could one hope to be fair at the university? Her professor friend had told her numerous anecdotes about the grading system. Once a student's mother had tried to bribe him with a bottle of Scotch, thrusting it at him in a brown paper bag near the bank of the elevators. "If not an A—a B? B+?" she had hissed, haggling over her son's academic future. The dean had many times cautioned the faculty against grading too harshly. He did not precisely say it in so many words, but instead spoke eloquently of the need for minority-group grants. It was possible to scan the long columns of grades posted on the upper floors and never see anything lower than a C+. Grace could not have tolerated such mendacity in a serious teaching job, but then she was hardly a serious teacher. She was merely an adjunct shepherding her little troupe through the mysteries of what the brochure called "Creative Writing," and she would simply have to practice creative grading. Yes, an A for Mr. García, because he moved her, and wasn't that what writing was all about? As for Mr. Buonsuccesso, whose turn was coming up, she could hardly justify giving him an A. Yet he wrote much more clearly than did Alonzo; perhaps there was even a future for him, once he had had the pretensions knocked out of him, on a magazine such as the one Jules had edited. If she gave Mr.

Buonsuccesso a lesser grade than Alonzo's, he would surely take the matter to the dean. If, that is, he could find the dean. And what of the two older women? Miss LoCasso? Mr. Ottway? Perhaps they should all get a C?

"Are you alright, Miss Peacock?" Mr. García inclined tremblingly toward her, looking concerned. Grace realized with a sense of alarm that she had allowed her head to rest on her arms, as if in despair, just at the culmination of Mr. García's reading.

"I was only thinking about what you've read us," said Grace. "I want you to know that, despite numerous grammatical errors, I'm very *fond* of your writing." This was extremely weak, but Mr. García beamed, then folded his papers away as if glad to remove them from sight. Mrs. Klein had compiled every instance in which Mr. García's cases had not agreed, but she was more concerned with a grievance of her own.

"I couldn't sympathize more with you about the noise," she said firmly. "I have a neighbor who is unbelievably selfish. His stereo is right against my living room wall, and when he turns the bass speakers up, it sounds just like thunder."

"What I can't stand," said Mr. Buonsuccesso, "is those little yapping dogs that are tied up to parking meters outside the supermarkets."

"At least you don't have to hear them in your own home," said Mrs. Klein.

"You do if you live right over the supermarket," said Mr. Buonsuccesso, hoping to get a laugh from Grace.

"Are we," she said austerely, "to hear more of your modern *Faust?*"

But Mr. Buonsuccesso was born to be upstaged. Grace saw a look of astonishment cross the face of Miss LoCasso, who sat facing the door. Turning to see what had caused it, she found herself staring at a frail black child who had apparently wandered into the seminar room by mistake. He was neatly dressed, and carried several university notebooks under one arm. She was about to ask what he wanted, when he smiled and she realized it was Mr. Ottway, shorn of his apocalyptic Afro.

"Why, Gilbert," she said, "I didn't recognize you."

"Does hair make the man?" he retorted smartly, and slid into a vacant seat. His strange appearance had a silencing effect on the entire company. Even Miss LoCasso smiled uneasily and would volunteer no comment. All during Mr. Buonsuccesso's reading, the focus of attention never shifted from Mr. Ottway's magical new person. The extreme slenderness of his neck was now revealed, and also his delicate eyebrows. He looked, thought Grace, like a *quattrocento* virgin done in black. There was something alarming, unseemly, about it. Where once he had disturbed the older women and Mr. García with his bellicose physical persona, now he invited comparisons with Bambi. When it came time for him to read, he briskly withdrew a single sheet of typewritten paper, squared it neatly on a clipboard, and began:

WHY I CUT MY HAIR

by Gilbert Claude Ottway

This morning I elected to play both Samson and Delilah in the privacy of my bedroom. Standing before my mirror, surveying the face which has greeted me mornings without number, I made a monumental decision. I would, by the simple expedient of removing most of my hair, deprive myself of the sense of power and comfort I now know to have been false. Although I quailed at the thought of the impending defoliation, I seized the shears and began to hack at my enormous, my glorious crest—my burning bush. As if viewed in slow motion, great hanks fell away and drifted to the floor. My hand seemed to move as if receiving instructions from some higher intelligence. My eyes wept at the desecration, but my arm smote again and again until I stood as you see me now. And this, my friends, is the real me. This small, rather ordinary colored boy who could easily play the part of an apprentice porter in a film of the forties.

Why, you may be asking, would I choose to do such a thing? Rob myself of physical distinction? Put away any thought of self-mutilation, self-hatred brought on by the cumulative effects of four hundred years of oppression. Also banish suspicions having to do with warped religious impulses. These do not apply in my case although they may, alas, have meaning for less fortunate members of my race. No. I cut my hair because I have suspected for a long time that black "Identity"—that any identity at all beyond that which might be tagged to one's big toe in the city morgue, is a terrible fake. I will repeat that. A terrible fake. "Black is beautiful!" they trumpeted at us in the late sixties, when I was only a child. "Black sisters are beautiful, Black brothers are beautiful, old Black men and women are beautiful . . . Black . . . Is . . . Beautiful!"

Directly the message had sunk in, ordinary people like myself, people of color, began to accentuate their "blackness." Clerks at the five and dime ran out to purchase nose rings. Professors of economics and night porters alike sported dashikis and fetish bags. My own aunt, a moderately fashionable woman in her day, took to affecting a do rag at all times. Afros bloomed out over the land like a hydrogen bomb; little girls crippled their fingers in the long and arduous business of fashioning corn rows. All in the name, gentle readers, of getting back to our roots, digging our blackness, snuggling up to the once-despised bosom of Mother Africa. This playacting was all very well for a time. It harmed nobody, or so I thought. It was a well-meaning manipulation; it did not smack of malice. It was like the games of dress-up children are urged to play when it's too rainy to go out—a notorious device for occupying children when they threaten to become sulky with inactivity. Everyone was charmed. And then, ever so slightly, it began to pall. Not, of course, for the children, but for the owners of the toy chest, the costume purveyors, the rulers. Confess it now: aren't you, white reader, bored to death when you read that a sister in Baltimore has hit upon a way to elongate black womens' heads with copper rings? Do you not sigh upon meeting a man named Joseph Poke who calls himself by some fancy Bantu tribal title? Here—in our great university—doesn't the very mention of Black Studies bring on helpless yawns? Don't you want to laugh aloud when, each September, some firebrand from Lenox Avenue demands, *demands,* that Swahili be required for incoming freshmen? I laugh frequently, although two years ago I would not, under the great persuasive canopy of my hair, have been able to.

I have been shorn and reborn. I will not claim allegiance to roots which pull me not at all. I will no longer hide beneath my hair. I am a dark brown man, and if I marry I will probably want a dark brown woman, this color being, to my prejudiced eye, the most pleasing. If a group of dark brown people and a group of white people were stranded at the top of a burning building and it were within my power to rescue some of them, I would probably choose to save the ones who looked like myself. Beyond that I cannot say. We stand alone. We will all die in a matter of a few decades and that—as they say—is that: the only identity I recognize.

Like a man who has given up alcohol or dope or religion, I miss my crutch. I pass my hands in wonderment over my reduced head, longing for my hair. In a few days, though, the pain will be less, and soon I will not feel it at all. In the meantime, I must ask you, my fellow students, to accord me the respect I deserve for discarding this last great illusion of my youth.

Thank you.

"Oh, Lord," said Grace, "who are you really, Mr. Ottway?" They were walking along the southern edge of Central Park, heading for the Oak Bar at the Plaza.

"I am Lucifer," said Mr. Ottway grandly, "or then again, I am the grandson of slaves, the first of my family to get an education. Actually, I'm pretty middle class." He was carrying Grace's attaché case, together with his own. Before the shearing of his Afro, Grace and Gilbert had stood almost eye to eye, but now he reached barely to her jawbone. "Why," he asked, "did you ask me to meet your friends? Rehearse me."

"Deveraux is my lover. He's a documentary film maker, very moody and paranoic. He'll be dying to photograph you, but of course he won't say so. Fiona's English. She's my cousin. Fiona's father was the sort of man who regretted the passing of the Raj, but she's not a bad woman. Very hearty and wholesome. Likes a good laugh."

"Hates wogs?"

"I shouldn't think so, although my uncle used to say 'the wogs begin at Calais.' "

"You realize," said Mr. Ottway, "that you're going back on your word, treating me like a person. I'm disappointed, in a way."

"I consider you," said Grace, "the son I'll never have."

This amused Mr. Ottway so much that he bent almost double in a brief spasm of silent laughter, then popped back up with agility to ask: "What will the film maker think I am to you?"

"My student, of course."

Fiona and Deveraux sat at a window table, talking with animation to a third party whose presence took Grace's breath away.

"There's three of them," said Mr. Ottway suspiciously.

"The other man, the blond one, is named Edward. I don't know how he came to be here, I swear I don't."

"Easy, easy, Miss Peacock. This isn't *Meet the Press.*"

Fiona, who had put on a long flowered skirt which she probably wore to Young Conservative dances in Wiltshire, saw them huddling together in the door and adjusted a momentary look of astonishment, replacing it with one of well-bred anticipation.

"Hello, everyone," cried Grace flamboyantly, before they had reached the table. "This is Mr. Ottway, one of my students. Edward? Nice to see you."

Edward rose, taking Grace's hand and then Mr. Ottway's. He and Mr. Ottway were well matched in the handshaking department. Both had slender, fine-boned fingers and elegant wrists; the two hands, ivory and sable, resembled an interior decorator's stab at something for Brotherhood Week. Deveraux lounged in his seat, nodding briefly and, Grace thought, rather sourly.

"Super to meet you, Mr. Ottway," said Fiona.

"Please do call me Gilbert," said Mr. Ottway. "I would be delighted. Only Miss Peacock is constrained to preserve the formalities."

"Why's that?" asked Deveraux.

Gilbert arched a delicate eyebrow and paused for a beat. "Why, to keep the student-teacher relationship in proper perspective," he said.

"What brings you here, Edward?" said Grace.

"I came to say hello. Fiona and Deveraux kindly asked me to join them."

He was, she knew, suffering acutely from the knowledge that Deveraux, at this moment stuffing nuts into his mouth with a bored and glamorous gesture, was her lover.

"They had ever such a good natter about the Arctic," said Fiona unfeelingly, "didn't you, love?" Grace noticed that Fiona, who had long ago been told the story of Edward's childhood, spoke to him as she would a recalcitrant child or a grown mental patient. Nevertheless, Edward brightened dutifully.

"Yes, we did," he said. "Have you ever been far north, Gilbert?"

"Just last night," said Mr. Ottway with a plum-pudding chuckle, "I was on 145th Street. That's about as far north as I care to go." Then he leaned back in his chair like an aging clubman and cast his eyes about for a waiter. Grace was just deliberating on the proper punishment for him when he abruptly smiled and said to Edward. "I'm sorry. That was rude. It's just that I have these irrepressibly high spirits."

Grace wished herself a thousand miles away. The evening stretched ahead, ghastly in its prospects. Drinks would be ordered and consumed, Fiona would continue to look game but bewildered, Edward would shake with misery and loneliness, and Deveraux would madden her with his sulky demeanor and monosyllabic, competitive remarks. As if he mattered! Mr. Ottway was a mistake, it had been wrong of her to bring him, and she thought briefly of resigning her post at the university. She was unfit to teach, even at so haphazard a center of learning; surely her bad judgment would doom her to a life spent in unwelcome situations—a span of years so dreadful to contemplate, so endless, it appeared to her like a long corridor in which snatches of misunderstood conversation were blown about, buffeted on some sluggish current until she, Grace, literally perished of the cumulative effect of her good intentions.

A despotic waiter now appeared to take their orders. Grace tried to amuse herself by comparing the individual to the drink it selected, but even this was too predictable to be of interest. Fiona, of course, was having gin and bitter lemon, just as she did on her rare visits to the local in Wiltshire. Deveraux wanted a proletarian ale; Edward a Scotch and water, pale and expensive, like himself. Grace asked for vodka and waited, mildly curious, to see what Mr. Ottway would have.

"A grasshopper," he said, with great dignity. The waiter looked offended and went away, and Grace, drunk before strong spirits had crossed her lips, gnawed her thumb and kicked a foot under the table in a suggestive way. She was not even sure whose foot it was.

VIII

Dear [imaginary] daughter,

Girls of your age often brood about death. It is profitless to think of one's own death, over which one has so little control, but the deaths of others are troublesome events. I should like to aid you in the selection of a proper attitude. I shall call this lesson: "Toys in the Car."

When I was eight years old, a friend of my mother's died suddenly and inappropriately. She was driving to a town some fifty miles away to visit her daughter, who had just given birth to a child. It was my mother's friend's first grandchild, and her car was packed with all manner of gifts for the baby. There were a number of stuffed animals: a rabbit, a kitten, a teddy bear, and—my own personal favorite—a plush chipmunk who clasped a leather nut in his little paws. There was also a musical carousel which could be hung above a crib and made to play a tune when activated by a kicking foot. I believe the tune was "Bye-Bye, Baby Bunting."

Although my mother's friend drove cautiously, she ran into some patches of ice near the Wisconsin border and skidded into the next lane. A large Chevrolet going sixty miles an hour hit her broadside, and she was killed immediately. The festivities she had planned did not, of course, take place. When my mother heard of this accident on the six o'clock news she turned quite pale and repeated various phrases the newscaster had used under her breath. She walked rapidly from room to room, lighting several cigarettes so that at one point I was obliged to tell her that three were burning in different parts of the house. Then she made herself a drink and spent a great deal of time on the telephone, talking to friends.

I was awed at the largeness of the tragedy, for it was the first time I had actually known someone who had died out of bed. I was violently excited, and wished that I had friends to telephone, cigarettes to smoke. My elation grew until I thought of running into the wall, head down like a bull, to calm myself. When my mother had at last exhausted the vast circle of her acquaintance, she turned her attention to me. "Think," she said with a peculiar intensity. "Just think, Grace. *Think of the toys in the car.*" When she said these words a true thrill of emotion seized me; so powerful was it that I felt a terrible pressure on my bladder and behind my eyes. My mother, too, was moved. Her lip trembled as she repeated herself, and tears came for the first time. Soon, with a few more incantatory references to the toys in the car, she was weeping openly, her head cradled in her arms and her shoulders heaving with sobs.

I pictured, obediently, the little shoe-button eyes which had gleamed so sweetly; I dwelt on the perky ears and cunning, rakish tails. I even allowed myself to hear the tune of the tiny carousel. Perhaps its mechanism had been released at the moment of impact. Oh, what if "Bye-Bye, Baby Bunting" had tinkled out over the thruway while my mother's friend lay dying, thwarted in her simple, joyous errand? Soon I was fairly shouting with grief. My mother's arms encircled me and together we whimpered and rocked, back and forth, back and forth, ecstatic in our release. It was, perhaps, the happiest moment of my childhood; certainly the happiest shared with my mother.

Much later, lying awake in bed, I made myself cry again and again, experimenting until even the tip of my tongue, flirting against the palate in the creation of the letter "T," produced tears. The shoe-button eyes were no longer necessary.

Do you understand? What we know of grief cannot possibly meet our expectations. Or put it another way: there is no grief, or none worth the name. There is only sentiment. Train yourself to respond to it; train yourself as rigorously as would an athlete. If you fail to do so you will know a terrible bewilderment and suffer much more than you can, at present, imagine. Heed my advice and you will simulate suffering so expertly that you yourself will be fooled!

Here is the most important part. *Learn this trick, and then forget that you have learned it.*

Your loving mother,
etc., etc., etc.

Grace had never seen Fiona drunk before. At the local in Wiltshire, Fiona had always taken a drink to be sociable, but she had never before, in Grace's company, packed away six gins in less than two hours. Now she sat, alternately chuckling to herself and staring straight ahead, looking like a wax candle that had been burning down. Remarkable, thought Grace, the effects of liquor. Fiona's cheeks glowed a more vivid red than they had done when Grace first spied her in the Oak Bar; her cousin's Wedgwood eyes, normally clear and sensible, glittered with a mad and histrionic cast when Edward, ever courteous, asked if she felt quite right.

"Two's my limit," she replied, intimating that Edward should have known as much. "After two drinks I'm not myself." Then she covered her mouth as if she had been guilty of an outrageous double entendre. "Ask Grace. Grace knows what I'm like." She laughed merrily, tossing her hair and darting conspiratorial looks in Grace's direction.

Deveraux was looking interested. "What does she mean?" he asked.

"I don't know," said Grace. "What do you mean, Fiona? What are you like when you have one too many?"

"Probably," Mr. Ottway said glumly in Grace's ear, "she's going to want to jump in the fountain."

Fiona wouldn't say. She continued to laugh knowingly to herself, inclining toward Grace as if to recall some long-ago occasion on which she had run barefoot through the county fields, or danced naked on tabletops.

"Perhaps we should go?" suggested Edward, the only one of them to feel genuine concern.

"Oh, please, no! No, no, no! I'm having ever such a grand time, really I am. It's what I always thought an evening out would be like, here in New York. All of us together, sitting inside with the great dangerous city pressing against the windows. Such a . . . motley group we are. Simply super. Fascinating."

"Motley," said Mr. Ottway, "means me."

Fiona leaned forward excitedly. "I didn't mean anything to do with your being colored," she said. "I meant our relations. Relations to each other."

"And what," said Deveraux with a glimmer of evil intent, "might those be?"

Fiona clasped her hands and looked lofty, a drunken scholar. "Grace and I," she said, "are cousins. Of course you all know that. Daddy and her father were brothers. We are related by blood, and yet we hardly know each other. Grace feels quite superior to me—oh, yes, you do, Grace, because I just poke around my dear little village and I'm not up to much and don't have interesting affairs—and I feel superior to her because of the letters to Aunt Winnie. Grace depends on me for those. You see? Are you beginning to see?"

"Oh, God," said Grace, "someone get her some coffee."

"Aunt *Winnie,*" said Mr. Ottway sonorously, as if testing the quality of his voice before a microphone. He bit his thumb to suppress laughter; his shoulders were shaking. Throughout Fiona's recital Grace could hear him repeating "Aunt Winnie" to himself in delighted disbelief.

"Deveraux is Grace's young man," continued Fiona. "Deveraux is Grace's—let's call it by its proper name—lover. He knows that Edward, here, used to be married to Grace, and Edward, here, knows that Deveraux makes love to Grace these days, and both of them know that Gilbert, here, is Grace's student, and Grace knows . . ." She looked momentarily daunted, as if the train of her thought had vanished in the bottom of her glass, but she made a swift recovery. "Grace doesn't know anything," she finished triumphantly. "Grace doesn't know anything about anything, and she never did. Grace is a hoax. A lovely, clever hoax." Fiona hiccuped gently, then stared at her cousin defiantly. "A hoax," she repeated.

In the silence that followed three things happened. Edward's hand shot out as if to ward off a blow, then crept along the tabletop to Grace's wrist. Deveraux applauded silently, urging Grace with his eyes to acknowledge the haphazard wisdom of Fiona's outburst. Mr. Ottway uncapped an old-fashioned fountain pen, made a brief notation on his cocktail napkin, and sat forward alertly.

Grace hardly knew what to say. She felt exhilarated, humbled. Never before had she heard anyone, with the possible exception of Sam Briscoe, whose venom was too extreme to be taken seriously, speak out like a character in a stirring, third-rate play. She had been pegged by her tipsy cousin, slotted and filed, and in exactly the words she privately reserved for herself. A hoax! Why, yes, how clever of Fiona to perceive her fraudulence. Accusations of coldness, frivolity, lack of charity or motivation—these she might have expected, but this attack from the rear, this altogether barbarous and amazing pronouncement from such an unlikely quarter, thrilled her. The unexpected could still happen, even in the Oak Bar of the Plaza Hotel; there was something in the nature of a revelation wrapped up in this silly incident, something to be investigated. And yet, even now, her time was not her own. Claims were being made. Edward's hand, cold and trembling, hovered on her wrist. He wanted to insulate her from pain where there was no pain—always an issue between them—and had to be reassured. She grasped his hand, returning the pressure of those slender, aristocratic fingers, and was framing her reply when Fiona's head hit the table.

"I'm fine," Fiona droned, speaking into her cupped palm, "perfectly fine. Make believe I'm not here."

They got her into a Checker cab, where she collapsed against Mr. Ottway's frail shoulder, still protesting. Deveraux and Edward took the jump seats, Edward austere and Deveraux obviously amused. The taxi jolted forward and Mr. Ottway said:

"My, my. How you folk do carry on."

No other words were spoken until the cab drew up in front of Grace's building, and then Deveraux announced in a loud, unnatural voice: "I'll get this, Woolas."

Woolas! Never had Grace imagined that Deveraux might know Edward's surname. It touched her that he would refer to Edward thus; it was so desperately manly, so unlike Dev, that she had a quick vision of him as unknown territory. She pictured him in his tent in Guatemala, squatting over a spirit stove and calculating lens angles, perhaps waiting for an Indian girl with conical breasts whose ancestors had eaten human flesh to present herself at the flap of his tent. Seeing him for the first time as a stranger, she wanted him wholly, physically, and without hope of immediate gratification.

Mr. Ottway was trying to rouse Fiona, who snickered into his shoulder that it had been a super evening. It took forever for them to disembark from the cab. Grace stood, alone and curious, while they emerged in sections. Deveraux clambered out first, leaning through to pay the driver, while Edward and Mr. Ottway maneuvered Fiona out the door and onto the pavement. Fiona's coat was buttoned wrong, rucking up on one side, and her eyes were unfocused. Nevertheless, she threw off the helping hands imperiously and began to reel toward the door of Grace's building. Edward hovered, looking tense and miserable, at one of her elbows.

"There'll always be an England," said Mr. Ottway.

Together, the five of them walked up under the long, canopied entrance. Grace was afraid that old Maurice might be lingering at the elevator or—worse yet—Mrs. Dorfman, returning from a filial visit to the twelfth floor, but the lobby was deserted and silent. Julio had waxed the floors earlier in the evening and they shone, proof that Grace had been capable of selecting a clean, fragrant building in which to conduct her fraudulent life.

"Coffee is in order," said Mr. Ottway. "The evening must continue." Nobody answered him.

The elevator crept to her floor without event, and all of them filed into the darkened apartment with a solemn, anticipatory air. It was not even late, as Mr. Ottway reminded them.

"It's the shank of the evening," he said quaintly. "The very shank."

Grace awakened feeling worse than she could ever recall having felt. There was a tenative quality, as always, to her awakening—she did not want to regain consciousness too quickly, to find the hands on her clock set at too early an hour, to know that great spaces of time must be lived through before she might find herself in some meaningful portion of the day. This morning—or was it afternoon? —carried with it extra anxiety, because she could not properly remember what had happened the night before. She did not know whom she might expect to find scattered around the premises and this, even for so dislocated a person as herself, was unusual. A body count, the police called it. Very well, she would prepare herself to make a body count.

She thought she could remember Fiona lying, fully clothed, on the couch in the living room. Well-bred child of the Empire that she was, Fiona had not wanted to make a fuss, to usurp the territory of another. She had made her nest where she believed a guest should lie, except, of course, that had meant the rest of them must go to the bedroom in order not to disturb her. Yes, that had been what had happened.

The texture beneath Grace's cheek did not speak of linen pillowcases; it was hairy, oily somehow, and abrasive. She was lying, it seemed, on the floor. She swept her hands out and about her person and encountered another body close by. Deveraux? Timidly she investigated the torso, finding it clothed and narrow. Edward, then, or Mr. Ottway. She opened her eyes, made them fly open all at once, and surveyed her bedroom. It might have been an air-raid shelter, or an ashram. To her left lay Mr. Ottway, his body folded in a supple Z, head sweetly cradled in his paws like a forest animal. His lashes splayed upon his dark cheeks, and he seemed to smile in sleep. To her right was the prone body of Deveraux, divested of his Indian sweater, which lay beneath her cheek, but otherwise decently attired. One of his arms lay outthrust, the forefinger pointing dramatically at the bed.

Nobody, however, lay upon the bed. The counterpane was smooth, undented. Even the pillows were plump and virgin; in the pale light she could not see them clearly, but she felt sure there were no indentations, no stray hairs or spots. Through the connecting door she could make out the sleeping continent of Fiona. One splendid leg was thrown outside the quilt which covered her, still wearing the flowered skirt which had witnessed its owner's fall from grace in the Oak Bar. Fiona was snoring fitfully, thrashing about in a vain effort to recapture the wholesome, nightgowned slumber she normally enjoyed. Where then was Edward?

Quietly, Grace gathered herself together for the effort it would take to rise. Her limbs creaked, audibly, and she was so stiff it seemed almost a cruel preview of old age. Was this how old Maurice felt in the morning? Did Mrs. Kriapine rise from her coquettish bed as from a rack, cursing the daughter who had ten good years left before she, too, knew her body to be a lightly covered skeleton, a sack of brittle sticks? Grace's head felt large and watery. Was this what it was like to waken after an orgy? Had there been an orgy? Her body informed her that nothing of a sexual nature had occurred, that nobody had entered her that night past, and yet she felt much as she had done on the day she performed the errands for the old people. Heavy with possibilities, or at least primed for possibilities. Mr. Ottway smiled more deeply as she stepped over him, and, wrapping Dev's hairy sweater about her shoulders, she moved toward the shadowy hallway.

As always, when she could not immediately locate Edward, her mind came alive with dreadful images. In the time they had lived together she had always expected to find him dead in some room of their flat. Without admitting it, ever, her inner eye had countless times prepared her for the sight of Edward hanging in the closet, or slumped over the rolltop desk, bleeding decorously into the double-thick blotter. Not for him anything extreme or unsightly. The gun properly placed in mouth or the person vertical, like one of his suits, in a cavern fragrant with sandalwood—these would be his style, his method of departing. He was far too considerate to cut a vein or leap into midday crowds; he did not believe in pills and although he drank constantly he never lost control. Unlike Jules, he could not meet his death through an error in judgment. Now she thought of the roof and pitied herself for having, always, to tremble for the sake of others. "Edward, Edward," she called softly, heading for the kitchen where a dim light burned. "Edward, are you there?"

He lay across the kitchen table, his head in the precise center of one of her confessions magazines, which was open to a story about an unfit mother. Grace could see the blurb at his temple; it seemed to issue from his head. IF JOHNNY DIED I HAD ONLY MYSELF TO BLAME—STAN'S HOT KISSES MADE ME FORGET ALL ABOUT MY INFANT SON! Although Edward's hands indicated a certain abandon, flung as they were at careless angles across the polished oak, his feet were crossed neatly at the ankle. His breath was even, untroubled; he was alive.

Grateful, jubilant, she smoothed back his hair and noticed with sadness that many gray threads had appeared, as if by magic, on Edward's head. She examined them with interest, lifting them against the light, testing their resiliency and luster. They were wirier, had, in fact, more tensile strength, than the others. She thought this might be a good omen for Edward, might indicate that he—in direct opposition to Mr. Ottway—was being regenerated despite himself. Mr. Ottway was young. He could afford to throw power to the floor in order to honor vague, metaphysical concepts. It was the appropriate gesture for one of his years.

Edward—older, sadder—slept on Grace's kitchen table unaware that a new day was approaching, unable to realize that he was being rooted, like it or not, to life. All his vast resources could not disconnect him. Like Grace, he was fated to stick around for the duration.

Much later, Fiona came rapping at the door. Everyone else had gone. Grace had lain, chaste in her own bed, feigning sleep, while they wakened and tiptoed about, trying not to disturb her. Deveraux had been the last to leave, although he was the first to stir. Grace lay immobile, one hand lightly thrown over her face so that she could squint through the fingers, undetected. Deveraux had looked at her recumbent form with what seemed, to her myopic gaze, a mixture of tenderness and despair. Nothing in his look indicated that he might be disgusted or angry and—as the evening's events came back to her in snippets—she realized there was no cause for shame. Deveraux's despairing look was merely the natural expression he assumed in his dealings with Grace. It was, of course, an overstatement. What he felt about her most, she thought, was bewilderment. He disappeared for a time, and she could hear water running in the bathroom, then the sound of muted conversation as Edward was roused from his kitchen slumbers.

Soon the smells of coffee wafted down the hall, but as much as she wanted some, she felt she must remain in bed, dead to the world in several senses, until the house cleared out. Besides, Mr. Ottway had begun to stir on the floor at her feet. She gave a mock groan and turned to her side, the better to observe his matutinal behavior. His lashes fluttered several times, then snapped open smartly. To Grace's discomfort he said: "Good morning." She continued to breathe, evenly and regularly, observing him through slitted eyelids. He sat up all in one nimble motion, smoothed his hands over his shorn head, and sprang to his feet. "I hope," he said, "I haven't outstayed my welcome."

Edward appeared at the door, solicitous. "There's coffee, Gilbert," he whispered, and withdrew.

Mr. Ottway approached the bed as Deveraux had done. "The trouble is," he said instructively, "when people are faking that they're asleep, they breathe too hard."

From that point onward, Grace kept her eyes shut and breathed as shallowly and convincingly as possible. Various footsteps approached the bed, Deveraux's firm and proprietary, Edward's hesitant. Fingers scrabbled on the bedside table, a note was written and propped near her alarm clock; Dev's Guatemalan sweater sleeve brushed her cheek, but Mr. Ottway never entered the room again. Only when all three had left did she fall asleep in earnest. She had forgotten that Fiona still lay across the passageway.

Now Fiona was entering her room, looming up as she had done in Grace's fantasy, except that everything was backward. Fiona's face was the last thing she saw, and when she focused on it she saw that her cousin had been crying. Her first thought was that Fiona harbored vague, maidenly passions for Deveraux and was coming to make a clean breast of it. Or could Dev have approached her in those hours before Edward surprised them and suggested Anglo-American relations of a sexual nature? Operating on malevolent and spiteful impulse, both of them unable to ignore an opportunity of expressing the secret contempt they nurtured for Grace, could Fiona and Deveraux have fucked away the afternoon, snickering together guiltily while Grace sat in her seminar room? That might have explained Fiona's outburst; armed with Dev's approval, she might have delivered her sermon on fraudulence with the memory of him still warm and frisky between her neatly crossed legs . . .

Fiona did not look sly. Nothing of remorse or triumph, either one, was present in her face as she approached the bed.

"Grace?" Fiona's weight depressed one side of the bed. "It's afternoon, Grace. Let's talk."

"Okay," said Grace. "How do you feel? You were very entertaining last night."

Fiona brushed away the topic of last night, as if it could not possibly interest anyone. "I couldn't help it," she said in a remote voice. "I get that way lately."

"How's that? Drunk, you mean?"

"Oh, look here," said Fiona impatiently, "I know I wasn't very nice. Ever so sorry and all that."

"You called me a fraud."

"Oh, for God's sake, Grace, can't you stop being so bloody self-centered? I'm trying to tell you something and all you can think of is that I made a few hostile bloody remarks."

Better and better. Grace had never heard Fiona use the word "bloody" twice in one sentence. It was so unusual that Grace sat up against her pillows and gave her cousin a shrewd and sympathetic look. "You have all my attention," she said.

"The thing is," said Fiona, "I'm pregnant. I'm going to have a baby."

If Fiona had struck her she could not have been more shocked. She let the import of Fiona's message sink in, and when it had she felt immediately and totally responsible. For almost the first time she felt what it must be to know guilt. She, Grace, was to blame. She had woven a confessions story about her cousin, placed Fiona in the tweedy arms of Richard Bowstitch, had them discard their native caution and decency as they satisfied their pent-up lust in the hedges and lanes of a Wiltshire village. *She* had impregnated Fiona, placed Farmer Bowstitch's throbbing cock in her cousin's body, directed his sperm, as it were, and willed life to grow where it was not wanted. She had knocked Fiona up, placing a squalling baby in Cygnet Cottage and ruining Fiona's life for a momentary whim, an act of fictional frivolity.

"It's all my fault," she said soberly. "I'm so sorry."

Fiona's reddened eyes opened wide, then drooped again. "Even now," she said with distaste, "all you can think of is yourself."

"No—you don't understand. I made up a little scenario, a story, just before I got your letter. I didn't have anything else to do, and it struck me you'd make such a good *True Story* heroine—you and Bowstitch were the perfect star-crossed lovers. You know what I mean, don't you? There he is, with that tragic drunken wife, mooning at you over the village green . . . You try to stay good and decent, but it's too much for you. One thing leads to another and you meet him in his Norfolk jacket on Market Day and, well . . . I *did* it, Fiona, I made it up! Not for publication, of course, just for my own pleasure. Your baby's name was Little Johnny."

Fiona was looking astonished. "Bowstitch? Richard Bowstitch? You thought I was having a thing with *him?*"

Grace lay quiet against her pillows, confused and terrified. "I thought you'd like to," she said. "It was all quite fictional."

Fiona laughed, arching her neck back and emitting peal after peal of silvery, mocking merriment. It was a trick all the Peacocks had mastered, all except Grace.

"Grace—Richard is bent! He's a pouf! He's always been that way. He's a terribly nice chap, of course, and utterly devoted to his children, but he's queer as a three-eyed codfish!" Fiona laughed again, shaking her head and bouncing slightly on the bed. "Crumbs, Grace, who'd ever think you could be so *naïve?*" She had recovered her idiotic high spirits. She didn't seem to recall, thought Grace with wonderment, that she was pregnant and unmarried. Alone and expecting a child, in a strange country and at the mercy of a naïve and fraudulent cousin . . . why was this woman laughing?

"Who is it then?" Grace asked.

"Oh," Fiona lowered her eyes, allowing her cheeks to become suffused with a becoming, bridelike flush, "someone I'm frightfully keen on. We've been seeing each other off and on for the past year." She smiled luminously. "He breeds dogs. His name is Emil."

"He doesn't sound very English."

"Well, why ever should he? He's Hungarian, as a matter of fact, but he's lived in England for donkey's years."

"Why the tears, then? What's the trouble?"

Fiona smiled maternally. "I wasn't really crying," she said. "I was having a bit of a throw-up. Pregnancy does that to you—alters the body alarmingly. I expect that's why I got so tiddly last night. I'm quite happy, really. It's just that arrangements have to be made."

Grace did not reply.

"Emil and I aren't going to be married, you see. He's got a wife already, and I don't much care about marriage in any case. If it weren't for Mother I'd have the baby in England and move closer to Emil—he travels to Winchester a good deal—and everything would be fine. But Mother is so conventional—you remember, Grace! It wouldn't be fair to her, she wouldn't understand, if you see what I mean. I went to Toronto half expecting to tell her, but when I saw her I couldn't. I simply couldn't."

"Abortions are legal in England," said Grace. "You didn't have to come to New York."

Fiona sighed patiently. "I want the baby, Grace. I intend to have it."

"I'm happy for you, then, but I can't understand where I come into all of this? Is there something you need from me?"

Fiona clasped Grace's unwilling hand, holding it firmly and looking at her cousin with an intensity which filled Grace with dread. "Try to understand," Fiona said in the tones of a barber-surgeon about to amputate a leg. "I've always been one for family ties. I'm not like you, Grace. I can't exist all alone at the edges of the world. I don't like deception, but in this case it's got to be. I'm going to tell Mummy I adopted the baby—single women do, you know—and she'll be very pleased once she gets used to the idea. But, Grace, I don't want to have the baby by myself, without anyone near me. Emil will help with supporting it, but he can't be with me, really *with* me, when I go through with it."

"You want to have the baby here?" Grace gestured feebly, hoping to indicate with one sweep of her hand the total implausibility of such a scheme.

"Good gracious, of course not! I'm going to Aunt Winnie. It's all arranged. Afterwards, I'll go back to England."

IX

I struggled up out of the darkness, my heart beating wildly. It was the phone again, shrilling through the peaceful night like a warning siren. One of these nights, I thought with dread, it would wake Kimberleigh. She would toddle to the hall stand and grab for the receiver with chubby, dimpled fists. "Me wanna talk to Daddy," she always gurgled when the phone rang during the day. How could I tell her? How could I explain to a two-year-old cherub that a sex maniac called her Mommy every night? That someone, somewhere, knew the desperate loneliness which tormented me now that Chet had left . . .

"Who is it?" I hissed into the phone, wrapping my worn robe around my body as if it could shield me. "Hi, baby," came the familiar voice, low and intimate. "Just thought I'd check in. I knew you'd cry yourself to sleep if I didn't call." There was a low, insolent chuckle.

I slumped against the wall, shivering. "Look," I grated furiously, "whoever you are—this has to stop. What sort of woman do you think I am?"

Again the laugh. "I'd sure like to find out, sweetheart. Just say the word . . ."

"Stop it!" I cried. "Why are you torturing me like this? I've never done anything to *you!*"

"I know what I'd like to do to *you,* though," my caller crooned. "First, I'd like to—"

"Stop!" I screamed. There was a sound from Kimberleigh's room. Automatically, I lowered my voice. "You're sick. You need help."

"Aw, come off it, lover. You're the one who's sick—sick from needing a man. You love it, baby. If you don't, how come you don't hang up?"

I wanted to scream, to rip the phone from the wall. Instead, heart pounding, I brought my lips close to the phone and said: "If my husband knew who you were, he'd kill you . . ."

The laugh at the other end was chilling now. "Tell him," he said contemptuously. "That is, if he ever comes back to you . . ." And then it began, the long, slow river of words—words that made me burn with shame. Words that told me which parts of my body he would linger over with his deft caresses . . . how he'd make me cry out with ecstasy . . . how I wouldn't be able to have enough of him. And all the while, beneath the burning revulsion, I was responding to his filth. The soft slur of obscene words seemed to wash over my starved body like little tongues of flame.

"Stop, stop," I sobbed into the phone. "Oh, please, please—" But I didn't hang up until his soft laugh told me he was through for the night. I sank to the floor, every nerve-ending jangling. "Help me," I whispered into the darkness. "Give me strength." I wasn't even sure what I meant. I only knew I wouldn't sleep again that night . . .

"I can't imagine," said Jenny, "why you should be so upset about it."

Grace cast a despairing eye at the next table, where a buxom woman in a jaunty knitted cap sat, head in hand, nodding down in the direction of her plate. No help from that quarter.

"My cousin is running off to have her baby in the company of my mother, who, in case you've forgotten, thinks I live in England, and you can't understand why I should mind?"

Jenny said nothing.

"Well, of course, put like that, I see what you mean. It's just so messy—so *familyish.* Why can't Fiona go to a nursing home?"

Jenny smiled, apparently enjoying Grace's fall from reason. They sat in the greasy spoon which had recently opened directly beneath Grace's building. It catered mainly to junkies and pimps and was a great source of annoyance to the old people. Even as Grace and Jenny sat, idly turning spoons in plastic cups of lukewarm coffee, a fight was erupting near the cash register. A woman dressed in numerous layers of clothing had attempted to leave without paying.

"Oh, boy," said Jenny, "the places you frequent." She said this without malice; Grace suspected she was enjoying herself immensely. When she returned to Sam they would be able to discuss Grace's penchant for the sordid to their heart's content.

"I didn't know you were planning to drop in," Grace said. She shrugged. "I didn't want to talk in front of Fiona. Anyway, it's convenient, right downstairs."

"Well," said Jenny brightly, "convenient for *whom?*"

Neither of them could finish the coffee. Jenny pushed hers away decisively; Grace buried her own cup beneath a paper napkin. She wanted it out of sight. Jenny, as Grace well knew, did not drop in for nothing. There was something she wanted to discuss, something which required Grace's presence as a sounding board. Jenny might not be so fond of Grace as she had once been, but Grace was the only person who had known her since her early, unenlightened days—the days in which Jenny had been so much nicer—and was valuable to Jenny as a sort of human diary. Jenny liked continuity, and in that was not so very different from Fiona, who needed to birth her baby near another Peacock. It was not an uncommon instinct. In fact, thought Grace, only she herself disturbed the order of things, breaking the circle and refusing to flow smoothly into the great sticky backwaters of their common experience. If I were Old King Cole, she thought, I would call for Chaos.

"In eight years," Jenny began abruptly, "I've never been really unfaithful to Sam."

Grace nodded. It was to be a confession, then. "Let's leave," she said. "It's not a place to discuss sex."

The remainder of the afternoon was spent in a detailed analysis of Jenny's affair with her therapist, a man so like Sam, it seemed, that the infidelity was lessened.

"Sam would really *like* Martin," Jenny said earnestly as they strolled up Broadway. "In some ways, he'd approve."

"Don't count on it."

"I've even thought of having Martin to dinner, but I couldn't do it. Not because he's my lover, of course, but because he's my shrink."

Grace sighed.

"I'm happier than I've ever been," Jenny said as they turned toward Central Park West. "Martin sees things about me that Sam has consistently blocked out. For example: about you. I've told him how I love you even though you're so impossible, and you know what he said? He said Sam is *jealous* of you because you've known me so much longer. It's perfectly obvious, of course, but I'd never thought of it that way. You knew me when I was always falling in love with fags back in college"—Jenny held up a gloved hand, ticking particulars off on her fingers as Deveraux was wont to do—"you saw me through my ridiculous suicide attempt, and my depressed periods, and my engagement to that rotten little pimp of a Dominican. Compared to you, Sam is just a Johnny-come-lately!"

Grace would not have described Sam in these terms, but she nodded judiciously. Jenny was so unlike a confessions-story heroine that Grace could not readily convert the adulterous tale now unfolding, but even so she tried out various titles: MY DOCTOR CURED MY LOVE-ACHE? MY HUSBAND'S BLUE CROSS COVERED THOSE AFTERNOONS OF ECSTASY? It wouldn't do. Jenny would never learn to sin and suffer and repent. There was no redemption for Jenny because she had been born redeemed.

They were turning into Naomi's building when Jenny confided, lowering her eyes and smiling slyly, that she and Martin had yet to know each other in the biblical sense. Their sex, she said, much to the interest of the elevator man, was strictly oral at this juncture. "It's terrible," she giggled close to Grace's ear, "but I don't really feel I've betrayed Sam. Not so long as we only do *munchies.*"

Naomi's apartment seemed densely packed with people, although in fact there were only Naomi, Alice, and Alice's friend Jennifer on the premises. From a back room a television blared, unwatched.

"Turn it off," Naomi said to Alice. "You're not watching it." Immediately the girls stomped off down the hall, entering a mysterious room in back. Presently the television's volume was escalated, and a heated argument could be heard in which Jennifer and Alice called each other "nigger."

"They all do that," said Naomi apologetically. "The word doesn't mean the same thing anymore." The grown-ups retired to Naomi's kitchen, safely sealed away from the children. Naomi rummaged in her cupboards and produced a can of mixed party nuts and a half-full bottle of sherry. She was not a drinker. She sat, massaging her ankles and smiling almost dazedly at her guests. "What a pleasure this is," she said several times. "Nobody ever just drops in."

Privately Grace thought this an enviable state of affairs. What would Naomi do if pregnant cousins and ex-husbands and seminar students trooped through her life and home as regularly as they did through Grace's own? On the other hand, Naomi had a family and could never be truly alone, so what would a few more bodies mean in the scheme of things? She could not envy Naomi any more than she could envy Jenny. She wanted neither child nor husband. She certainly didn't want to pay seventy dollars an hour for oral sex. She could think of nothing she wanted, only of things she did not want, and these were many. She wanted Fiona not to be pregnant, or rather not to run to Winifred Peacock for her confinement. She wanted not to quarrel with Deveraux about Edward's continued presence in her life. She wanted not to hear, sometime in the future, of Edward's death. She most emphatically wanted not to have to correct and comment upon the huge load of papers her students would shortly be turning in. If asked at gunpoint to name one thing she wanted, she would surely die before scraping up an answer. "Yes," she might shriek in the final moment, "perhaps I want to be the woman in I COULDN'T HANG UP ON MY OBSCENE PHONE CALLER!"

"Do you still want to go to the Midwest?" Naomi asked.

Immediately Jenny sat forward, scrutinizing Grace hawkishly.

"To the Midwest?" she echoed. "Grace hates the Midwest." Then, as if to atone for making Grace a witness to Sam's betrayal, Jenny embarked on a series of anecdotes about Sam's grant.

"The reason a thirteen-year-old kid can knife an old lady without the slightest remorse," she concluded, "is that he doesn't see that old lady as human. He's been knocked around so much himself he can't conceive that extinguishing another life means anything."

"I think Alice suffers from anomie," said Naomi pensively. "The other day she was looking out the window and when I asked her what was so interesting she said: 'There's a man on the roof across the street. Maybe he's going to jump off.' "

"Oh, my dear, no," protested Jenny. "That's normal childhood ghoulishness. The people Sam's studying aren't normal at all. Not by our standards, at least." She popped a few cashews into her mouth and told them about a young mother who had thrown her baby down an airshaft to stop it from crying, and then about some boys who had set an old derelict on fire.

"That happened years ago," said Grace.

"These are new cases," said Jenny. "And how about that double suicide? The old couple who'd been mugged twice in a month? The second time she didn't have any money, and the kid plunged a fork into her face. After that, she and her husband just didn't want to live anymore."

Naomi shuddered. "That reminds me," she said gloomily, "of what happened to Joe's cousin." The cousin, a middle-aged man in the rag trade, had been hospitalized after an automobile accident.

While he recuperated, he sat near his tenth-floor window gazing down into the northerly reaches of Central Park. Here he could observe, with great clarity, the stalking of lone figures who had ventured into the park hoping to take a shortcut to Fifth Avenue. "He said it was like something at the bottom of the ocean. First there'd be the one person, floating along, and then out of the bushes would come other figures, circling in on him like sharks, and then they'd be on him. Pow!" Joe's cousin had been powerless to prevent what he saw. Day after day he was drawn to his window; sometimes he found himself staring down at night, even though he could see nothing. "When he was released," said Naomi, "he was afraid to go out. He had a breakdown, became quite suicidal."

"At least," said Jenny, "he would have done something if he hadn't been so far away. Lots of people just stand around scratching their noses when people are murdered in subway cars. Now *that's* anomie."

Before they left, Grace asked Naomi's opinion on the Fiona situation. Naomi was more sympathetic than Jenny had been, but the stories and the unaccustomed sherry had affected her powerfully. "I don't know," she said, tears in her eyes, "I just don't know."

Deveraux's expression, even as he laughed, warned her serious business was in the offing. Here, in his own apartment, Deveraux always seemed more dignified. For one thing, proof of his professional self was everywhere—still photographs showing him with Bushmen on the plains of central Africa lined the hallway, and an emormous blowup of Dev in Zuni ceremonial garb dominated the living room. Pictish runes transferred to batik served as window curtains; Grace thought they came from the Orkney Islands where Deveraux had spent six weeks working on a film about the Ring of Brogar. Everywhere, at present, lay relics of his Guatemalan trip, including an intricately knotted length of fabric which was intended to make a dress for Grace.

Grace still felt the physical yearning for him which had been so much stronger on the previous evening, when it could not be dealt with satisfactorily. She wanted to ask him about the events of that evening, but feared the repercussions. Edward, the fact of Edward, rankled, and Dev would surely reproach her for "encouraging" him. He would call Edward effete, played-out, ephemeral, thin-blooded—all the adjectives everyone chose in describing Edward—and Grace would feel obliged to come to his defense, to speak of him in terms which could not fail to make Deveraux jealous. Conversation was out of the question. Best to opt for sex and have the conversation afterward; Grace and Deveraux argued far less ferociously when they were naked.

She crossed the room and sat on Dev's lap, feeling suddenly coy and overgrown. She thought of Jenny and her therapist—did they make a pretense of thrashing through Jenny's problems or get right down to business? Did Jenny remove all of her clothes or simply shuck her panties and sprawl on the therapist's Barcalounger? That Jenny wore panties she knew—Jenny had confided to her that going without them made her feel hollow. Thoughts of Jenny gave way to thoughts of Lou-Ann, the woman who received obscene phone calls. Grace thought she knew that Lou-Ann's estranged husband was the culprit, but she had been forced to stop reading when Jenny arrived.

Deveraux traced the line down Grace's back. He was intrigued by backs, preferring them to be strong and well muscled. He had once confessed to Grace that many womens' backs displeased him because their extreme fragility made him think of chicken bones. "I'm very fond of your back," he said, as always. He slipped his hand up under her shirt and stroked her back with strong, slightly calloused fingers. Grace had once read a story in *My Confession* in which the heroine had been excited by her lover's rough-edged fingers—rather daring for a confessions piece—and although the fictional lover had come by his calluses doing construction work she still felt proud of Dev. Irritating or not, he was the sort of man who could arouse a Lou-Ann or a Terri; this was not true of most of the men one met. Would a decent, God-fearing housewife, struggling to plan the week's menu, stop dead in her tracks, abandon her moral precepts, for the likes of Sam Briscoe or Martin the therapist? For Edward, despite his generosity and stony beauty? Deveraux was coddling her breasts now, smiling happily against her shoulder and humming under his breath, a childhood trick, he'd told her, something he'd always done when he was happy. The lap she straddled grew larger, more resistant. Did men who suffered from anomie get erections? They must, how else rape women? Suddenly she thought of Mr. Ottway. His face loomed up vividly and she was startled. She was not a bigot; rape should not immediately remind her of gentle Mr. Ottway. And then she realized that she had been staring over Dev's shoulder at a wooden head, carved in Western Africa, without really seeing it. How like Gilbert's the fluting nostrils were: fastidious without smacking of prissiness.

"What are you thinking?" asked Deveraux suddenly, his voice close in her ear. She turned and kissed him full on the lips, pleased to be there, at that moment, safe from the demands of others and about to make love. She thought herself immensely fortunate. Her feelings about the Mr. Ottway head were companionable rather than lascivious. She had never cherished fantasies about people looking on, but the sudden presence of Mr. Ottway in her sex life was cozy and oddly reassuring. It was like discovering an old friend in new surroundings. She and Dev slid down to the floor, not wanting to break the connection for mere comfort's sake, and lay toe to toe. Deveraux continued to hum lightly as he helped Grace out of her jeans. The last clear thought she had, before he entered into her, was a fervent wish that the large dog in the courtyard not bark. Having an orgasm was a chancy thing at the best of times, and if the dog barked she would surely lose it.

Deveraux paused discreetly, allowing the waiter to remove their plates before he continued. He was treating the subject with more deference than Jenny or Naomi had done.

"Shouldn't you go with her?" he said, pouring wine for her with an extra solicitous flourish. "Isn't it the perfect opportunity?"

"For what?"

"For, oh, making your peace with your mother." Dev looked embarrassed. "You wouldn't have to stay long. And isn't that what you've been talking about—going to the Midwest?"

"I don't have to 'make my peace' with my mother," Grace said disdainfully. "She doesn't even have to know I'm not in England." She felt slumbrous, unable to deal with so many wrongheaded concepts.

"How about your pilgrimage?"

"Wrong Midwest. I need small towns, rural areas. My mother lives in an enormous house. She shops in Chicago; she doesn't know anyone who suffers."

"I know that," Deveraux said, indulgent. "But wouldn't it be a good time to get it out of your system?"

As if, Grace thought, she needed to be detoxified. Dev scarcely concealed his opinion, which was and always had been that Grace's aberrations were serious. He might have been talking to a mental patient when he said: "Look, baby, give it a try. Can't hurt."

She felt suddenly alert, crafty. Deveraux wasn't trying to dispose of her; of his continuing infatuation she felt quite sure. Her momentary jealousy over Fiona (fantastic, that!) had been inspired by the mystery of her cousin's pregnancy, not known to her at the time. It had turned Fiona into a formidable adversary, but Grace had mistaken the cause. No, Deveraux had another reason for wanting to ship her off. He was ordering more wine, priming her for one of his small lectures, setting the scene. Their impetuous lovemaking had mellowed him, made him feel that he might, after all, meddle in her life with impunity. She allowed him this illusion—she too had been pleased, more than pleased, had held him in her arms most fiercely for a long time afterward. It was too easy to be in love.

"Grace," he said, "I think you ought to leave New York for a week or two. I think"— he winced, plunged in—"you need to get away from Woolas. Edward." He blushed.

"Edward would never hurt me."

"Hurt you? Who said he'd hurt you? I only mean it's not healthy to have him hanging around."

"I don't think he'll hang around much longer," she said gently, trying not to laugh at this strange new manifestation of Dev's jealousy. "He has a girlfriend. Christine."

"I know. He brought her around to meet me, earlier this afternoon."

Now he had her. Grace felt astonished at the things which might happen in her absence. While she and Naomi and Jenny had traded ghost stories in the kitchen, Deveraux had been having adventures of his own. She felt her mouth hanging open stupidly; she hated Deveraux for witholding information and Edward for meddling so audaciously. She could think of nothing to say.

"It was pretty clear what he had in mind," Dev said uneasily. "He's a subtle kind of guy, but it was clear anyway. A sort of trade. You for her."

At last Grace found words. "Whatever made him think you'd want Christine?"

"What a pimp he'd make!" Deveraux shook his head admiringly. "What balls! When Christine went to use the bathroom he said 'pleasant girl, Christine,' and I said yeah, she was, and he said—just slipped it in, very casually—'if you ever find our Grace gets to be too much for you, I'd be pleased to have her back.' Just like that."

"As if I were a library book—something you'd borrowed."

"Or a pet, maybe. He's outrageous, Grace. Still, I can't help liking him. A little."

Grace excused herself and went off to the restaurant's small, ill-lit ladies' room. She felt enraged and exhilarated, both, and needed to cool herself. What would Mr. Ottway have to say about a situation like this? What would Lou-Ann do if Chet, her straying husband, confessed to having hired the obscene phone caller? The door and walls of the single toilet were covered with graffiti—

densely packed messages, scrawled in pencil and ink and lipstick, bloomed on the field of cracked paint. WOMEN ARE GENTLER THAN MEN appeared over the door handle, just beneath BILL'S DICK IS TOO SKINNY. A small, modest script proclaimed: I GIVE GREAT HEAD! The authors of HELP ME I'M CRACKING UP and PUSSY POWER! had been upstaged by someone of a literary bent, someone Grace felt sure she'd like, who had penned firmly, and in black felt-tipped marker:

MALT DOES MORE THAN MILTON CAN
TO JUSTIFY GOD'S WAYS TO MAN.

"When's Fiona going?" asked Deveraux when Grace had returned.

"Day after tomorrow."

"Where is she now?"

"Having dinner with a friend who works for the UN."

"Well," Deveraux shrugged as if to make small of his next words, "I still think you should go with her. At least think about it."

The restaurant's bank of windows, cloudy and steamed and partially obscured by the heads of other diners, were set high up. Occasionally one could glimpse the legs and feet of passersby, trotting toward Greenwich Avenue at a rapid pace. It had grown quite cold since the afternoon; people did not dally in the streets. Grace became aware that one pair of legs had passed the window more than once, had loitered by several times, in fact, and were even now framed, motionless, above and beyond Dev's head. She put her prescription sunglasses on and studied them carefully. They were surely the same legs she had noted while Deveraux was ordering the wine. In a sea of boots and frayed denim jeans they were a standout. Gucci shoes, neat trousers of some dark stuff, the hem of a coat barely visible—could it be that Dev's fears for her were not ridiculous after all? She felt that if the legs pivoted about and descended the three steps to the basement restaurant, that if Edward appeared in the doorway, smiling hesitantly, feigning surprise at seeing her there, she would lose control, run amok. "Let's get out of here," she said.

Dear [imaginary] daughter,

I am sure it has crossed your mind to wonder how I have supported myself before securing my present position at the university. Since Jules died penniless and I can only take money from Edward as a gift, you may well wonder. On the whole, people have been very kind to . . .

Dear [imaginary] daughter,

You may have wondered if I am a feminist. I find it useful to define myself as a feminist, but rarely have anything to do with what is called "the movement." So much have I existed outside the framework of normal society that . . .

Dear [imaginary] daughter,

Perhaps you find it odd that I have nothing to do with Grandmother Peacock? You imagine, no doubt, that there was once some great offense, a terrible situation, which created the unbridgeable gulf between us, and in this you are wrong. I would like you to know that . . .

*I*t had not been Edward at all, of course. The phantom legs had belonged to a woman who was waiting for someone outside the restaurant. A trick. Why, then, did she feel so uneasy about Edward? An unpleasant, prickly feeling behind her knees and between her breasts prodded her back to consciousness, jogged the adrenalin so that she lay against Dev's bare warm back rigid with sleeplessness. Through his window she could see a high, cold quarter-moon riding the skies with a brisk, no-nonsense aloofness that was infuriating, maddening to the insomniac mentality which takes everything as a personal affront. Fucking moon. It illuminated, no doubt, the room where Edward lay with Christine and plotted new ways to officiate at the borders of Grace's untidy life, it silvered innumerable unspeakable acts of anomie even now being committed on stairways and streets, in subways and bushes around the city. What the hell did it care? Officious, irritating, odious. All the same to me, mate, it would say if it could speak—all the same to me.

There had been a splendid moon on the night Winifred Peacock flew to New York to meet Edward. Her plane had been delayed an hour or so; nevertheless she came straight to the restaurant in the East Sixties where Grace and Edward waited for her. Grace commanded the scene to unroll—perhaps something in it would reassure her, would call forth some small and friendly detail which could unknot her body and send her off to sleep . . .

The scene opens in a small, expensive French restaurant on the East Side. A woman is approaching a table, walking down the long corridor between banquettes, smiling hesitantly. She is approaching two pale and pretty children (they are in their late twenties, but this takes place in the days when anyone under forty felt entitled to consider himself or herself a child) who sit close together against the wall. The male term of this couple is both more relaxed and better groomed than the female. His light hair is well cut; his suit is English. The female is wearing purple woolen knickerbockers, long boots, and a buccaneerish shirt. Her black hair is clean and straight but needs to be cut by an expert. Both of them are from the Midwest, but one would never guess it—only an anthropologist might discern beneath his blondness and her pallor the possibility of Indian blood, so common in the northern Great Lakes area, which has endowed them with high, curving cheekbones and brushed them with an air of melancholy distinction. They are both drinking vermouth on ice. "Here she comes," says GRACE. "That one's my mother."

"Yes," says EDWARD, half rising, "I thought it would be." The woman who approaches is clad in a navy suit and a short fox jacket. Everyone in the restaurant has heard her tell the bored coat-check girl that she will keep the jacket because it is chilly. She is smiling determinedly as she advances; when she is still twenty feet away she can keep still no longer and calls "Hello, hello, I'm here!"

WINIFRED PEACOCK is introduced to Edward, and there is such visible relief at Edward's suitability, such naked gratitude in her eyes, that Grace feels insulted. Momentarily she knows a pang for Jules, remembers with affection his comportment in the same situation at Reuben's Restaurant. Edward will not seem exotic to her mother, not even if she connects his name to the newspaper headlines a decade earlier, because the son of a mass murderer is less alien to her mother than a Jew. Mrs. Peacock orders a vodka gimlet and sighs luxuriously. She will continue to sigh like this throughout the meal and in all her dealings with Edward. It is as if a mighty burden has been lifted from her shoulders. There is also another factor. She thinks Edward very sophisticated and is conversationally inhibited; their dialogue, when there is any, goes something like this: MRS. PEACOCK: I can't tell you how nice this is, how glad I am that you two young people have decided to get married! EDWARD: I'm so glad you're pleased. MRS. PEACOCK: I certainly am! Indeed I am! And what do you say, Grace? GRACE: I'm glad you're happy, Mother.

Occasionally Grace is aware that Edward would like more authentic emotion to flow at the table, at least from her. He is passionately in love with her, insofar as his immaculate sensibility will allow him to experience love, and can easily be made to suffer. She does not wish him to suffer, but his passion for her excites her immensely. In some ways it is more arousing than the feverish, doggy love she and Jules shared. It is unknown territory. Other men have loved Grace, but none have been so certain of victory, so determined to have their way. "I can't allow you not to marry me," Edward has said to her. Such strong-arming thrills her—it is splendidly courageous and naïve. It makes her think of Edward as an older man, though he is not much older than herself. His money confirms it, sets the seal on his otherness, the quality that causes Mrs. Peacock to overflow with approval, to all but dance on the table in a primitive release of maternal joy. Grace looks at her mother nervously. Mrs. Peacock is twirling a strand of blonde hair with such vigor she seems almost insane. "Will you be establishing a business here?" she asks shyly. She has read the old newspaper clippings; she knows the score. "I'm considering other ventures," Edward replies with a fine ambiguity. Mrs. Peacock bites her lip to keep the questions from popping out—anything this well-bred boy wants is good enough for her, good enough—certainly—for Grace. He will not be writing unwholesome articles for low-grade magazines. He will not force her to eat delicatessen foods with his mother. He will not render her daughter a widow at an awkwardly early age.

Together, Edward and Mrs. Peacock bend the force of their love toward Grace. Mrs. Peacock twinkles at her, screwing her mouth in little heart-shaped moues of outraged tenderness when Grace boorishly lights a cigarette between courses. Edward is hostlike, charming, attending to their needs, but if Grace so much as touches his hand he goes pale with emotion . . .

Later, when they are alone, they take a bath together. Edward's bathroom is the jewel of his well-appointed, five-room, cooperative apartment. Large enough to accommodate a family of six, it reminds Grace of the hotel in Tuscany where she and Jules experienced the Breakthrough. The towels are beige and chocolate brown and there is a cunning mosaic of swimming deer worked into the terra-cotta tiles of the floor. Edward will not be coaxed into making unkind comments about Mrs. Peacock. All he will say is: "How unalike you are—you and your mother." Grace is keen on making love then and there, as soon as they step from the tub, but Edward is afraid she will be chilled. Courteously, he ushers her from the bathroom ahead of himself, down the hall and into the warmth and safety of his bedroom. Edward makes love to Grace with single-minded intensity. He is reverent. His fine, thin flanks work with the precision of an expensive watch, tensing rhythmically; and although he murmurs continuous words of endearment, encouragement, even, he never says "I love you." The fact of his love is so pressing, so clear to him, that he does not think Grace will respect him if he gives voice to it. Almost always, when Grace and Edward fuck, she thinks of Hansel and Gretel in the forest, holding hands . . .

It wouldn't do, Grace thought, turning toward the wall, away from Deveraux. Her scenario was not even a proper one. Being connected with a documentary film maker had its disadvantages, and one of them was that she could no longer instruct her mind's camera to PAN in, ZOOM in, with any confidence. The expressions were likely to be wrong. Dev's sleeping back reproached her for her ignorance.

Thinking of Edward only made her sad and, admit it, jealous. She had always been jealous of Edward's friends Juana and Bettie, whom she suspected were hookers. She knew they had been treated less reverently than herself in the days before she and Edward had married. She could imagine Edward and Juana and Bettie taking a bath in the colossal tub on East Sixty-eighth Street; doubtless Edward would not have scrupled at cold tiles with them. She allowed herself to wonder if Edward and Christine were well matched, sexually. She didn't think Christine was aware of Edward's plans to trade her off, but one never knew.

She knew what she was longing for and almost laughed out loud. She wanted her portfolio of papers from the university. How pleasant—just for once—to sit beneath the calm and level gaze of Deveraux's Mr. Ottway sculpture and make judicious markings in the margins of *Johnny Faust* or turn, with breaking heart, the pages of *The New World: Pathway to Despair.*

Dear [imaginary] daughter,

The time has come to talk of Grandmother Peacock. It can hardly be put off. The moral lesson I should like you to draw from this letter is unclear, even to myself. Perhaps you will be able to extract the proper inference if you attend carefully.

Winifred Peacock is a winsome woman still. In her youth she was glamorous, vivacious, a quintessential American Sweetheart. Her beauty was far different from mine—so different that she sometimes seemed bewildered at having hatched me. She was, if I may say so, a relentlessly cheerful woman, and it may have been just that quality which drew my lawyer father to her when they were growing into adulthood in the Midwestern city of my birth. By allying himself with her, with her silvery voice and persistant commands to "look on the bright side," he was able to shore up residual gaiety for those moments when he himself could not keep up the illusion of happiness, for he was a melancholy man. With Winnie by his side, people would not notice his silences. Charles Peacock, except when he was utterly consumed by the demands of his profession, looked into the middle distance with an expression of profound sorrow. He once told me it was the legacy of his Chippewa great-grandmother, that he could not help his eyes and that they had nothing to do with him, but I knew better! When he fell victim to an abnormally early heart attack—the first of his family to do so—I blamed his death on his efforts to appear happy, well-adjusted; to deny the melancholy which was so patently his constant companion was to invite Death. One cannot cheat one's nature.

My mother and I were left comfortably provided for. It was, in some respects, as if my father had never been. He had appeared briefly on the scene to beget me, to establish our credentials as a family, and then almost stealthily departed. My mother and I were sad at this defection, but our sorrow was not nearly so extensive as it had been during the earlier, "toys in the car" episode. I waited tensely for her to give some sign. I thought she would be able to find the proper incantation to release the torrents of suffering I had come to expect in the wake of sudden death, but she failed. There were no dog-eared copies of *Ellery Queen's Mystery Magazine* to remind us of husband and father, no abandoned coping saws and drill bits hanging forlornly in the basement, no tobacco pouches or well-loved pipes. My father had had no hobbies, no vices. He had had no interests, really, except the law, and one could not say, "Think—only think of the briefs in his study!" My mother and I felt an acute embarrassment in each other's presence. Charles Peacock had been our only link, and now that he was gone we were simply two dry-eyed women who lived together in a large house on Lake Michigan. She was thirty-four and I was ten. There is less difference between the two ages than you may think, but hers was the advantage. She should have given a sign.

Perhaps my only lesson is this: Blood ties are all nonsense, the Family a sham. Acknowledge one must—remember my father's great-grandmother—but beyond that, there is no obligation to prolong acquaintances based on consanguinity alone.

Your loving mother,
etc., etc., etc.

Cygnet Cottage
Wiltshire

Dear Mother,

Since Fiona will soon be with you, I am sending my weekly letter along with her. I wish I could come, too, but the book of poems I have been working on is nearing completion and I can't leave England at present—not until I have a definite commitment from my publisher.

Fiona looks marvelous! Her pregnancy barely shows at seven months, and I attribute this to the healthy, wholesome life she has led. I almost believe she could have the baby squatting in a cornfield and walk away! (Only joking, of course.) I quite understand her compulsion to return to Family in her situation, although why she should do so a full two months (!) in advance of the event eludes me. Emil is a very nice bloke and will, I'm sure, stand by her and the child.

There's a real nip in the air these days and we should have frost soon. Old Reg has advised me to "cut yon dahliers soon or they'll 'ave 'ad it, Miss." Wish you could see them—they're a riot of color.

Don't worry if I don't write as often in the next few months; the book of poems on life in rural England occupies nearly all my time. Maybe I'll give you a call! Bye for now—

Love,
Grace

At LaGuardia, Fiona chose two tubular packages of mints and a copy of *Mon Tricot* to take with her on the plane. She was dressed in the same neat costume in which she had appeared at Grace's door in the middle of the night. That event now seemed to have transpired a lifetime ago. "I say," said Fiona to Grace, "don't hold it against me—what I said at the Plaza that night."

"About my being a fraud?"

"Did I say that? I *must* have been tiddly! No—I meant when I mentioned the letters to Aunt Winnie." Fiona withdrew the blue airmail envelope Grace had given her from her bag and waved it archly. "I don't think any of the others caught on, though."

Grace explained that the others were aware of her scheme, except for Mr. Ottway. "He'd like the idea," she said.

"Do you think so?" Fiona pursed her lips. "I must say I doubt it. He's got his head screwed on right, Gilbert has. I was rather taken with him."

Grace eyed the pale blue envelope nervously. It seemed possible to her that this new, powerful Fiona might be planning to betray her. Even if her cousin's intentions were not malicious, a thousand perils, mainly conversational, awaited her in the Midwest. She might blurt out the truth under the influence of scopolamine, at the very moment of birth; but no, Fiona was surely planning on natural childbirth and in any case had secrets of her own now more daring than the matter of Grace's method of communication with Winifred Peacock. Grace shuddered as a new image assaulted her inner eye: Mrs. Peacock and Fiona girlishly attending Lamaze classes together, going for ice cream frappes afterward and giggling over the panting exercises.

"The point is," continued Fiona, eyeing departure schedules as she spoke, "you can't send letters from the UK if I'm not there, can you?"

"I might know someone who's going over," Grace said vaguely. "I've prepared my mother for a silence. I might even call." And then, reliving the fantasy in which she had discussed the hair-dryer plan at Cygnet Cottage, Grace explained. Fiona neither flushed nor fainted as she had done in the scenario—had Grace imagined nothing right?—but her lips tightened a bit.

"You're daft," she said. "What a fuss over nothing."

"It's my fuss. Let me be the judge."

"I don't suppose you'll ever tell me what started the feud."

"There was no feud, Fiona. I don't want to have to play at Mother and Daughter. It depresses me. It doesn't signify."

"You want to be careful, Grace. You're picking up Third World language from that university." Sighing, she tapped the letter back smartly into a compartment in her bag. "I'll give her this when I arrive," she said. "But if you call her—if you actually do that ridiculous thing with the hair dryer—" Fiona narrowed her blue eyes, looking fiercer than Grace could ever remember her, and then finished weakly, "I just hope I'm not there to hear it."

Grace nodded meekly. Even with the upper hand, Fiona could not really be a bully. After all, she herself was hardly a model of probity these days. Who'd have thought she'd have so much guile in her? Fiona had arranged to dupe her own mother far more daringly than Grace had done. She'd chosen the unfortunate woman's sister-in-law as her accomplice, and she had planned her adventure with the efficiency and vigor she had formerly expended on more innocent pursuits. Perhaps, thought Grace, Fiona regards me as a master criminal might a petty thief.

"Tell me," said Grace, pretending to watch a group of women with name tags pinned to their breast checking their luggage at the Ozark counter, "how have you arranged things with your Mummy? Won't she wonder why you don't write?"

For the first time Fiona looked slightly put out. She made a great flurry of motion to indicate that it was time to get to her gate, but Grace sat idle, amused. "Have you borrowed my scheme?" she said softly. "Let me guess. Good old Emil is even now tenderly fingering a small packet of letters which he has promised to dispatch, one by one, when the time comes."

"I would never," said Fiona hotly, "burden Emil with a chore like that."

"Seems to me he's burdened you with more."

"My child is not a burden, Grace." Fiona said this dramatically, but her look was one of great suavity. "If you must know, Richard Bowstitch has agreed to mail the letters. He's ever such a good bloke, really. I can trust him."

"I see," said Grace with a smile she hoped was infuriating.

"Look here," said Fiona. "There're worlds of difference between you and me. I'm doing what I'm doing for the very best motives in the world. That's what distinguishes us, Grace."

"You and I get our better traits from our great-great-grandmother. The one who was a Chippewa."

Fiona looked puzzled. "What are you on about?" she said. "I don't have any red Indians in my past."

A deafening announcement rolled through the hall, and Grace bent quickly to take Fiona's hand luggage. The walk to the gate was fairly long, and she didn't want her cousin to go into false labor at LaGuardia Airport, four thousand miles from home and nine hundred miles from Winifred Peacock. They walked swiftly toward the departure gate, heels clicking so importantly that for a moment Grace felt exhilarated and wished that she, too, were going away, going somewhere.

"Ask Aunt Winnie," Grace said as they approached their destination. "Ask her about my father's and your mother's great-grandmother. She'll tell you."

"Nonsense," said Fiona. "Not," she added, "that you don't look it. I've always thought you looked foreign."

"Recessive genes," said Grace. "That accounts for it."

They parted with a show of affection, kissing each other's jawbones lightly in farewell. "Good luck," called Grace. "Good luck, Fiona!"

Fiona gave the British thumbs-up signal and then turned, surrendered her bag to the hijack inspectors, and walked through the small, domestic checkpoint. No electronic warning sound pierced the air. It was a slow afternoon, a half-empty flight, and the attendants stood about looking bored and dispirited. Fiona disappeared into the corridor which would lead her to the plane; she did not look back again.

For one moment, and without understanding why, Grace felt close to tears.

"What is it, honey?" Madge Risotski and I were in the restroom together freshening up. She was looking at me with a worried expression. "You look so tired and washed-out," she said anxiously.

I sighed. "It's nothing, really." I was afraid I'd burst into tears if she said one more kind word . . . It seemed ages that anyone had worried about me or even noticed me. "You can't fool old Madge," she said, applying a fresh coat of lip gloss to her pouty mouth. "Tell me. It helps sometimes."

And that's how I came to spill the whole story to tough, kind-hearted Madge Risotski, my coworker at Burton's Department Store, the only human being who'd realized I was alive for so long I'd lost track . . . I told her how Van and I had taken his mother in to live with us, how Van was working two jobs now to help make ends meet. Mother Hodges had Parkinson's disease, and I had to wait on her hand and foot when I got home, feet aching, from the store. "I sound like a heartless monster," I whispered. "She's old and ill and I ought to welcome the chance to help Van's mother, but . . ." I broke off, my shoulders shaking with sobs.

"Honey, you're not a saint," Madge said, stroking my lifeless hair with tender fingers. "You've let yourself go, Holly," she continued. "When you first came here you were a pretty girl! Look at yourself now." She was right. The mirror gave back the image of a drawn, gray-faced woman with stringy hair and shadows under the eyes. I looked ten years older than my twenty years, and what was more important, I looked unloved. "Aw, honey, have a heart," Van would groan when I cuddled close to him at night. "I'm too darned tired." And then he would roll to his side of the lumpy daybed and be asleep in minutes while I sobbed into the pillow. The walls between our rooms were paper-thin—if we *did* manage to make love we had to stifle our cries of ecstasy so Mother Hodges wouldn't hear.

"I'll bet," said Madge, like a mind reader, "things aren't so hot in the sack, huh?"

If I'd had any brains I would have walked out of that restroom then and there and kept my troubles to myself . . . then my life might have been something I could talk about without a burning sense of shame. I would still be married to Van, and somehow, some way, we could have worked out our problems together . . . It would be easy to brand Madge as guilty for her part in my disgrace, but it wouldn't be truthful. I was ready for her shameful suggestion. Ready and willing . . .

Grace closed the magazine, sighing. HOUSEWIFE HOOKER . . . THE EXTRA DOLLARS HELPED, BUT IT WAS THE SEX I CRAVED had failed to engage her.

She found herself thinking of destinations on the trip home, thankful for the taxi driver's silence. Most of the men Grace had taken up with were native New Yorkers. They had thought of her, dark hair and brows and all, as a daughter of the plains, wholesome and blonde in her heart.

Only she and Edward had come from the middle of the country, wandering along on their separate paths and meeting, instantly recognizing each other as kin, in the dim city which had welcomed them so extravagantly. There were other Midwesterners in New York—Grace had heard their flat, friendly voices countless times in the streets and salons of her adopted city, seen them plodding toward her in the aisles of stores and extending metaphorical hands in the crowded elevators of mighty buildings. Always, she had avoided them as one might avoid a food—shellfish or loganberries —sure to bring on an uncomfortable chemical reaction; she was afraid she might have known them in childhood, or that they might prove to be emissaries of Winifred Peacock. They looked and sounded so much alike to her; how was she to tell?

In the case of Edward she had known that he, like herself, had come to New York for no discernible, certainly not schematic, reason. He was not keen to see his name in lights, he did not lope, scarves billowing behind him, through the monkey puzzle at Lincoln Center, sheet music ostentatiously displayed, singing snatches of obscure songs and yearning for someone to see, mark, his youthful eccentricity. He had not been the lone homosexual in a hamlet so tiny that decamping was his only hope for comradeship, nor had he secretly plotted revenge at the high school reunion. He had come for the same reason as Grace. Both of them were obeying, in their migration, the law of their tribe, which was simply to go as far as the outlines of the continent would allow, to perch at the lip of the landmass, knowing that nothing more lay beyond. To go west would have been to obey deeply rooted American traditions, pioneering traditions, which had no meaning or allure for them. Both she and Edward would have been embarrassed to admit to expectations, to think that any New World awaited them, but still they needed to put some distance between themselves and the land where they were born. The East was the proper place for them. They had no great expectations.

The music she could hear in her living room, a Brahms violin concerto, both pleased and startled her. She could not remember having left the radio on. It swelled dramatically as she rounded the corner of her long hall and burst into one of its most exquisite passages as she entered the room to find Edward, hands neatly aligned on the arms of her swivel chair, sitting at her desk.

"Hullo," he said, smiling at her, "I let myself in."

She would not let him see the astonishment she felt at finding him there; somehow it seemed of great importance to remain detached, neutral. "You haven't got a key," she said.

"I used a credit card. It's easy. You really should buy yourself a good lock, Grace."

"You're the only person who's ever broken in," she said, allowing the comment to float in the air between them, an accusation and reassurance both. She took off her coat and stood uneasily in the center of the room. She could not offer him a drink, since he had, she noticed, already helped himself. Why not? He'd paid for it. The Scotch resting on the blotter near his elbow, the crysanthemums and dahlias at the window, even, if it came to that, the copy of *Vogue* with *True Story* hidden in its pages—all came from the money he had left on the night of the Briscoes' dinner party. She spent his money on small and pleasing things, buying them as fast as she knew how, so that the money would be used up quickly, relieving her of obligations. Had he noticed, on his secret visit to Deveraux, that his rival had a set of new coffee mugs, lacquer red and frivolous, purchased with his own money? All this she thought as the silence lengthened between them and the Brahms filled the room with artificial joy.

"Are you glad to see me?" he asked, not smiling.

"I don't like to be surprised like this."

"I know," said Edward, "and I'm awfully sorry, but I had to see you. I couldn't pace around out in front until you came back, could I?"

"You could do as other people do," said Grace. "I don't know what they do, but they don't break in." Her voice almost trembled. She was breathing hard, either a slackening of the rage she had felt on first seeing him or as a prelude to some larger rage. "Will you make me a drink?" she asked. She didn't want a drink but she needed to see him move from the chair.

"Certainly." He rose immediately and disappeared down the hall; she could hear him cracking open an ice tray in the kitchen. She thought of rushing to the telephone and calling—whom? And what would she say? For the first time since she had known him she felt afraid of Edward. Always before her fears had been for him, for the breaking of that slenderest of threads which connected him to life and to her. Never had it occurred to her that he, like his father, might wish to wipe the entire slate clean. He had wept when Grace had left him, but he had not tried to stop her then. Often she thought of Edward's tears which had, in the balance of things, more power to stir her than the death of Jules. Jules had died happily enough. By the time he had reached the West Side Drive, pumping along past the Cristoforo Colombo's berth, the long, profitless hours at the typewriter must have assumed their proper place, become humorous, even. Jules would have been exhilarated, happy in his plan to cycle back to Perry Street where his wife waited on the fire escape, and take her to a party. There had been no real sorrow in Jules, and if he had lived, Grace thought, nothing in his life would have so pierced through him as Grace's leaving had done Edward.

"What is it?" she asked as Edward reentered the room, carrying a tumbler in one hand. "What's happening, Edward?"

"Grace, my love," said Edward, kneeling before her and offering the glass, "nothing at all is happening. Why are you so tense? Was it seeing Fiona go off?" He smiled tenderly. "You see," he said, "you do need me after all. What if you'd come home alone with no one to look after you, depressed and shaky? Isn't it good that I'm here, darling? Isn't it?"

She did not awaken in the dark. The room was illuminated by a small, ornate lamp in a far corner. The room itself was familiar, and so was the bed in which she lay. She rolled over the large expanse of it and touched her bare feet to the thick carpeting. She discovered that she was wearing a white batiste nightgown, very chaste and quite expensive, and that an apricot silk kimono had been thrown over the foot of the bed. There was a tray on a small table which contained three pieces of fresh fruit, a plate of biscuits, a silver pot of coffee, now tepid, and a bottle of Perrier water.

She walked slowly across the room to the half-open door, which confirmed what she had known all along. The bedroom had been altered, but the bath with its frieze of swimming deer remained exactly as it had been in the days when she had lived here. Even the towels, which she had left behind, were monogrammed GWP. It had often occurred to Grace how false was the popular concept of pondering alternatives before arriving at an obvious truth. She neither wondered if she had fallen into a time warp nor considered that she might be dreaming, although she had, on occasion, dreamed of this very room. Instead she knew instantly, and with a feeling almost of awe, that Edward had managed to spirit her here. He had put her to bed, undressing her and slipping the nightgown on over her helpless body, perhaps smiling as only a lover could do at the ungainly sight of his beloved—drugged, cumbersome, mouth agape; perhaps she had drooled on the pillow or snorted her gratitude when he drew the coverlet over her. She thought of him in her kitchen, slipping something expertly into her drink and carrying it to her, knowing that soon she would complain of sloth and discomfort and need to be taken for a walk. She did seem to remember the cab ride over with Edward holding her against his shoulder; even then she had known that he had played a trick on her, but she was past caring. Had he transported her to the elevator with the doorman's help, indicating with a secretive male smile that his companion was intoxicated and needed assistance? Come to that, the doorman had probably remembered Grace and figured she and Edward were celebrating a reconciliation.

She bathed her face in cold water, noting that her eyes were swollen from what her watch, neatly reposing on the marble stand, told her had been eight hours of torpid sleep. It was now eleven o'clock at night. She brushed her hair with the hairbrush Edward had thoughtfully provided, disdained eau de cologne, and rinsed her mouth with something strong and medicinal, reflecting that she was very calm for a woman who had been kidnapped. The rage she wanted to feel would not come, and she smiled when she thought of Edward's tenacity. Fear could be dealt with later, when she confronted him and took the measure of his intentions.

She went back to the bed to think about her situation. Her clothes were not in evidence, but she did not want to go to the closet to see if they were there. She ate a pear and smoked a cigarette, finding the cigarettes in the small malachite box she had always admired, and then she returned to the bathroom to rinse her fingers. She allowed herself to peer briefly into the closet and there, like old friends, were the clothes she had been wearing. Only her boots were missing. At last she went to the door and tried it gently; it had not been locked and swung open with the ease and silence that Grace's own doors, badly fitted into the jambs, never managed. To her left were the library, living room, and a second bathroom, all in darkness. Light glowed far off in the other direction, where there were a dining room, kitchen, and a tiny maid's room which—in the days of her tenure here—had been fitted out as a sort of writing room for Grace. She set off in the direction of the kitchen, walking on the balls of her feet through the dim dining room where she had once confided to guests that it was Edward who had prepared the meal, not she, and stopped at the swinging door with its diamond-shaped pane of glass. The diamond was lit from within. She peered through but could see only a section of kitchen cabinets and one corner of the large table, where a glass of milk—frothing as if freshly poured—rested near the evening paper. Her abductor was in the kitchen. She pushed the door quietly and stood blinking in the dazzling light. The milk drinker sat, neat blonde head bowed over a crossword puzzle, wearing a quilted robe and bunny slippers.

"Hi, there," said Christine, acknowledging Grace's presence and filling in a horizontal word. "Feeling better?"

"I thought you'd be Edward," said Grace. "Where is he?"

"Are you hungry?" Christine asked. "I could make you an omelette, or a sandwich."

"Where's Edward?"

"Or would you like some cocoa? Tea? I'm just having a glass of milk." Christine rose, clearing some magazines from the chair nearest her and making room for Grace. She inclined toward the refrigerator, awaiting Grace's pleasure.

"What I'd like," said Grace, "is my coat and boots and some money for a cab." She considered Christine, who was looking at her guilelessly. Christine sipped at her milk and regarded Grace over the rim of the glass with a friendly and somewhat curious gaze. "You can't go out," she said. "It's late, almost midnight. You ought to stay the night. You don't look at all well."

"That's nothing compared to what I must have looked like when I came in," said Grace.

"Gosh, you were in terrible shape. Ed said he was afraid it was food poisoning, but you seemed to want to sleep."

"So would you if you'd been drugged."

Christine ignored this. "You know," she said, "it's odd you should get sick and come back here like this. It gives us a chance to get to know each other. I told Ed I liked you the moment I saw you at the Briscoes'."

"Look," said Grace, trying valiantly to keep her voice steady, "it would be awfully nice to have a comfy pajama party and set each other's hair and eat popcorn and all that, but right now I want to go home. Please get my coat." Her voice, intended to ring out commandingly, sounded feeble, pathetic. She was at a terrible disadvantage. She was never at her best when she first woke up, even after a normal sleep; at the happiest of times she found conversation intolerable in the morning. How was she to parry and thrust with Christine, who reminded her more than ever of a capable stewardess, when her body ached with disuse and fatigue and her tongue felt thick and dusty? She was now shivering in the thin gown and regretted her imperious rejection of the kimono.

"You're cold," observed Christine. "You forgot your robe."

"I'm going to leave now," said Grace. She walked past the refrigerator, heading for the service door and the back stairs. Christine rose and pushed a bell which sounded through the entire apartment; then she positioned herself in front of the door and shook her head decisively. "Edward doesn't want you to leave," she said. "He's been having a nap in the library, but he asked me expressly to let him know if you woke up." Grace considered making a run for her, but already she could hear Edward's footsteps in the hall. "She's up!" cried Christine loudly. Edward entered the kitchen with his usual air of competence, although his shirt was rumpled and his eyes still heavy with sleep. Evidently kidnapping her had been exhausting, thought Grace; she had rarely seen him look so tired. When he saw her his entire expression softened and he came to her, wrapping her in his arms and murmuring that she was cold but looked much better, and how did she feel? "Get her kimono, Christine," he said quietly, and then he stroked Grace's hair and told her how sick she'd been that afternoon, how helpless. "I was so worried," he whispered. "Are you alright, darling? Do you think it was something you had to eat at the airport?"

And a strange thing happened. Instead of accusing him, laughing at his lunatic, meddling ways, demanding to be set free, Grace felt herself leaning into the warmth of his body, beginning to cry with exasperation and the power of her feelings. Only the smallest fraction of her sudden wild outburst could be attributed to the fatigue and frustration she had felt moments earlier; chiefly she wept because she felt with certainty that whatever remained of her heart was now broken. Edward had broken her heart, as she had broken his. She would never forget that he had kidnapped her, would think of it always and be forced to envy him the strength of his passion. As she cried she felt his body tremble with her, as if in sympathy. While they were thus engaged, Christine entered the room, held out the kimono with eyes averted discreetly, and then retired to the maid's room, shutting the door. Edward wrapped her in the robe, absorbed in his task now, and frowned when he realized her feet were bare. Somewhere, she felt sure, there were slippers laid out for her, but he did not want to leave her. For a moment she was afraid that he might command Christine to remove her bunny slippers and thrust them through the door, but instead he lifted Grace to the kitchen counter, opened his shirt and —taking her ankles in his hands—held her icy feet to his breast.

"Something you learned from the Eskimos?" said Grace.

But Edward, who had closed his eyes, did not answer.

Dear [imaginary] daughter,

Would you believe me if I were to tell you that the heart does not break? It is appropriate for one of your years to imagine the opposite, is it not? I think it is important to distinguish between the feeling that the heart might break and the certain knowledge that—although to lack this feeling is something like lacking an arm or an eye—the heart is merely a metaphor we have invented in order to . . .

Dear [imaginary] daughter,

Do you imagine yourself to be immortal? When I was your age I believed that I would never die, or conversely that I would surely die before I was twenty-five. It is all the same thing, all a metaphysical striving after dignity which does not, really, exist. The sufferings of the mind are as nothing to the potential anguish of the body. Luckily, neither you nor I has yet . . .

*I*n the morning, Christine brought breakfast to her on a tray. Grace did not want to acknowledge Christine, nor did she feel safe in feigning sleep, so she lay staring straight ahead, stony-eyed and ungrateful. Appealing to Christine would be worse than useless; she would have to deal with Edward alone, and her softness of the night before was something she now bitterly regretted. If Edward thought her tears, her submissiveness, the obvious relief with which she leaned against him, meant she had acquiesced to his plans—whatever they might be—he was mistaken. She would have to set things straight immediately.

Christine turned back at the door. "I'm going to work now," she said. "If you need anything, Edward will see to you." Since there was no answer she smiled professionally, as a nurse might to a sulky convalescent. "See you tonight," she said, and vanished. Grace ate two croissants and drank three cups of coffee. Hunger strikes were all very well for people of strong character, but she could not prepare herself for the ordeal with Edward unless she felt strong, well fed, and clean. She began to draw a bath and sat beside the tub, feeling out her state of mind, fingers twitching with nervous energy. The drowsiness and languor had abruptly fallen away sometime in the small hours of the morning, and she had passed the night examining her situation from every conceivable angle. Edward had not, as one might have expected, treated the foot-warming incident as a prelude to lovemaking. He had guided her down the hall to her bed and tucked the quilts around her with care. He had remained, holding her hand, until she had fallen asleep again. Her last thought had been an unpleasant one and she had briefly struggled to articulate it, but she had been sucked into a period of blank unconsciousness which ended just before dawn. Her first action had been to test the door, which her mind had insisted in those moments before sleep would be locked this time. It was, and for the first time she felt really angry. Christine's appearance with the tray had alleviated some of the panic, but her rage was nicely stoked; she wanted to preserve it. She lay in the deep tub, scene of so many connubial frolics in the past, and considered the same set of facts for the tenth time. Today was Friday. Deveraux had gone to Washington for a fund-raising party yesterday and would not return until Monday. Fiona, as all the world knew, had flown off to the Midwest, necessitating that Grace miss the Washington weekend in order to be present at the airport. Deveraux had urged her to come down on the first shuttle after Fiona's departure, but she had declined, wanting a weekend to herself. Now she regretted the erratic nature of her affair with Deveraux; a more conventional woman would have aroused his concern by not being at the other end of the line when he called. Deveraux would simply assume she was being moody and wonder, not for the first time, why he bothered with such a bitch. Her seminar did not meet again until Tuesday, and there was no one in all of New York who would sense cause for alarm if she did not appear all weekend. Therefore, she could remain imprisoned in Edward's house for three days, four at the most, before the world began to search for her. No doubt Edward had researched all these points, depending on the blank weekend as an ally to his cause. Edward! She leaped from the tub and locked the bathroom door. If he should appear now, brow furrowed with concern over the comforts of the bath—did she need more oil? was the water warm enough?—she would kill him. The mere thought of such a confrontation sent adrenalin pumping through her—oh, for some of the warlike animosity she was experiencing now last night! She relapsed into the water and buffed her toenails, pretending to herself that his intentions were harmless. She thought she knew what he wanted, and this was simply a chance to win her back, to convince her that the communal arrangement with Christine could be pleasing to all parties. If he could not have Grace alone, perhaps Grace would consent to live in his house—relieved of the onus of being sole love object, she might learn to love him once more in her limited way and, being the vain and idle creature he took her for, become addicted to the easy life he could provide for her. Certainly this was no small consideration. She had lived badly, badly, in the years since they had parted. The trouble, Grace thought firmly as she stood up and turned the shower on her hair, was that Edward had no confidence in her ability to choose the life that best suited her. He mistook her for one of life's casualties rather than seeing her as she was. Since she could find no proper words to describe exactly what it was she felt she was, she pushed the whole business from her mind and began to sing a song which had been popular the year before, but her voice sounded pathetically brave and poignant under the circumstances, so she went to sit on the bidet and dry her hair with a high-powered machine which was, evidently, a new acquisition.

When she had dried and powdered her body, brushed her hair with vicious strokes, and kicked the wet towels into a corner of the bathroom—let Christine earn her keep—she was confronted with a new problem. She could hardly put on the bridish batiste of last night's weakness and hope to impress Edward with her rational arguments. Even with the kimono on she would appear to be an invalid or a concubine; better to don yesterday's clothes which, even without her boots, suggested that she was her own woman. She dressed herself and, going directly to the locked door, pounded against the panels with the bottle of Perrier water. She had made two satisfying scratches in the oak before the scraping of the key announced that her captor was ready to grant her an audience.

It did Edward credit that he neither flinched nor ducked when he saw the Perrier bottle in Grace's hand. "What's all this?" he said in an avuncular tone which did not fool her. "Why are you dressed?" He peered at the tray and nodded with satisfaction when he saw that she'd eaten her breakfast. "Shall I take your tray away?" he asked.

Grace kept quiet. When Edward ran out of banal things to say he would wind down, leaving her with the advantage. She did consent to put the bottle on the dresser. "Would you like more coffee?" he said and then, catching the scent of emollients from the still humid bathroom, "You've had a bath." He was dressed in pajamas and a robe and had obviously been awakened by her frenzied attack on the door; he was trying to give the appearance of having been awake for hours. He sneaked a look at his watch, probably to see if

Christine had left for work, and met Grace's eyes uneasily. "You look well rested," he remarked. He picked up the tray and headed for the door. "Think I'll have some coffee," he said loudly, as if to himself.

Grace was free to follow him if she so desired. He was her sole jailer now that his accomplice had left, but since the apartment's two outer doors were kitchenward he apparently felt safe. Grace headed for the library, feeling ridiculously grateful for even this small favor. She saw that the convertible bed was rumpled, slept in, as she had suspected. The curtains were drawn, leaving the room in gloom, but a malevolent trick had caused a shaft of daylight to penetrate the chinks and illuminate the oil portrait of herself which she had always hated. She had not thought of it for months, but here it was, a snide and hateful likeness of herself smirking down at her and seeming to say: Forgot all about me, huh?

The artist had conceived of her as a sort of gum-chewing cheerleader in disguise, an all-American cocktease, and the painting, for which Edward had paid an outrageous sum, was a piece of outright mockery. She stepped closer, surveying it with fresh hostility. Here was a false Grace, wearing a simple black dress, her hair quite straight and falling to the level of her breasts. The artist had managed to get her legs into the picture—surely unnecessary!—painting them in their high boots as he might have painted the prize object in a still life. The flesh tones gleamed above the dark bootline; the legs seemed flexed as if poised for flight, even though Grace was demurely seated. The bastard hadn't troubled to paint her eyes, merely rendered them shut in crescent shape, and he had accentuated the fullness of her lips so that she appeared to be pouting and smiling nastily all at once. The crowning insult was the large pompom flower Grace held in one hand across her lap, completing the cheerleader image and sealing Grace's enmity toward the painter for all time. She had never discovered why he had done it. Once, at a party, she had asked him. "It's one of my best," he said. "You'll love it when you're older." Edward had loved it then and there. She gave the painting her middle finger and went to see if the phone was working. The one in the bedroom had been unplugged from the jack, of course, but there was a slim chance that Edward, in his dim, precoffee state, might have forgotten that she was loose in other parts of the house. The library phone was nowhere to be seen, so she plunged into the living room.

If the rest of the apartment was much as she remembered, this room was alien territory. All the furniture had disappeared, along with the carpeting and curtains and incidental pleasantries. Hard morning light poured through the windows on a chilly menagerie of soapstone walruses, musk oxen, caribou, polar bears, sea terns, seals, and foxes. One piece seemed to be fashioned of ivory—she could not be sure. Several ceremonial masks of a quite breathtaking fierceness glared from the walls. The room seemed many degrees colder than the other rooms. Either it was unheated or its Arctic inhabitants produced the illusion of extreme cold. Of course there was no telephone.

Edward was brewing coffee, standing in the kitchen with an alert, jailer's look. Grace took a seat and remained, chin in hands, staring at him. At last she said: "Why do you keep the Eskimo room so cold?" Edward shrugged. "I like it like that," he said.

"They're very nice."

Edward brightened. "Aren't they? I'm so glad you like them."

"Of course," said Grace, "you didn't have to drug me and drag me here to see them. I would have come on my own if you'd asked."

"That's not why I did it," said Edward. "And it wasn't really drugging you. It was only a sleeping pill or two."

"I believe that qualifies," said Grace, "as drugging." She was determined to ignore the pained look which had crept over Edward's features as soon as the topic had been introduced. "What about Christine? Has she been trained in hospitals? Women's jails?"

"Christine," said Edward, "is a secretary. A very capable one. I'm sorry you think of her as a jailer."

"What am I supposed to think? She wouldn't help me to leave

last night, and when I threatened to go anyway she rang a bell for you. Both of you could get in a lot of trouble for this."

"Not Christine," Edward said promptly. "She thinks you're having an *episode,* a sort of breakdown, you know, and that I'm helping you. She thinks you need a rest. She thinks"—he brought it out determinedly—"you called me and asked if you could stay for the weekend."

"Jesus," said Grace admiringly, "you've really got things under control, haven't you? But you know the truth, Edward. I could have you put in jail."

"Maybe," said Edward, pouring out his coffee and mutely offering her a cup. "But I don't care."

"When Deveraux comes back," Grace said spitefully, "he'll probably want to beat you up."

Edward's face convulsed with pain and distaste. "Let's not talk about him, Grace. What's he got to do with anything?"

"He's my lover," said Grace. "We don't always get along so well, but he has a certain interest in my welfare. He told me I ought to stay away from you. He warned me."

"He's jealous," said Edward. "Would you like another croissant? I have some Robertson's jam, or honey. I noticed Christine didn't put any on your tray." This black mark against the efficient Christine emboldened Grace. "Why is Christine willing to play slavey? What's wrong with her?"

"She's not selfish the way we are, Grace, not proprietary. If it makes me happy to have you here she's happy, too. She doesn't feel jealousy. She *wants* me to be happy." He said this last with an air of such wonderment that Grace wanted to pour coffee in his lap.

"She's after your money," Grace said. "Secretaries are always after people's money."

"Don't be such a snob. Anyway, I don't have enough to attract fortune hunters."

"More than anybody that boring little toady could ever get close to," said Grace. "Christ, Edward, where's your brain? Three words out of Christine could put an entire roomful of people to sleep, for God's sake—who'd want her?"

"She's pretty," said Edward judiciously. "Quite pretty in her way."

"She's freeze-dried," said Grace. "She wears double-knit pants."

"That's just what I meant about her being different from us," said Edward eagerly. "She'd never talk about you that way. She thinks you're beautiful, fascinating. She told me so after that night at the Briscoes'. It was quite voluntary."

"She's probably a dyke, then," said Grace. "Are threesies a part of this arrangement?"

Edward looked shocked, then amused. "No," he said.

"Does she like to watch? Is there a peephole in the maid's room? Was she breathing hard at the other side when you were doing the foot-to-bare-chest routine last night?"

"Certainly not."

"She calls you 'Eddie'," said Grace. "Anybody who can do that is up to no good."

"Would you like to see the *Times?*" Edward asked.

"If I were to walk out the door, now, would you stop me?"

"You haven't any shoes on," said Edward.

"Will you get them for me?"

Edward lowered his eyes, as if momentarily shamed. "No," he said.

"When can I leave, then? I have to go to my seminar next Tuesday." Instantly she cursed her lack of inventiveness in moments of stress. Why hadn't she said there was a special meeting of the faculty today or tomorrow? Edward, whose education had been good as far as it had gone, would never dream that the university knew her only as a social security number. He would have believed her.

"I'm sure you'll be able to get to your seminar," he said. "You'll have stopped being so emotional by then. In the meantime, I brought your briefcase. You can mark your papers here."

Nothing he might have said could have unnerved her so much. She began to retreat from her aggressive position, bargaining for his goodwill. "As you see it, then," she said, feeling unreal, fathoms deep in unknown water, "I'm to stay and rest here this weekend?"

"Why, yes," he said. "That's all I want, Grace. I apologize for using unfair tactics to get you here, but it seemed the only way." He looked across at her. "I've got to live, too," he said, "and I've missed you so . . ." He stood up abruptly, banishing emotion, and beckoned to her. "Time for you to get to those papers," he said. He settled her back in the bedroom with her briefcase and three neatly sharpened #3 red pencils for correcting. He also gave her a small bell to ring if she required anything, refilled the malachite box with her brand of cigarettes, and placed a stack of magazines on the table next to the bed. "I bought these, too," he said, "they're the latest ones."

True Story lay on top with a tantalizing lead feature emblazoned across its pulpy cover: I WAS A MIDDLE-AGED GROUPIE . . . I THOUGHT ROCK AND ROLL WAS FOR KIDS, UNTIL MY DAUGHTER INTRODUCED ME TO CADE!

"Thank you, Edward," she said. "That was very thoughtful."

It wouldn't do. For whole minutes at a time she could occupy herself without feeling desperate, but eventually came the realization that there were hours, days, more of this to live through. She read the "Middle-Aged Groupie" story and sighed with irritation over the randy hero, Cade, who bore as much resemblance to a rock star as her janitor, Julio, did to Manolete. True, Cade said "far out" and turned the heroine on to hashish (cocaine was too pricey a substance to mention in blue-collar love stories), but essentially the story was false from its trumped-up beginning to the infuriating end, in which the adulteress realized she had become the laughing-stock of Central City, USA, and went back to a life of Christian endeavor, hoping her husband would find it in his heart to forgive her. Pah! She did not buy confessions magazines to read about penny-ante fools, and the housewife wanton in this story was so much a fool she didn't even realize that anyone who played her hometown café was not a star. Celebrity fuckers made poor heroines, degrading the entire market.

She graded Miss LoCasso's latest effort, marking it a B because it was well written enough, but she found herself making petulant marginal notes so often that two of her red pencils were worn to nubs. She considered writing "Help—I am a Prisoner" and Edward's address on Mr. Ottway's paper in the event that she was not freed in time for her seminar, but Mr. Ottway—for the first time—had not turned in any work. She buried Chapter III of Buonsuccesso's *Johnny Faust* at the bottom of the pile and turned to Mrs. Klein's short story about her mother, a Lithuanian immigrant who had borne six children and educated the young Mrs. Klein to accept only suitors who "rang the door with their elbows,"

> The idea being that they should be so laden down with gifts that only their elbow would be free! I told myself that when I grew up I would not be materialistic, that I would marry only the man who struck that common, mutual, interest in me, no matter how poor he might be. True love must never be measured by material wealth the poets say, for it springs up so suddenly it takes you by surprise. Who has time to think?

Had Mrs. Peacock counseled her, ever, about the manner of husband she ought to select? Grace thought not. She did recall that once, in her second year away at boarding school, her mother had tried to press upon her, at vacation time, the son of a friend. They had spent the whole evening driving aimlessly around the town's lakefront, finally parking near the lighthouse and discussing their parents. He—Glenn? Gregg?—had said his father was having an affair with the daughter of the hospital superintendent. "It pisses me off," he repeated over and over. "My mother's so dumb she can't imagine stuff like that going on." Grace had volunteered that her own mother seemed to be chaste, but how could she tell, away at school half the year? "You're lucky your father's dead," Glenn/Gregg had said morosely, and then they had kissed with hot open mouths, simply to console each other, and he had asked, no less morose, if she ever got frustrated away at girls' school. They were the only two young people in town who went away to boarding school; that was undoubtedly why they'd been propelled toward each other by Winifred Peacock.

Some time later her mother had warned her not to become too friendly with the boys she might meet at school dances—this warning was put in such a vague, amusing way that Grace had felt no need to reply. At her school there was no opportunity to become familiar, since one's partner at a dance was selected by cross-indexing the respective heights and religions of the prospective partner, resulting in the sort of match which inspired lust on neither side. College, of course, was a different story, but by then Grace had grown so aloof that Mrs. Peacock hardly dared to offer advice.

She gave Mrs. Klein a C– and suppressed a desire to scream. Already she had smoked half the cigarettes in the box and drunk so much coffee her nerves fairly danced. She considered ringing the bell and asking Edward for another sleeping pill, but she was sure he wouldn't come across. It was not yet one in the afternoon. She could guess by the clattering in the kitchen that Edward was preparing a bumbling, endearing lunch for her. She seized the bell and rang it.

"I need to make some calls," she said when Edward appeared. "I have to cancel some engagements if you're going to keep me here."

"Well, I suppose so, Grace, but no tricks," said Edward. He brought in the phone and plugged it in the jack. "I'll have to stay here while you talk," he said apologetically. "Don't say where you are." Grace had guessed that he would monitor her calls, but she had a plan. She dialed Naomi. After three rings her friend answered. The sounds of Robert and Alice quarreling in the background rose and fell, a *leitmotif.*

"Speak up, Grace," said Naomi. "Robert has chicken pox and so does Alice. I can barely hear."

"I just wanted you to know," said Grace craftily, "that I can't make it tonight. I've got so much work to do."

"What's tonight?" shrieked Naomi. "Were we supposed to do something? Joe's in Baltimore and I'm going crazy."

"We were supposed to go to the ballet," said Grace, "but if the kids are sick I'll give our tickets to somebody else."

"Ballet? Are you kidding? They're on strike again."

"Yes, exactly." She rang off quickly, hoping Naomi would sense her desperation. She had done it badly, though. Practice makes perfect. She dialed Jenny.

"Hello?" The voice was Sam's.

"Is Jenny at home?" asked Grace, making her voice clipped and English.

"Grace, you loon, how are you?" Sam chuckled with pleasure at having seen through her vocal disguise. "Jenny's at her shrink," he said. "Shall I have her call you back?"

Edward, who could hear Sam's voice clearly from across the room, shook his head no. "I was just calling to say I couldn't make it tomorrow night," said Grace. "Be sure to tell Jenny! I wouldn't want her to be disappointed."

"Grace, Grace," moaned Sam with pseudofondness, "you've confused your schedule again. Jenny and I are going to watch a taping of the show tomorrow night at Morgan's private screening room. I hope you're going to watch it. It's on regular TV"—he said this condescendingly—"Sunday night at eleven. Might teach you a thing or two."

Morgan White, whom Grace and all her friends had always called the Whited Sepulchre, hosted a weekly TV show on which experts in various fields argued points heatedly for two hours, invariably arriving at no conclusion. "Is the topic anomie?" said Grace.

"You bet your sweet buns it is," said Sam. "I think I made some really good points. Be sure to watch."

"Grace," said Edward, when she had rung off, "you're not being honest with me. You're canceling imaginary dates." He walked toward the jack. "All you'll do is make your friends think you've gone crazy."

"Edward, I'm sorry, truly I am, I just got a little impetuous there for a moment. I have to make one more call, please; no tricks. I have to call Mr. Ottway to tell him he can't pass the course unless he submits this week's work. Could I have a telephone directory, please? I don't have his number."

Edward took the phone with him, returning with it and the phone book. He replugged the instrument and handed her the directory, open to the O's. There were three Ottways, one of them a firm of lawyers, and none could conceivably be Gilbert. She tried Caroline Ottway on West Ninety-fourth Street and was informed that she had a wrong number; she even tried to phone the university, but of course there was no reply.

"Think of it!" she cried, summoning up all the considerable art she had possessed in her brief career as an actress. "Think of that poor, sweet kid failing a course he can hardly afford because I couldn't reach him! He's black, Edward, and poor and young! He's from a stinking *ghetto* and he comes to class faithfully, and he can *write!* He's my best student, Gilbert is, my very best, legitimate, A student! He's got real *talent!*"

"Then don't fail him," said Edward, removing the phone. "I'll bring you lunch now."

Johnny Faust walked slowly toward the social club. Part of him was eager to see Don Mephisto and find out what was on the kindly, gray-haired old man's mind, but another part of him seemed to say —Hey, wait a minute! Maybe you are getting in too deep!—From the tenement windows high above the teeming streets of Little Italy came the sound of many voices calling him. "Johnny! Hey, *Johnny! Buon giorno,* Johnny! How's things?" Yes, he was popular with his lithe, rippling body and gleaming dark hair and eyes. Popular, and not conceited about it. On the fire escape above him sat Helen Troiano, combing her long blonde hair. She gave him a secret smile.

He could see the lines of her magnificent body very clearly, for she was wearing short shorts and a T-shirt with no bra. Helen gave him the come-on regularly, but so far nothing had come of it. Some of the guys said she was frigid and narcissistic. "Boy," thought Johnny, "what I wouldn't give to kiss that chick just once." He'd laid plenty of girls in his twenty years, but with Helen he'd settle for a kiss. As he was imagining what it would be like to take Helen's voluptuous body in his hard, muscular arms and press his well-chiseled, slightly cruel mouth to hers, he realized he had arrived at his destination. The Social Club. It was reputed to be evil, a place where Deadly Sins were committed, but he couldn't see it that way.

"Ah, *buon giorno*," said courtly old Don Mephisto, coming to meet him. "I've been expecting you . . ."

"Mr. Buonsuccesso—One cannot be popular with one's body!" Grace wrote vehemently in the margin. Actually, if she and Edward were not on such peculiar terms, she would have called him in and read him this latest addition to Mr. Buonsuccesso's best-seller. "I want to write a blockbuster," Mr. Buonsuccesso had announced on the first day of class. "I want it to be sort of like *The Godfather,* but with moral content. People can read *Johnny Faust* and come away with a moral lesson—it has something to say to everyone." Good luck to him. Even as she shuddered at his writing, she had to admire Mr. Buonsuccesso's self-confidence: the race, as everyone knew, was not to the swift but to the plodding and blessedly thick-skinned, and it was determination like Mr. Buonsuccesso's which founded dynasties, settled the wilderness, and—for all she knew—wrought best-sellers. In ten years she might see his name climbing the list at the back of the Book Review.

It was almost four o'clock, and Edward had promised to let her out for a walk through the apartment at four. She was becoming impatient for this small treat, which alarmed her. In less than twenty-four hours she had developed an invalid's mentality. Perhaps by next Monday she would not want to leave, would smile ingratiatingly when Christine brought her breakfast and ask for the *Times*. She was so relieved to hear the sound of the key in the lock that she had to force herself to be cool to him. "Have you brought a leash?" she asked.

"I've brought you some slippers," said Edward. "I thought we'd go to the gallery, and it's cold there." He held out a pair of suede and sheepskin slippers which she realized, with an unpleasant shock, had belonged to her when they had been married. How many Relics of Grace did he possess? It appalled her to think that odd wads of cotton and fingernail parings might be secreted away somewhere in these rooms, to say nothing of actual garments she had left for Goodwill. "Put them on," said Edward encouragingly. "I bought them for you when I knew you were, ah, coming to stay. They're the kind you like." And then she saw that they were new, unworn, and laughed at her self-important imaginings; there was no need to make Edward crazier than he was.

They strolled through the library, which had been tidied and aired. The convertible bed was a couch once more, the heaping ashtrays of Edward's vigil-night had been emptied, and the curtains drawn. The hateful portrait snickered over everything. "I'm not an invalid," Grace said crossly. "We don't have to shuffle along." The gallery was colder than she remembered, and everything in it more alien. The primitive pieces were not arranged or displayed in any noticeable order; it was as if Edward had brought them back from the North and left them wherever there was space. Yet they were not neglected. No speck of dust had settled. A squat figure, a hunter, stood nearest the door, harpoon raised. The hunter was carved of soapstone but his weapon had been fashioned separately. "Bone," Edward said, "the same as the real harpoon would have been." She asked if she might touch the figures, and chose a walrus first, experiencing such delight at the feel of the long, curving back under her hand that she shivered.

Edward brought her a small seal and placed it in her cupped hands. It almost seemed the seal had grown there, between her palms, been fashioned expressly for her. "Are they very old?" she asked, and Edward told her that it didn't matter which had been crafted with modern tools and which scraped with stone and bone, drilled by antler—they were all, he said, much the same. There was a polar bear about eighteen inches high, carved, so Edward said, in a time of famine so that a real bear might appear. The smaller, ivory figures were, she supposed, most valuable, but it was the soapstone she wanted to hold, marveling at the cosmic curve of it, the smoothness so free from imperfection her own flesh, surrounding it, seemed coarse by comparison. Edward, cheered by her attitude, began to instruct her. "This fellow's made of caribou antler," he said, "and this seal with two heads—do you see?—is by the same artist. The bird is a little auk—bone—and just near your foot is a narwhal. This is an Inuit piece, not old, but exactly like one I saw in a museum in the Canadian Arctic that was ancient. And this, this is the frame for a drum, *ayayut;* it's played by striking the frame, and poems are composed to the sound of it. Do you know what the period of silence before artistic inspiration comes is called? The Alaskan Eskimos call it *qarrtsiluni."*

Edward looked expectant, as if waiting for a reply. When none came he said: "What it means, *qarrtsiluni,* is 'waiting for something to break.' "

"Yes," said Grace, "I see."

"How did this happen, Mrs. Benson?" The young doctor's eyes seemed to pierce through to my innermost being. I couldn't meet his glance. "I ran into the kitchen door," I lied, biting my lip as soon as the words were out. It sounded so phony! I had never been a good liar. Dr. Connell lifted his eyebrows slightly. "Do you do that sort of thing often?" he joked. I had to smile. Often? I couldn't even count the times I'd had to wear dark glasses to the supermarket to conceal the marks of Chad's fists. "I guess I'm just naturally clumsy," I said, trying to laugh. The pain made me wince.

"You're going to have a beautiful shiner," the doctor said. "There are lacerations and contusions along the right cheekbone, and your lip is cut." His gentle hands traced the outlines of my swollen, battered face. "That must have been some door."

I thought how shocked he'd be if I told him the truth. Sometimes I could hardly believe it myself. I felt as if I was living a nightmare—one that *nobody* would believe. When Chad came home in one of his dangerous moods I had to remind myself that this was the gentle, loving man I'd married only three years before. The first time it had happened I had believed his apologies, melted under his tears of regret and warm kisses. We'd made love then and there, hot, passionate love that transported us both to the uttermost peaks of ecstasy. "Tracie, Tracie," Chad moaned, "my precious wife . . . I swear it won't ever happen again . . ." But it had. Again and again. Gradually, I learned to harden my heart to Chad's tearful pleas the morning after. I no longer believed him, but I was too humiliated to tell anyone, to ask for help . . .

Dr. Connell's capable, blunt fingers were swabbing my lacerated cheek so gently that I felt tears of gratitude well up. It had been so long since I had felt a man's hands that weren't brutal and rough that I sighed. "Is something wrong Mrs. Benson?" I shook my head and closed my eyes. Last night had been the worst yet . . .

Chad had been drinking when he got home. "Don't look at me like that!" he yelled, slurring his words and spilling what remained of his weekly pay check on the kitchen floor. I said nothing, but began to move toward the door. "Don't move away from me," he thundered, "I'm your husband." Then his fist caught me a glancing blow on the side of the face and I went spinning across the room. He hit me again and again, until I fell in a heap at his feet, sobbing out my pain and misery, cursing him and myself and the universe that permitted such things to happen . . . There were words for what I was. I knew—I had read about it. I was a Battered Wife. I thanked God that we had no children yet, sobbing my thanks that the miracle we had always wanted hadn't come true . . .

"Mrs. Benson." Dr. Connell's deep, kind voice jarred me from my bitter memories. "Are you sure you wouldn't like to talk to me? It looks to me like you're in trouble . . ."

How could he understand the shame, the scalding, wrenching shame I would feel if I shared my terrible secret with him? "No," I replied almost violently, "I'll be fine." And then, remembering my manners, I added, "Thank you, doctor. You've been very kind."

His hazel eyes darkened a shade, with concern and something else, something I couldn't quite put my finger on. "Call me Dave," he said quietly . . .

"Have another veal bird," said Christine.

Edward poured her a third glass of wine. They were certainly taking very good care of her. She had come to the table, sullenly, refusing to wear the pretty gown Christine had laid out for her; tramping flat-footedly in her sheepskin slippers to her place at table, she had been reminded of aching moments from her childhood, of times when an unexpected kindness of her mother's had so moved her that she was forced to redouble her efforts at seeming ungrateful. She had to remind herself, after her second glass of wine, that she had nothing to be grateful *for* at present. Did they think they could keep her on bread and water?

"Where did you learn to cook?" she asked Christine.

"I'm from a very large family. I was the oldest of six children."

"Funny—you don't look ethnic," said Grace, helping herself to wild rice.

"Ah, but appearances are deceptive, aren't they?" Christine laughed merrily. "Actually, I'm Estonian."

This stopped all conversation for a time, and when Christine cleared away the plates and brought them salad Grace changed her tack and commenced an outright interrogation.

"Where were you born?"

"D.C. My father has a dry-goods store there."

"How old are you?"

"Twenty-seven."

"Why did you come to New York?"

"To be with my husband. He was in graduate school here. Psychology."

"Are you divorced?"

"Two years ago. I helped put him through school, and then, when he was ready to set up practice, we found we had nothing in common. As long as he was in school we got along just fine. Funny, isn't it?"

"You got screwed."

Christine looked prudently at Edward. "No," she said at last, "I wouldn't say that. It wasn't a case of his throwing me out—I left. It was my idea."

"What did you do next?"

"Grace, sweetheart," said Edward, "aren't you being a little preemptory?" He turned to Christine. "It's not usually like this," he explained, as if they were discussing a failed soufflé. "Grace is a very delicate conversationalist."

"I don't mind," Christine said. "If there's anything you want to know about me, Grace, just fire away."

"What," said Grace, "do you suppose Edward sees in me? I never made him happy, couldn't in a thousand years. Why does he want to recapture me? Couldn't you make him see the light?"

"There's no use in telling people what makes them happy," said Christine. "Nobody has the right to do it. Edward—forgive me, Ed—is in love with you. He will not feel complete until he has you back again. His love is quite unselfish, but perhaps you don't understand that?"

"What about me?" said Grace, pointing a fork for emphasis, glorying in her new, brutish attitude. "What about what I want? You call Edward unselfish? Taking an unwilling prisoner, shutting her up in his house, making his mistress wait on her?"

"Oh, pooh," said Christine. "You're not a prisoner here. You can go anytime you like."

Grace rose promptly. "Will you excuse me? It was a lovely dinner."

"Oh, not *now,"* said Christine. "Wait until tomorrow at least."

"Why not tonight?"

"Tonight," said Edward, "is Halloween."

"The streets," said Christine archly, "will be full of ghosties and ghoulies and long-legged beasties."

Grace looked at them in astonishment. Were they unhinged or was this simply their stiff way of making light? Humorless people were difficult to gauge. Or—happy thought—perhaps they were planning a surprise for her? More than anything she longed for other people—Mr. Ottway, please God, come to trick-or-treat in a Devil costume from Woolworth's. "Do kids come to trick-or-treat here?" she asked.

"The doorman doesn't let them in," said Edward. "I always keep some Hershey bars around for the children who live here."

"On the West Side," said Grace, "they put razor blades in kids' apples. Junkies ring your bell."

"I think," said Edward, "Grace could use some coffee. Shall we have it in the library?"

Grace thought of going home, of the point she had meant to press, but a sudden image of her apartment, its studied bareness, chilled her. Her handbag, left behind when Edward kidnapped her, the two glasses they had drunk from, the ringing phone, the old people, layer after layer of them barricaded behind police locks lest the trick-or-treaters tramp in with long, lead pipes—all these suggested themselves with a frightful clarity. She did not want to go home. Tomorrow, or Sunday, she might regret her decision, but for the present there was nothing to do but pretend to be drunker than she was. "I want," she said, "a pumpkin."

Christine had just brought the coffee in to them. Edward hesitated, then rose and walked toward the phone. "I'll order one up," he said.

"You can't," Christine said, "you'll have to go out."

Edward came to Grace and took her hand. "You'll behave?" he asked. She nodded, and he got his coat and left.

"The worst Halloween I ever had," Christine said pensively, "was in Silver Springs when I was seven." She was sitting cross-legged in the leather chair and seemed to want to make up for the long silence which had engulfed the room during Edward's absence. Neither she nor Grace had been able to converse; it was as if they needed Edward's presence to bring them properly into focus, each for the other. Christine had tried, of course, but her neutral remarks fell so quickly into silence that both of them had lit cigarettes (rare for Christine) and smoked together like two old gentlemen in a London club.

"Tell us about it," said Edward, who was spreading papers on the carpet so Grace could carve the pumpkin he had bought, for a greatly inflated price, on Lexington Avenue.

"It was at a party, given by a cousin of mine. We were about the same age, but I didn't know her very well. When it came time for the games to begin we formed a line, and each child was blindfolded and led, one at a time, into a little curtained alcove. I could hear them shrieking and squealing in there—it sounded like fun. I thought it would be like the tunnel of horrors at an amusement park."

Grace cut through the top of the pumpkin, fashioning a jaunty cap. She angled the knife so that the top would fit snugly; she was an expert at carving jack-o'-lanterns and felt the calm authority which accompanies the performance of a task one does well. "What then?" she asked.

"When it was my turn my cousin led me in, blindfolded, and told me to hold my hand out, palm up. 'This is the witch's eyeballs' my cousin said, and something round and cold and hard fell into my hand. Grapes, probably. 'This is her tongue' and then there'd be a long, dry horrid thing—maybe bacon or a beef jerky, more likely—and finally she plunged my hand into a bowl of what must have been cold spaghetti and shrieked: 'And this is the witch's GUTS!' " Christine shuddered. "I was outraged! It was so ugly, so unnecessary. I remember I started to cry and all the others thought I was afraid and made fun of me. Nobody understood I wasn't afraid."

Grace, whose hands were poised over the gaping crater in the pumpkin's head, found herself looking at Christine with amazement. A few more stories like that and Christine might find herself the sole beneficiary of Edward's love. She, who was about to plunge her hands into a pulpy cavity and pull out great hanks and strings of slimy material, felt barbarous by comparison. "You're very fastidious," she said at last.

"I suppose so," said Christine, pouring herself a second cup of coffee and looking off into the middle distance. Suddenly her chin lowered with military precision and she shot forward in her seat.

"Oh, heavens, Grace, I see what you mean! Goodness, I don't mean to put you down for rummaging in that pumpkin! I cook a lot—anyone who cooks gets awfully dirty in the process—raw meat and liver and so on, frightful textures sometimes! No, no, I don't mind getting my hands dirty. It was the ugliness of it. And being blindfolded."

Grace plunged elbow-deep into the pumpkin and began to draw forth the innards with zest. Pumpkin seeds squirted through her fingers and onto the carpet; shreds of pulp clung to her cheekbone when she pushed back her hair. "I myself," she said, selecting a long-handled spoon with which to perform her curettage, "have never had a bad Halloween. Once I burned up a road with kerosene, another time I broke windows. I loved every minute of it."

"How about you?" Christine asked, addressing Edward. He cleared his throat and glanced nervously about him. "There *was* an incident," he said, "but I'm afraid it's not awfully amusing." Christine and Grace gave him their full attention; there was no escape. "It was when I was about ten, I believe. Yes, ten. A group of us were bobbing for apples at a small party. A boy drowned." Edward smiled apologetically. "I warned you," he said.

"But how could he drown?" whispered Christine. "Didn't anyone help him?"

"It was one of those freak accidents," said Edward. "Somehow he swallowed water. We thought he was joking, clowning around. By the time we saw he was blue in the face and tried artificial respiration, he was gone. He had a weak heart; I suppose that complicated matters."

They were silent, then.

She did not dream that night. Rather, she had a series of images before the steep descent preceding sleep which were so clear, so jolting, that when they were over sleep was impossible for some time. She supposed the inactivity coupled with so much wine had prompted them, these ghoulish faces which hovered vaguely at the borders of her consciousness and then rushed steadily toward her until they occupied all of the red-black field which lay behind her closed eyelids. They were faces to frighten a child, not a full-grown woman, and she was annoyed and terrified together, in equal measures. Edward and Christine had allowed her to keep the jack-o'-lantern in her room. Its candle was guttering now, burned down close to the end so that the smell of scorching pumpkin filled the room. She breathed quietly and deeply, lying with her hands folded on her chest as she had seen Deveraux do, and shut her eyes once more. For a time all was well, and then she felt the air around her shift and move, grow cold, colder, as she was transported to a hut somewhere in the far North, an igloo perhaps, where an Eskimo sat carving a pumpkin with a pointed tool made of caribou. His expression was bland, neutral, but she knew his face would come closer, altering as it zoomed toward her until—when it was so large it took up all the available space behind her eyes—he would be grinning with infinite malice, homicide in his heart. When he had gone the canvas was smooth again; ever so slowly it took on the familiar little cracks and fissures of the hallway in her own apartment, and when a shaft of moonlight struck the walls she could see the shadow of a multitude of long weapons quivering there.

Two o'clock, All Souls' Eve. Across the park Naomi must be asleep, a worried furrow between her brows, alert even in slumber to the claims on her life. Beside her Joe might be locked in some fearful dream of water—misty seas looming up where he had thought no water lay, tidal waves bearing down upon them from the Hudson River. Deveraux, in Washington, might travel to the Mato Grosso and back before room service wakened him in the morning. Old Maurice. What did he dream of? Crystalline winters in St. Petersburg before the tsar had fallen. Ellis Island. His wife, long dead. The tyranny of dreams made them all equal in the night, and no one ever thought to rebel, to question the necessity of nightly torture or its worse reversal, sweet delights which vanished in the bleak light of awakening and yet seemed more real than the bedpost, the blanket and the light at the window.

She would stay awake forever; she would not surrender.

She wondered what Winifred Peacock and Fiona had done to celebrate Halloween. Perhaps they had driven out to a sedate roadhouse for a cheeseburger, a dimly remembered treat from Grace's own youth, but no, the roadhouse would surely be gone now. All that had been field and woodland surrounding the town of her birth would now glow as brightly as a Wurlitzer jukebox with motels and fast-food palaces and multilevel movie houses. The old traveler's hotel on Main Street had been pulled down in the first year of her marriage to Jules; she remembered that a smart new motor lodge had been erected in its place. She pictured her mother and Fiona in the restaurant of this establishment, debating rhetorically whether or not to make a second trip to the salad bar. Both know they will do so, but Mrs. Peacock has always thought it ill-mannered of restaurants to force their clientele to seek out food. All the world can see one prowling back for seconds; a modest notoriety is the price of greed . . .

There is a centerpiece of gourds, Indian corn, and small pumpkins on the buffet table. It is identical to the seasonal centerpiece used by the old traveler's hotel many Halloweens ago. Waitresses in whose bosoms bloom hankies folded to resemble exploding flowers move briskly between the tables, replenishing glasses of ice water and thrusting friendly faces close to ask if diners would "care for some hot rolls?" Piped music plays continuously. The most popular drink here is something called a Harvey Wallbanger, but both Winifred Peacock and Fiona have chosen gin and tonic. Even this choice has not been made without deliberation. "Technically," says Mrs. Peacock, "it's too late in the year to drink gin and tonic, but the weather's so warm . . ." Fiona remembers her drunken orating at the Oak Bar in Manhattan but blames it not on the drink or her condition but on the company. "Let's!" she says. "It's Indian summer," says Mrs. Peacock. Fiona remembers what Grace has said about the Chippewa ancestress and makes a mental note to ask, later. Her aunt is flushed with pleasure, glad of the companionship of this well-bred English niece. Fate has taken Mrs. Peacock's daughter away but rewarded her with this cheerful and infinitely more pleasing young woman who is, after all, her blood relation, or her dead husband's blood relation, which is almost the same thing. Fiona is much better company than Grace ever was! Mrs. Peacock wishes to tell Fiona something of the sort but restrains herself for fear that it would seem unnatural.

What's this? Fiona has risen to go to the salad bar and reveals the body of a pregnant woman, clad in a voluminous overblouse purchased at the British Home Stores before her departure. In New York Fiona's pregnancy was barely discernible; here, in the Midwest, in less than two days, it has bloomed out prodigiously. Her belly seems immense. Grace first attributes it to the garment Fiona is wearing but soon realizes that her cousin's body has relaxed and expanded under the more genial skies of Winifred Peacock's hospitality. With Grace, in enemy territory, Fiona's pregnancy had gone into hiding. Grace marvels at the many talents of Fiona, who at this moment is being encouraged by a waitress to ladle more chickpeas into her brimming bowl. The words "eating for two" are never spoken, but they appear high over the buffet as in a cartoonist's balloon.

A woman has stopped at Mrs. Peacock's table to chat. When Fiona returns introductions are made. The woman looks perplexed. "Where's your daughter?" she asks. "She's in England," Fiona and Mrs. Peacock say in unison. Something in the alacrity of their reply chills Grace. Mrs. Peacock's eyes are dancing wickedly as she darts a glance at Fiona, and when the woman returns to her table both Fiona and Mrs. Peacock begin to giggle helplessly together with guilty merriment. "Oh, dear," cries Mrs. Peacock softly, pressing her napkin to her lips and trying to stem the tide of her hilarity, "Oh, dear. Poor Grace." Her shoulders are shaking.

"I had to tell you," says Fiona between fresh spurts of laughter. "I couldn't keep it a secret any longer."

Mrs. Peacock rearranges her face. She is about to say something serious. "Grace was always secretive," she tells her niece. "I don't know where it comes from. I'm an open book. Charles was too. Grace is so . . . *theatrical.*"

Fiona smiles compassionately. "If it makes her happy . . . ?" she suggests.

"Yes," agrees Winifred Peacock, "who am I to spoil the poor child's fun?" They laugh again, blonde heads tucking together in gentle conspiracy, pitying Grace with all the affection and good humor at their command . . .

Edward heard the bell and came immediately. He had not been sleeping either. He lingered at the doorway of the room like a discreet manservant—was there anything he could do?

"Yes," said Grace, "stay with me."

"Did you have a nightmare?"

"No. I was awake."

Edward advanced warily into the room, suspecting a plot. "Your jack-o'-lantern's burned out," he observed. "Would you like a fresh candle?"

"Get in bed with me, please. And take off your bathrobe."

Edward removed his robe and laid it neatly on the chair next to the bed. He was wearing maroon silk pajamas. Grace moved aside to make room for him. "I remember those pajamas," she said. "You take good care of your things, don't you? You must have had those pajamas for ten years."

"Actually," said Edward, "I have several pair in this color. These wouldn't be the ones you remembered."

"I've been thinking about that Eskimo word," said Grace.

"It's a good word."

"Tomorrow will be Sunday. On Monday I'll leave."

Edward sighed. "I know."

"I think we should make love. I've been thinking about it. It seems the only proper thing to do. It will make things more natural."

"Natural?"

"You can't just kidnap someone and have her lie around all weekend and not make love to her. I wouldn't want to be forced, but as long as the suggestion comes from me . . . it's *appropriate,* don't you think?"

"Um," said Edward, turning toward her, "I don't like the sound of it. It's too much like striking a bargain."

"But there aren't any qualifications. No strings."

"I would rather," Edward pointed out, "there be strings. That's the whole point, Grace."

Grace stretched forth her hand and allowed it to rest, palm downward, on the slippery material of Edward's pajama top, over his heart. He winced. She stroked him gently, as she might a kitten, careful not to move too suddenly.

"Grace," said Edward in a strained voice, "why are you doing this?"

Her hand slipped down the length of his chest so lightly they could both hear the sound of the silk sighing beneath her fingers. His head turned away from her on the pillows; she reached across and cupped her other hand around his cheek, drawing his face around so she could look into his eyes. They were closed to her, lashes cast down sullenly. She smiled at the familiarity of it, of Edward once more, after all this time, in her bed. His bed. Edward's thigh tensed beneath her marauding palm, his eyebrows knitted briefly and then smoothed out again. She turned on her side and drew the sheets down to survey his body, which lay like a shrouded continent under the pajamas, full of unexplored terrains, possible dangers. She began to unbutton the pajama shirt, slowly so as not to startle him, and thought how obedient he seemed, how pliant and virginal. Always before, it had been he who had made love to her—although never as freely as she might have wished—and now he submitted, in his confusion and his guilt, to being seduced. His pale chest gleamed from between the burgundy lapels; it was as clean and hard and white as bone. His pale nipples rose beneath her hand, so small and endearing compared to her own large, woman's nipples, so useless and pretty. He stirred irritably. "Hush," said Grace, hooking a thumb beneath the elasticized belt of the pajamas, "hush, Edward."

She thought she sought to exorcise him of his futile passion for her, but she could not be sure of her motives. It was possible that by taking the initiative and coaxing forth Edward's reluctant excitement she might divest herself of all that made her valuable to him. "There is nothing," she murmured, loosening the strings of his pajama trousers, "mysterious about me." His face remained impassive, but now and then he shook his head, as if in disapproval. His sex stirred under the silken fabric, moving fretfully beneath her hand. There was an advance and retreat to it, a resistance which made Grace feel she might fail in her mission. It seemed very important that she succeed. His penis swelled under her nurturing touch until it filled her hand. It reminded her of the Eskimo carvings she had held earlier—smooth, seamless, telegraphing a sense of tranquility, it seemed to have been created by an artisan expressly for her hand, her mouth. All of Edward's body, it occurred to her, had the consistency of one of his carvings. Perhaps that was why he so liked them, her strange soapstone lover.

He made no struggle when she slipped on top of him; taking him into her, she discovered that this connection, too, seemed perfectly crafted. Her triumph precluded sexual pleasure for herself, indeed prohibited it. She experienced great aesthetic pleasure and was able, in this high-minded and controlled state, to ruminate on the varieties of names for the male organ and reflect that Edward's was a thing of beauty in the Victorian sense—a true shaft of ivory if not precisely an engine of bliss. She looked down at his face. His eyes were too vehemently closed and his teeth grinding, but otherwise he showed no sign of life. He was not participating; no slightest upward thrust of hip or tensing of thigh indicated that he was being fucked. Only the unwilling cock demonstrated, by its helpless throbbing, that something was going on. At the last moment, when he came, his eyes flew open and he looked straight at her. The expression in his eyes was one of betrayal.

Dear [imaginary] daughter,

Will you think it indelicate of me if I broach the subject of sex? My own mother did not talk to me of such things when I was your age, but that had as much to do with the recondite nature of our relationship as with any conventional reluctance to introduce the topic. Of course, if you have taken my earlier advice you will be saving yourself for your husband (Donald or Ted) and need read no further. If you have written me off as a crank—and I suspect you have—then I still have much to teach you. Alternatives. Once again, an illustration from my own youth may serve to elucidate as well as anything . . .

When I was a girl, well-meaning strangers often asked me what I planned to "do" when I grew up. It is irritating, is it not? I myself enjoyed telling such people that I planned nothing at all. They smiled unpleasantly and thought private thoughts on the rudeness of adolescence. Yet I meant what I said. I could think of nothing important enough, or rather nothing with a proper label, to describe my intentions. These were simply to lead a full and adventurous life, to take many dares and travel widely. Love affairs seemed to be a desirable, indeed necessary, ingredient of the life I planned, but I could not tell these earnest adults that I envisioned sexual congress with a number of interesting people.

At the university I had a fine time. Nothing was required of me except to attend classes and lectures occasionally; I was not pressed to hew to a standard of excellence by any of my professors or to visit with counselors and establish mythical goals which they, and I, would from that day on pretend to be working toward. I had no interest in marriage. I did not wish to enter a profession, since this latter held attraction in inverse proportion to its possibility for a young woman in those days. Overprivileged as I was, I had no desire to study medicine or law because there would have been no barrier to this objective.

The real pressure came from young men who wanted me to surrender my body to them in parked cars, fraternity houses, wooded parks, mountain chalets, abandoned mineshafts, dormitory lounges, and once, in the costume room of the university theatre. This I refused to do, not out of moral conviction or fear or prudery, but because I believed my first sexual experience should be memorable. Once I had allowed myself to believe in my right to lose my virginity to a blare of trumpets, it became difficult to select the proper partner. I was prepared to give myself to an art teacher who perplexed me by his lack of interest in my sacrifice; he proved to be a homosexual. Another time I was ready to go the length with a morose boy from Oklahoma who read the plays of Eugene O'Neill, but he sabotaged himself by drinking too much beer and confessing to a sneaky liking for inferior authors. One candidate smoked a pipe ineptly, one was too much impressed by psychoanalytical homilies, and so on. Time was passing. My university career was being spent in a search for a lover worthy of myself. My studies, such as they were, went neglected. I failed to realize that I was just as reprehensible as the most foolishly determined husband hunter; the only difference was that I merely sought a lover, a first. Do you see? *Anyone would have done.* Would the Oklahoman's preference for shoddy writers have mattered one jot when we were horizontal? Would this one's unfelicitous voice or that one's protruding ears have impeded him from initiating me to the bracing nonmystery of Sex?

By the time I selected a mate—and need I say it is difficult to remember his face?—all impulse toward study, meditation, self-improvement, had atrophied. The trust fund established by Charles Peacock for my education was entirely taken up by the pursuit of love; my chosen career was the laborious one of procuring admiration, lust, loyalty, and fierce sentiment from members of the opposite sex. I had the decency not to take a degree—I did not wish to solemnify the sham—and embarked upon real life with no credentials other than those I have mentioned. I was, if you like, a Bachelor of Intrigue. My lesson is this: get sex out of the way early so you will not be obliged to waste your academic life in vain pursuits. Acquire skills, as they say.

Your loving mother,
etc., etc., etc.

Promptly at 11:00 that night they turned the TV on. It was time for Morgan White's Anomie Show and Grace didn't want to miss a single word. "Why watch it?" Edward asked with the slightly detached air he had assumed ever since last night's sexual escapade. "Really, Grace, if you hate Sam Briscoe and you can't stand the Whited Sepulchre, there's not much point, is there?"

"I'm very interested in anomie," said Grace primly.

"Oh, do let's watch it," said Christine. All evening she had gone out of her way to endear herself to Grace. It was almost, Grace thought, as if she knew what had transpired the night before, knew and understood the altruistic motives which had prompted Grace's rape of Edward.

Edward obediently addressed himself to the television, upon whose face the name of Morgan White was now written large. The familiar musical signature filled the room, the letters faded, and White's face in fearful close-up usurped every available inch of the screen. "Good evening," he intoned. "Tonight we'll be talking about anomie—a word some of you will be learning for the first time."

"Christ," said Edward. "What a beginning."

"With me tonight are a variety of people from all walks of life who share a common concern—the decline of a shared moral code, of the rules which govern our society, and the feelings of alienation this collapse produces in the individuals who must *live* in that society." He paused for breath, looking beleaguered at the mere thought of the acres of anomie they would explore that evening. "All of us have felt, to greater or lesser extents—"

"Let's watch an old movie," said Edward.

"Let me introduce our panelists," said Morgan White, reluctantly turning to acknowledge the presence of others in the studio.

"Panelists! It's not a quiz show."

"Quiet, Edward, here comes the good part."

"To my left is the Rt. Rev. Benjamin Otto, pastor of the Good Shepherd Reform Lutheran Church in Flint, Michigan, and author of *Flaccid Christianity: Why We Don't Care*. Next to him is Dr. Emily Bodgett, a practicing psychotherapist in New York City and a volunteer coordinator of Scorekeepers, a militant organization which keeps track of unredressed crimes against women."

"She does look fierce," said Christine.

"At the end is Mrs. H., who is wearing a mask because she does not wish her identity to be known. She has been the victim of three separate muggings and is currently undergoing treatment for the symptoms of extreme anxiety she manifests whenever she is forced to leave her home." Mrs. H. dipped her head quickly by way of acknowledgment. She looked, in her dark mask, quite ominous.

Quickly, the camera flashed back to Reverend Otto. Occupying the space where the minister's knees should have been was the top of a familiar head, and as the camera lowered Grace saw that Sam had hunkered down boyishly dead-center, legs crossed Indian fashion. "Sociologist Samuel Briscoe," continued Morgan White, "is the recipient of the prestigious Inner-Cities Studies Grant, which this year is concentrating on anomie in the urban ghetto." Sam gave what appeared to be the peace sign, then returned to hugging his knees. He looked larger and puffier than usual. Morgan White completed the introductions. A Jesuit priest, an elderly rabbi, a young woman who was identified as a member of the anti-Samaritan movement, and a concerned housewife from Astoria took their bows. "And finally," said Morgan White, "we have a reformed gang member from Harlem who is currently studying to be a poet. Say hello to Gilbert Claude Ottway, seated at the far right."

"No!" cried Grace. "No!"

Mr. Ottway inclined his head with dignity. He was wearing the sort of cut-rate dashiki he never wore in real life. He also sported an Afro wig which returned his frail features to the fierce demeanor they had worn when Grace first saw him in the seminar room. Even Edward gasped. Morgan White leaned back, closing his eyes with the strain of choosing the first speaker. At last he nodded, sipped purposefully from the tumbler at his elbow, and said: "Let's start with the acknowledged expert on anomie, shall we? Sam—you've been doing the spadework—" (the merest twitch of White's upper lip showed that he recognized the infelicity of the phrase)—"and we'd like to know what you've come up with."

The camera cut to Sam. SAM BRISCOE flashed across his opening mouth; the necessary alterations were made and the letters hovered briefly at his midsection, then faded.

"I think," he said, "we should start with a literal definition of anomie. What does it mean? What are its roots?" He shifted his haunches. "Anomia—lawlessness. From the Greek. A: without. Nomos: law. But are we speaking of a mere matter of lawlessness? Or are we speaking of the vague malaise we all suffer as a result of this condition of lawlessness?" He paused rhetorically, too raw to know that reflective silence was not allowed on Morgan White's show. Quickly the Jesuit leaped in.

"Our old friends, cause and effect," he said silkily. "Teilhard de Chardin discusses, in a moving passage from *The Divine Milieu . . ."* He in turn was interrupted by the Astoria woman who wished to state that her burgeoning resentment of a certain "element" (something she would never have dreamed possible a decade ago) was surely caused by the rash of crime in the streets. "Cause and effect!" she declared heatedly. "Oh, please. If some knife-carrying animal *causes* me to give him my hard-earned money, the *effect* is I'm gonna resent him—am I right?"

At the words "knife-carrying animal" the camera indulged in a close scrutiny of Mr. Ottway's face. It remained judicious, impassive.

"That's not quite what Father Carroll meant," said Morgan White, inviting the others to snicker at the Astoria woman's impassioned ignorance, but the Jesuit had seized the ball and was prepared to run with it.

"Actually, Morgan, she's put the case very well. The ambiguity of remaining a good Christian in the twentieth century, as Teilhard de Chardin knew so well, is aggravated by our relative sophistication as well as by the terrible pressures exerted on us daily in our urban centers. Indeed, Mrs. L. may ask: How can I feel charity for those whose mere existence robs mine of the modest peace I had thought a birthright? How can—"

"Did you know Ottway would be on this show?" asked Edward.

Grace shook her head. The amazement she had experienced on seeing Gilbert had been total, yet she had quickly accepted his presence. Of course. How he had managed to become one of the group, or even whether he had already known the night he had called her from the party, was unimportant. She was grateful that he was there; indeed, the sight of him filled her with delight.

"I'm a forthright individual," cried Dr. Bodgett in a bid to capture the camera. "I say what I think, and what I think is—how the *hell* can there be respect for human life when one-half or more of all humanity has never commanded respect from the other half? I am speaking, of course, of women."

Morgan White groaned audibly. He was famed for his impatience with feminists; it was rumored that he had once told a radical lesbian activist that all she needed was a good plumbing job.

"Women," continued the therapist, "have felt anomie throughout the ages. Where were the laws and social codes, what possible meaning could they have, when the leaders of the church could compare Woman to an open sewer? As St. Paul did?"

"St. Bernard," murmured the Jesuit.

"Or, to be ecumenical about it, take Martin Luther." She spun in her chair to face Reverend Otto. *"He* said if a woman dies bearing a child it doesn't matter! That's what she's there for!"

"Tell me," said Morgan White, smiling unpleasantly, "does your organization, Scorekeepers, propose to redress wrongs committed by Martin Luther? How will you go about it?"

"Have we really advanced so far from those days that we can afford to *joke* about it?" Dr. Bodgett spoke in level, measured tones, as if to a child. "When women are being raped, beaten, deprived of their civil rights by the mere fact that they can't walk down the streets without fear? My organization exists so that women will know that someone is keeping an eye out for them. The police don't care. The courts still send wife beaters and rapists back to the streets with a fatherly pat on the back. Crimes against women are too quickly forgotten crimes, absent a celebrity's involvement, but Scorekeepers *never forgets.* We have a large dossier at our headquarters . . ."

"I feel," came a gentle, fastidious voice, "that we've strayed off the track here. We were discussing—" It was the rabbi, who seemed about to initiate a scholarly and reflective discussion and then inexplicably began, instead, a long anecdote about his nephew. "Time to pause for a station break," said Morgan White. "We'll be back."

"A Tower of Babel," said Edward.

"I like the priest," said Christine, "he's real suave."

"I wonder if they really have a dossier?" said Grace. "It's quite a good idea." Privately, she wondered if Edward's kidnapping might qualify, in Dr. Bodgett's eyes, as a crime against women. She was prepared to sit through almost anything in order to hear what Mr. Ottway might say. Sam was totally forgotten, his presence negligible. It was with a feeling of supreme irritation that she saw his face hogging the screen when the break was over.

"The feeling of anomie can be likened," he was saying, "to that of malaise and despair in the depressed person. Anxiety, a sense of helplessness, lack of will, inability to care about what goes on around you . . . when enough people experience these symptoms of a social, er, disease, we have incidents like the Kitty Genovese stabbing . . . many neighbors heard her cries for help, yet none aided her . . . in its final stages, of course, a society suffering from anomie fails to perceive that every member of the community is a human being, worth protecting as much as, ah, oneself."

"Sam never could get out of sentences," said Grace.

"What you're saying," contributed Reverend Otto, "is that the danger of a communal, spiritual listlessness is in the ultimate dehumanization of the sufferers themselves."

"Yes, exactly, yes, that's what I'm getting at here. In my studies on the subject, time and again we meet the perpetrator of a crime who is unrepentant because he fails to realize the life he has taken is worth as much as his own."

"More," said the woman from Astoria. "Usually the life he takes is worth *more* than his own."

"When will Gilbert say something?" demanded Grace impatiently.

"I thought you always called him Mr. Ottway," said Edward, "to preserve the proper student-teacher distance."

"I can vouch for the story I'm about to tell you," said the rabbi. "I know the young people concerned, personally, and I am acquainted with their parents—"

"Excuse me, Rabbi," said Morgan White, "but we haven't heard yet from two of our members. I'd like to get your views, number fifty-seven, on the subject. Perhaps you'd begin by explaining why you are identified by a number rather than a name?"

Number fifty-seven was perhaps twenty, and had a countenance of such placidity that she seemed to have been sculpted of Crisco. Her lips barely moved when she spoke, and the voice that emerged was as thin and pure as the hum of high wires. "The anti-Samaritan movement does not believe in names," she explained obligingly. "We think that having a name tends to, you know, personalize our existence too much. I'm number fifty-seven because I'm the fifty-seventh person to become a member in the Greater New York area. There are 103 of us now, and we're growing fast."

"And your beliefs? Is it true that members of your sect take a pledge *not* to help other human beings in distress?"

"Well, yes, that's it. I mean, you only have like a limited number of years to be alive in, and you owe it to yourself to spend your time getting to know yourself." She produced a sheet of paper and began to read: "We believe that any act of kindness is, in the end, an act of evil. It distracts from the true goal of Knowing Yourself Perfectly, and makes you a Less Good Person. Every distraction from Self-Knowledge is dangerous and counterproductive. Crimes happen because people are outerdirected. One who seeks Perfect Self-Knowledge does not rob, steal, murder, rape, or wage war. If all people abided by the principles of anti-Samaritanism, the world would be a better place." She folded her paper and smiled radiantly.

"You believe that?" Morgan White all but winked at his unseen audience.

The girl nodded.

"You're content to let the world go to hell around you in the name of nonpersonalized existence? What about . . . sex?"

"Sex," said the girl, referring to her paper again, "tends to obscure Self-Knowledge. We permit sex only after the age of twenty-five, and then only for a period of five years. This is so that women can provide future members of the anti-Samaritan movement during peak bearing years." Dr. Bodgett groaned. "Before twenty-five," continued number fifty-seven, "humans are not sufficiently advanced in Self-Knowledge to withstand the distractions of sex."

"So," said the masked woman in icy tones, "if you or one of your cult members passed me bleeding in the gutter you'd just walk on?"

"Yes," said the girl. "We would."

"And if you were the one lying in the gutter?"

"Because our theory hasn't caught on yet," said the girl disarmingly, "one of the uninitiated would probably help me."

"Very neat," said the Jesuit. "It is, of course, nothing new. Christian cults have always existed which hold that man's only proper business is the adoration of God. This young lady's generation merely substitutes self for God, something which—"

Edward correctly predicted the gist of the next three comments, which came from Dr. Bodgett, Morgan White, and Sam Briscoe. There was a sudden commotion in the studio as the masked woman and the therapist walked out in protest. "Stay and fight!" cried the woman from Astoria, but Dr. Bodgett gave the camera a final, disdainful look and swept away, her arm firmly around the shoulders of her companion. "When you want serious talk," she announced by way of a parting shot, "call me back."

Morgan White shrugged, although courtesy dictated that all of them dwell belatedly on their sympathy for the masked woman.

"Here we have an individual under terrible stress," said the rabbi reflectively.

"Clearly," Sam explained, "the breaking point came when she was actually confronted with a representative of our alienated culture. Here is a mild, nonviolent young woman who espouses total indifference to the plight of her neighbors. Not a knife-toting, swaggering—"

Again the camera cut to Mr. Ottway. His face was impassive but Grace thought she could detect a glimmer of amusement in the fawn eyes. "Why doesn't he *say* something?"

"Was he really in a gang?" asked Christine.

"Of course not. I mean, I don't think so. With Gilbert it's hard to tell. He's an enigma."

"At least," said Edward, "you know why he didn't get his paper in on time."

"—crime statistics are much exaggerated," the minister was explaining. "Or rather, they are no worse than they ever were."

"That's not true!" declared Astoria. "I read the other day where murder, rape, and assault and battery are up from last year."

"I mean in the larger sense—as history views crime. Naples in the seventeenth century, Paris in the fourteenth, were more dangerous than New York in the twentieth, but with this difference—"

"Gentlemen, ladies," said Morgan White suavely, "we aren't disputing about violence through the ages. We're here to talk about why nobody *cares.*"

"Ah, Morgan, that's not quite the way to put it," said Sam. "I would rather compare anomie to a religous crisis of faith—"

"Accidie," said Father Carroll, "is that state in which man remains indifferent to the love of—"

"—we plan to get into street theatre," said number fifty-seven. "You know, to illustrate our point."

"Here you are emulating Diogenes of Sinope," said the priest affectionately. He seemed taken with the girl. "With his lantern he effected *chreia*—a moral epigram, a means of teaching by illustration."

"Shall I make some popcorn?" asked Christine at the next break.

"He's got to say something soon," said Grace. "The program's almost over." And just then, as if on cue, Mr. Ottway's face was before them, inscrutable and wearing an instructive, infinitely tolerant expression. "My function here is ambiguous," he said, his voice assuming the grave, resonant pitch it had employed when ordering a grasshopper at the Plaza. "It must have occurred to the viewing audience, when Mr. White introduced us, that I was the only person present without credentials, without a philosophical, spiritual or personal stake in this business."

He bowed slightly to the Astoria woman. "It might be said that Mrs. L. is in a similar position, but since she feels wronged by a society which has caused her to feel unpleasant emotions toward some of its members, her case is rather more clear-cut than mine. I have no complaints, no grievances to air. Why, then, am I here at all?" He smiled engagingly. No one interrupted him. "I am here because it is necessary to have one representative of my race present whenever discussions of an ailing America take place." There was a muted flurry of protest, presumably from Morgan White, but Gilbert held up a slim and talismanic hand and continued: "Why me?

In lieu of the black sociologist who would have been here except for a last-minute illness, you see before you a reformed member of the criminal element which so oppresses society; indeed, I may be said to have represented, in my street-gang days, the very force which produces anomie. You have spoken of the sacredness of human life. The value I placed on human life was no higher than the value mankind has placed upon it from the very first, which is to say: human life is, was, and always will be, cheaply got and easily destroyed. It is an error to think otherwise."

"Goodness," said Christine. "I don't agree, but he's certainly articulate."

Grace silently expressed her wonder. Was this the put-on artist from class?

"My chosen milieu, violence, had two things in its favor. The first was the total lack of self-consciousness experienced during the performance of a violent act. One does not think about it while it's going on, and this is a great blessing to the mind that will not, in popular parlance, quit. The second attractive feature of violence lies in the romantic nature of the violent act; it is the last formal action left to us of which society wholeheartedly disapproves." He paused and looked about, as if welcoming questions. Morgan White and Reverend Otto spoke together. The minister won out.

"I have counseled youths like yourself," he said. "You, of course, appear to be exceptionally intelligent, but aside from your choice and mastery of words, what you say is exactly what they have said. Violence is exciting, and boredom is the curse of our age."

"Ah, but in the end violence is boring, too. Extremely boring. I always had to be mindful of my reputation as a ruthless and unbending warlord, which in itself became quite a strain. As soon as I perceived that my life as a romantic depended upon public relations, I ceased to find it amusing. I had never enjoyed cruelty; if ever I'd found myself liking it I would have stopped at once."

"Did you rob? Kill people? Rape women?" The Astoria lady

asked Mr. Ottway these questions with an air of deference, as if he were a celebrity.

"Certainly I robbed. I never killed another human being, but it was the merest chance that prevented me. As for raping women, I did not. It seemed a graceless thing to do, and unfair too. It did give me a certain pleasure to frighten white girls, though."

"Excuse me," said Morgan White, "but you're not a very fearsome figure, Gilbert. You're on the small side, aren't you?"

"Oh, definitely, very small. My wrists are like chicken bones. Nonetheless, it was easy to frighten white girls. Walking down the street, I simply retreated into my blackness; that did the trick. I have no animosity now—I'm not sure I could do it anymore."

"Gilbert," said Sam unexpectedly, "tell us what made you give up your street life? You must be aware that it's a cop-out to say you got tired of it. We human beings are motivated by deeper things than boredom, you'd agree? Let me make a guess, an educated guess . . ." Sam steepled his fingers and puckered his lips. "Let me say that something happened—an epiphany—which led you to realize that violence is two-edged. That by harming others you harmed, brutalized, yourself. This realization—simple on the face of it, no?—is the first step toward . . . "

Edward made a marking on his paper napkin. He was keeping, he had told them, a cliché-count.

"—a link in the long chain of humanity, struggling desperately, and with pain, to make some sense of your existence?"

"Oh, no," said Gilbert, "it was never anything so grandiose as that. Even if I believed all of what you said, I couldn't count on a sufficient number of others to believe it, and if enough people don't believe it then it isn't so." The Jesuit shot forward in his chair at this last remark and nodded forcefully. "I do believe," continued Gilbert, "that life is unreasoning and unreasonable. In this sense I must be said to subscribe to anomie in its first definition, that of lawlessness. What I cannot accept is the principle that people who exist in a lawless world must feel . . . alienated." He pronounced the last word gleefully; it was, Grace thought, the first concession he had made to his youth. "Like Giacomo Leopardi, a great personal favorite of mine, I cannot understand the arbitrariness of those who attempt to show why evil must exist. It does, that's all. Once you've come to terms with it, once you accept that life is likely to be lavish with pain and chary of felicities, then you can get on with the important things." Gilbert smiled in the direction of Sam. "I haven't answered your question," he said, "because there is no answer. It would be very nice to feel myself a link in a long chain, but there is only me. One day I tired, as I have said, of romance. I decided to deny myself the luxury of mindlessness and determine whether or not virtue could please me. It was not easy, of course. I missed—violently, at first—the bracing sense of society's disapproval. It had been such a tonic! And then, gradually, the pain of loss vanished and I found an almost equally bracing pleasure in the new freedom I had achieved. Society takes no notice of a virtuous man; he is free to come and go as he pleases."

"Does that mean," Sam put in hastily, "that you take no notice of society? Because if you don't, then we're back at square one. Anomie."

"To take no notice of society would be foolhardy in the last degree," said Gilbert. "My gentle ways do not exempt me from calamity and random horror. Unlike Leopardi I do not say: 'Of what value is my life, except to despise it?' I should be very sorry if my life ended too soon, but not a bit surprised."

They were running out of time. Morgan White thanked all the members of his symposium. The camera played briefly over each face, and it was with an effort that the majority of the anomie panel composed their expressions for a suitable farewell. Sam looked bewildered beneath his angry smile; the woman from Astoria and number fifty-seven appeared to have wakened from a catnap, and the rabbi, who had never followed a single anecdote to its conclusion, merely nodded. Reverend Otto nodded emphatically. Only the Jesuit, whose whole body remained inclining in the direction of Mr. Ottway, missed his cue. The final vision presented to the studio audience was that of Gilbert, in the act of raising a hand to his enormous Afro. Was he planning to pluck it off? The camera reverted to Morgan White, who told anyone still listening that next week's discussion would be a lively examination of child abuse, and then they were gone.

Grace, Edward and Christine retired soon after, each in their separate chambers.

The next day she was allowed to leave, without incident. Her shoes and handbag were returned to the closet in her room, and she said goodbye to her hosts with a measure of true affection and gratitude, exactly as if she had been a weekend guest.

On the crosstown bus she noticed her knees trembling slightly, and when she tried to press them down they jumped back against her palms. This manifestation of the fear she'd suppressed during her captivity surprised her, but when she thought about it she saw she had a lot to fear. Edward was more unstable, to put it charitably, than she'd realized, and Christine seemed capable of anything. At least, she thought, her ordeals were getting more genuine. In the space of a few days she'd passed from Ordeal by Pity to the real article.

XIV

Dear Grace,

This is just a brief note to let you know I've arrived safely. Aunt Winnie is in excellent health and looks quite marvelous. I think she's rather keen on the idea of the "b." Thanks for allowing me to stay with you. This is such a beautiful house—how could you bear to leave it?

Yours, Fiona

Feckless Grace—Thought I'd write to say: bet you don't miss me at all. Why do I bother?—Love, Dev

Grace:

Must talk to you immediately! Sam has found out about Martin and everything's horrible! Is your phone off? You can reach me at Naomi's. Don't, repeat, don't, watch the Morgan White show!

XXX Jenny

Dear Dr. Peacock,

I am sorry my paper is late. Here it is. Please accept my sincere apologies. Perhaps you would consent to watch the Morgan White show this Sunday night? I am delivering this by hand, as you can see, and I thought you would want to know that one of your neighbors —old dude—was taken off in an ambulance just now.

Sincerely,
G. C. Ottway

These messages, together with Mr. Ottway's paper in its large manila envelope, and the November issue of *True Stories,* strained the limits of Grace's mailbox so severely that she had to rip a portion of Fiona's letter to get them out. Ordinarily she would have been vexed at this disorderly proof of the many claims upon her attention, but on the first day of her freedom it seemed touching. The world had missed her, after all.

She read Fiona's note on the elevator and smiled at the reference to the "b." Clearly her cousin felt that Grace left her mail about for anyone to see and was protecting her privacy. Deveraux's message had been scrawled on a postcard which featured the Washington Monument in full erection as seen through a screen of cherry blossoms. This, too, made her smile. Her apartment stretched before her, limitless in its familiar shabbiness and all the more welcoming after the enforced luxury she had endured at Edward's. She noticed with some appreciation that Edward had removed all traces of his crime. The glasses they had drunk from had been wiped clean and returned to the kitchen; even the ashtrays had been emptied. She carried the rest of her mail through to the bedroom and selected Jenny's letter next, leaving the best for last. Had Sam discovered Jenny's perfidy before or after taping the Morgan White show? She thought that her friend was in no real danger, but she could not be sure. She was too anxious to read what Mr. Ottway had to say to dwell on Jenny's problems. When she came to the part about her ailing neighbor she felt with certainty, and sorrow, that it was old Maurice. Gilbert's manuscript—it was entitled "A Talk With Giacomo Leopardi"—would have to wait until she had scouted out Julio and determined which of the old people had faltered over Halloween. Perhaps it was not Maurice. Her judgments, instincts, of late, had been far from infallible.

She found Julio resting in his basement chamber. His feet were propped against a tiny refrigerator which sweated and grumbled in a corner, and he was leafing through a back copy of *National Geographic*. He looked up from a full-page color photo of a tree toad and motioned her to step inside. "These pictures," he said, "remarkable, no? Look how the small frog is so clear in every detail."

"Very nice," said Grace. "Very good photography."

"I can always get this magazine from 10C," said Julio. "They throw it out the first of the month."

"Can you tell me who was taken off in an ambulance? I was away for the weekend."

"That was the old man on the eleventh," said Julio. "Mr. Bolovsky. His heart's no good for years now."

"But he's alive? Where is he? Which hospital?"

"I don't know," said Julio, flipping the page to admire a tripartite foldout of tropical insects. "They take him away in the police ambulance. He's maybe still alive, but he is old."

Grace shifted her feet, feeling awkward, suddenly, and intrusive. "Do you think he will die, Julio?"

"Sure. He will die, probably."

"I liked him very much."

"Sure," said Julio. "I too. I known Mr. Bolovsky longer than you." He made this seem an accusation, a censure of Grace's rash, headstrong affections on such short acquaintance. She felt she might actually be blushing and did not know why. "Look," said Julio suddenly, smiling broadly for the first time Grace could recall, "look—don't be afraid of dying. Life is the thing to be afraid of, not death." And then, with the air of one offering a special treat to a fretful child, he took her up to the lobby in the service elevator.

The hospital, unlike the country-clubbish one Grace had visited when Naomi's son was born, was old, dim, and cheerless. There were no pretenses here; it seemed to guarantee misery and discomfort from the moment one stepped inside. Prowling the corridors in search of old Maurice, she saw an astounding display of feet. In one room a woman lay propped against pillows, doing needlework. She looked robust enough, plying her needle with a firm brown arm; only the fact that her feet, which were strong and somewhat circular in shape, were bare, betrayed the fact that she was confined to the room, a patient. Her neighbor sat with skinny legs dangling over the edge of the bed, scrabbling for her slippers with prehensile toes. She wore an inappropriate lavender nightgown which intensified the pallor of her skin. It was a whorish gown; Grace had seen racks of them in the open-air stalls on Fourteenth Street. Soon enough, a corner turned, the tenants of the rooms became old men. They too displayed feet which were spidery and blanched from long disuse. Those who were able to move about were all in the process of shedding, or donning, their slippers. The flurry of activity heralded the beginning of visiting hours. Grace had timed things correctly for once, although—in her haste to get to the hospital—she had neglected to bring an offering.

Mr. Bolovsky, when she found him, lay flat, head reposing on a stingy pillow, eyes shut, feet pointing upward beneath the thin blanket. The veins in his eyelids showed like the veins of autumn leaves through the delicate parchment. They were as blue as the Adriatic Sea, perhaps drawing color from the unseen eyes themselves. His hands were out of sight beneath the covers, but a long tube attached to an IV entered him at midarm. He was breathing regularly. The other bed in the room had been recently vacated, the covers thrown back and a pile of magazines scattered over the surface as if the tenant had tired of them and flung them aside.

Grace looked about nervously, wondering if the occupant might come shuffling out of the bathroom and demand proof of her rights to visit, but the door stood ajar and she could see that the room was vacant. A weak light came through the single window. It had been sunny when Grace arrived, but the hospital room's mysterious alchemy absorbed and thinned the light as if to tell the patients they were missing little. There were no flowers in the room, no books by Maurice's bed. She brought a straight-backed chair close to his side and sat in it. She was prepared to wait. She did not know what she would say to him when he awakened, nor even why she had come, precisely. It was possible that he would not recognize her, or even that he would recognize but not welcome her.

The sounds from the corridor were becoming louder as visitors arrived. The well hailed the sick in loud, cheerful voices designed to reassure, and the collective clamor of their separate deceptions came rolling through the halls like thunder claps. Still Maurice slept on, pushing closer to oblivion with every breath he drew. He did not look sick, merely very old. This in itself was a novelty to Grace. She had never seen an old person *in extremis.* All the deaths in her life had involved young people. Charles Peacock had been the oldest, a teenaged girl—once a baby-sitter to Grace—who died of polio the youngest. She had never been obliged to look at Jules's body, but he too had been young. This habit of death, of taking to its bosom those who made attractive hostages to the living, she had never questioned. And now Maurice, a man of eighty, whose only importance to Grace had been one of a chiefly imaginary nature, was dying. Of this she could have no doubt. His seltzer hair already lacked the icy lustre she had observed in the lobby of their building on the day the elevator failed. His face was drawing inward, toward the bone, and with his eyes obscured in sleep there was no hint of the wry male spirit which had so engaged her.

She continued to sit by his side, keeping him company while he slept through what would perhaps be his last day. She never questioned her right to claim that privilege, although she knew she had none. She thought instead of Jenny's foolish plight, of what she might say to Mr. Ottway when the seminar met again, of Edward and Christine gathering up the linen she had used and dropping it into the laundry basket. When these thoughts had lost their charm, she reached into her bag and withdrew *True Story,* careful to hold it in such a way that passersby would not be able to see what she was reading. She leafed through the cover stories, studying the photo layouts. She had been reading confessions magazines for so long that she recognized many of the models. Here were several familiar faces—the girl in shorts and running shoes under the title I JOGGED MYSELF OUT OF MY MARRIAGE was the same who had appeared, more poignantly, in a tale of infant mortality in a rival publication not long before. This jogging story seemed to be a tongue-in-cheek piece about a married couple whose ideas of physical fitness clashed. Grace was not pleased to see the note of mirth, barely concealed, which surfaced in her magazines these days. It was as if nobody took the stories seriously anymore, even—to judge by the enthusiastic reader response reported for the trendier items—the readers.

Jules had warned her that the letters to the editor were frequently written by the editors themselves. She turned now to the readers' forum and saw, with sinking heart, that most of the letters were signed anonymously: "Mrs. L.R." or "Sheralee K.," which seemed to corroborate Jules's story. On the other hand, the women who wrote in would hardly want their names published in full. It was anyone's guess. Mrs. L.R. had written to report that she sympathized "with all my heart" when she read of Cara's troubled marriage in the August issue. "It really struck a chord in my own life, for very often I have experienced the same emotions as Cara. Bless you for making me feel like I'm not so alone." This seemed genuine enough.

But what of Mrs. T. J. of Mendota, Wisconsin, who saw fit to announce: "Like Mary Jo in the August bonus-length story, I too have had a breast removed. But where Mary Jo's husband learned to love her just as much minus her breast, my husband can't bring himself to touch me since I got back from the hospital. I truly feel that I am Half a Woman and wish my husband was more like Paul. I am trim and blonde and people tell me real attractive for my age (41) but as far as my husband is concerned I might as well be dead." This had a false ring, smacked of smart-ass fabrication. If an editor had made it up, where did her responsibility end? Having invented Mrs. T. J., mightn't she have also invented a set of anxieties and set them loose in Mendota, Wisconsin, without heeding the consequences? She thought of testing *True Story*'s probity with a letter of her own: "I have been feeling very depressed lately and look forward to your magazine each month to cheer me up. My doctor says I have a bad case of anomie and need to read about the lives of real people who suffer real problems. Thank you for providing me with therapy."

A nurse looked in, scrutinized Grace, and made a notation.

"Where is the other patient?" Grace asked.

"Gone for X-rays."

"Do you think Mr. Bolovsky will wake up?"

"Hard to tell," said the nurse. "Maybe yes, maybe no."

"I am his granddaughter."

"Fine," said the nurse. "Visiting hours will be over in half an hour." She went to check on Maurice's IV bag, turning back the covers to get at his arm. He was wearing blue and white striped pajamas with darker blue piping at the collar and breast pocket.

"Who brought him here?" said Grace.

"Ambulance," said the nurse.

When she had gone, Grace shoved the magazine deeper into her handbag and made contact with something heavy and smooth at the bottom. She drew it out, knowing before she saw it that it would be the soapstone seal she had admired. It settled into her hands exactly as she had remembered, like a part of her body returning after a temporary estrangement. Light spilled from its silken surface and gathered in a pool in her cupped hands; the corner where she sat was brighter now than it had been. She was pleased at Edward's simple generosity; she had always been good at accepting gifts. She sat holding the seal, perfectly content, for some time. Gradually she became aware of voices again in the corridor, diminished, weary now, worn down by the hour of reality they had safely negotiated, and she understood that soon she would be forced to leave.

Maurice, too, seemed mindful of the time, because he stirred delicately and came awake. His gaze was fixed not on her, but on the carving. Slowly, his eyes made the journey to her face and she could not immediately tell whether he knew her or not. She pressed the seal into his unencumbered hand, closing the fingers around the heavy smooth stone. His flesh, by contrast, was as weightless and dry as a grasshopper's. She had expected it to be cold, but it was quite neutral and pleasant in temperature, like a weatherless day.

"Thank you," he said in a faint but steady voice. "Have you been waiting long, Miss Peacock?"

"No," said Grace. "It hasn't seemed long."

He was studying her with care, and with a hint of the amusement he had found in her presence that day in the lobby. "Why have you come?" he said at last. There was no rudeness in the way he had voiced the question, only genuine curiosity.

"I told them I was your granddaughter," said Grace.

He nodded, but his eyes remained unsatisfied. "That does not answer my question," he chided. "I did not ask how you got in, but why you came?" His voice was remarkably strong now, not the quavering reed she had expected. She admired and feared him.

"I came because I like you," she said. "From the first moment, by the elevator that day, I liked you."

He nodded again, smiling now, pleased. "I know."

"I wish," said Grace uncertainly, "that we had known each other better."

"You put it in the past, this friendship," said Maurice. "You think I am dying?"

Grace remained silent. She was in uncertain waters now; nothing in her past life had taught her the etiquette for conversing with moribund persons.

"Yes," sighed Maurice, "you are right. This time I am dying. I have been sick before, but this is the last time for me. I will die." He loosened his hold on the soapstone seal, then grasped it more firmly, hoisting his hand to his chest. "I knew when I saw you, sitting by my bed when I awoke, that I was a goner. Otherwise, you would not be here."

"Oh, no," cried Grace, appalled. "I would have come if you had only broken your leg—" Both of them reflected on this remark, smitten by its possibilities. "I was away, you see. I discovered you'd been brought to the hospital when I got back. A friend put a note in my mailbox. I wanted to come, to see you. I would have wanted to see you even if you'd been well." And then she told him about being kidnapped, and how it had been accomplished, and described the comfort in which her captors had kept her all weekend. "I thought of you several times," she concluded, "and also of the person who happened to see you go off in the ambulance." And then, because he seemed interested, she told him about the Anomie Show and about Mr. Ottway's unexpected role in it.

"Giacomo Leopardi was rachitic," Maurice said instructively. "He had a humped back and he died at the age of thirty-nine. What does your Mr. Ottway find in him to so identify?"

"He's black," said Grace, "but that's stretching a point."

"No," said Maurice, "it is a confederation of the dispossessed. Or so your young friend thinks."

Grace asked if she were tiring him and he confessed that this was so. "But stay, stay," he urged. "This will be the last chance for us to be together, you and I."

"I could come back tonight," said Grace.

Maurice shook his head sadly. "No. It would be no good tonight. My daughter will be here then. She is coming from California."

"I'm glad," said Grace.

"No, no," he shook his head irritably, "don't be glad. It is a mistake to think a man must have his family about him. I don't need to see her, don't want to know . . ."

Grace waited for him to finish, but he watched her shrewdly, daring her to supply the words. "You don't want to know she'll be alive when you're gone?" He nodded. "You don't like her?" He thought it over.

"I am too old to like my children," he said at last. "When they were young I loved them, and when they grew up I felt the loss of them—as they had been—and then, one day, when they were fully grown I realized how foolish it was that we must continue to know each other, year after year. I wished them well, I was pleased when one had children of her own, but all of it was playacting, beyond that. There was no meat to it, no passion. My son died long before me, when he was a man of thirty, and I felt such sorrow, such sorrow! But only," he shut his eyes briefly, "because it reversed the order of things." He opened his eyes and looked at her with a fierce and contemptuous expression. "You think I am a hard old bird?" he asked.

"No," said Grace. "I think we are alike."

"Now my wife," said Maurice, his voice softening, "I loved her with my heart. I loved her also with my body, even when we were no longer so pretty to look at, and I loved her with my mind and soul. When *she* died, I can tell you, I was furious—mad with rage. I could not look at my daughter for wishing it had been *she* who had died, and it made me ashamed. I could not love my grandchildren, because the link was missing."

"Now you are beyond me," said Grace. "I envy you."

"I also," said Maurice, smiling again, "had mistresses—other women—before and after my wife died. I loved them all, and one was very like you to look at, but none could I love as I loved Sophie. She was so funny."

"I think I'm going to cry," said Grace.

Maurice nodded. "That would be okay with me," he said. "I would cry, myself, only the tears won't come. The body fails in many ways, you know. If I were only strong enough I would pummel my body, punish it for failing me, but this is an impossibility."

"What shall I do?" said Grace. "What shall I do?"

"Say goodbye to me now and leave. My daughter would not like you, we wouldn't be free to talk."

"But what shall I do?"

"Ah, such a silly question. Go home. Have a good time. Live your life. Try for everything, expect nothing. This is where it ends. Only this. Think of me sometimes; I am superstitious."

Grace bent close to him, letting her tears fall upon his cheeks. It seemed the only service she could perform for him at this late date. She felt the hugeness of her young face, hovering over his small and wasted one, and was ashamed of it. "Don't kiss me," he murmured, so softly she wondered afterwards if she had heard him right. "It might make me dream."

"Goodbye," she said, but he had closed his eyes again and appeared to be asleep. The fingers of his right hand, the one which clasped Edward's soapstone figure, fluttered a weak farewell.

"I warned you," said Deveraux heatedly. "I told you not to have anything to do with him." Grace had described her weekend with Edward, omitting the intimacies which had passed between them on Halloween. "What do you want me to do?" asked Deveraux. "Shall I call Woolas?"

"No. It's none of your business, really. It's between me and Edward, and it's over." Grace said this placatingly, aware that the words themselves would be unpleasing.

"He's a maniac, a fucking nutcase," said Deveraux. "It's partly your fault—oh, yes, it is, Grace—but all the same he's certifiable." He pronounced this last word with satisfaction. He had been uncomfortable and oddly unmoved at hearing of her visit to Maurice. "I don't like hospitals," he said. He had dismissed her account of the Morgan White show with a shrug of impatience. Only the saga of her kidnapping had interested him, and this she had saved for last. They were on their way to Naomi's, where Jenny had taken refuge. "You sure she won't mind my being there?" Dev asked, with the bewildering swing from passion to good manners which he occasionally displayed.

"Jenny loves an audience," said Grace.

Deveraux began to describe a speech he had given at a Georgetown fund-raiser. Without warning he stopped and pushed Grace roughly against the doorway of a Broadway poultry shop. "He didn't hurt you? Didn't try to screw you when you were helpless?"

Grace was so astounded by this unrelated train of thought that she could only stare at him, mindful that two scrofulous types were watching with avid eyes from a nearby bus stop. Slowly, she shook her head. "He was the soul of kindness," she said. Still Dev refused to relinquish his grip. The onlookers, used to livelier disputes, turned away. "A million women in the world," said Dev at last, "and I have to meet you." He rearranged her coat and took her hand and they continued up Broadway. "I'm sorry," he said, when they'd gone a block. "It's just I feel like a fool. I don't know what to do with you. It's like adopting a kid, a kid you're allowed to make love to, and having to worry about it all the time."

"There's no need," Grace said. "Honestly, there isn't."

A cold wind had sprung up off the Hudson and whipped bits of paper around their ankles as they turned east. Pumpkins had been put out for the garbage collectors and stared sightlessly from the tops of trash cans, their indistinct features halted in the decomposing process by the threat of frost. Grace wanted to be inside in the warmth of Naomi's kitchen where she could call the hospital and check on Maurice. She walked more quickly, pulling Dev along with her. "It's creepy on these side streets," she said. "Hurry, Dev."

Ahead of them a shadowy group of young men loitered in the deep gloom of a brownstone doorway. They fanned out across the sidewalk and then reassembled in a cluster, a movement of such potentially warlike meaning that Grace wondered if now could be the moment, the moment everyone dreaded, when she would be jumped upon, her clothing ripped, handbag stolen, her body trampled and broken by pounding feet as they retreated toward the park. What match would Deveraux be for five grown boys as large as himself? Rape never entered her mind. They would have to lay hands on her, wrestle her to the ground, despatch with Deveraux, unbutton themselves in the November chill and somehow maneuver her unwilling body into the proper position—no, rape was too cumbersome an act to accomplish in public at this early hour of the night, but a simple act of violence could take place with appalling ease. She looked up at Dev, whose eyes were narrowed against the wind only; no fear there. Perhaps she was imagining danger. Prompted by the discussions of mayhem she had listened to the night before, jarred by the emotional experience she had undergone at Maurice's bedside, she thought that coming as close to death as she had done that afternoon might have stamped her, set her aside in some way, as an appropriate victim.

The group was straggling out over the pavement again, surging forward and then back in unison, and then she heard the music, coming from a low-tuned transistor radio which had been propped on the stoop. The boys were learning to dance the Hustle. She could hear their leader urging them, softly: "Back, back, one two . . . side, side . . ." One of them looked up as she and Deveraux passed and smiled at her with the abstracted sweetness of one whose concentration was elsewhere.

"False alarm!" said Naomi at the door. "You don't have to worry." Grace looked perplexed. "Chicken pox," Naomi explained. "The kids don't have it after all."

The television was droning away from the back of the apartment, but the children were nowhere in sight. Jenny was sitting in Naomi's living room, huddling in a large Italian rocker. She had an afghan around her shoulders and her nose in a glass of brandy. Her eyes were swollen and red, but they brightened noticeably at the sight of Grace and most especially of Deveraux, whom she had never met. Naomi hugged Grace and muttered, without moving her lips: "Joe's still away. Jenny's been here all weekend." They advanced into the living room, where Jenny was smoothing her hair and checking surreptitiously at the corners of her eyes for bits of silt brought on by weeping. She extended a graceful hand to Deveraux and then resumed her rocking, staring with tragic intensity into the middle distance. Naomi felt obliged to whisper when she asked if Grace and Deveraux would like a drink.

"I brought all this brandy with me," said Jenny. "Three bottles. It cleaned me out. I've been staying at a hotel since we taped the Morgan White show, but I ran out of money on Friday."

"How did it happen?" asked Grace.

Jenny looked pointedly at Deveraux. "Look," he said, "if you want to be alone I can go back and watch TV or something."

"No. No." Jenny extended quavering fingers in his direction. "It'll be all over town soon. I might as well get used to it. Actually, you're probably the last people in New York to hear about it."

Grace thought this claim more histrionic than even Jenny could carry off, but she said nothing.

"I know what Grace is thinking," said Jenny. "You're thinking I'm a self-important nobody, aren't you? It may interest you to know that Sam talked the whole thing over on the Morgan White show. He sat there"—Jenny shuddered, genuinely, Grace thought "—and announced that his own wife was so alienated she had to get her sex from a *shrink.*"

"We didn't hear it," said Grace. "You must know they bleeped it, Jen."

"They didn't *bleep* it," said Jenny scornfully. "You can't *bleep* a whole dissertation like Sam's. They didn't use it, that's all. Mostly, Sam talked about me during the station breaks, and then when he was back on camera he talked about anomie, and there I was, shivering out in the audience, afraid he'd start in right in front of the whole world!" Fresh tears rolled down Jenny's cheeks and she scrubbed at her eyes impatiently. "It was the first I knew. I didn't know he'd found out about Martin. He didn't even have the kindness to tell me, he just stored up his anger and let it loose *right on camera!"* This last was a wail, and Grace felt torn between pity and the need to laugh.

"Hard to believe, isn't it?" said Naomi. She looked dazed, and delivered her clucks and sighs of sympathy as if by rote. She'd heard the story more than once, obviously.

"It's exactly the sort of thing Sam would do," said Grace. This was a tactical error, since if anything could make Jenny appear more foolish than she had already been made to seem, it was the implication that Jenny's husband was also a fool. To smooth things over she asked: "How did the others react?" More than anything, she wanted to hear about Mr. Ottway, but Jenny would have to be gentled along first.

"Morgan was an absolute saint," said Jenny. "He's a wonderful man, Grace, so humble and unassuming. I've been in touch with him since that awful night, and he's terribly anxious for me to make it up with Sam. He just can't see that I'd never be able to look Sam in the face again. Not after this sort of betrayal. Never."

"And the others?"

"They ate it up, of course, adored every minute." She closed her eyes in agony and then whispered: "Sam mentioned Martin. By name."

For the first time Deveraux spoke. "I don't think you have to worry about it getting around. From what Grace told me they were mainly clerics and professional people. They won't gossip."

"Won't gossip!" shrieked Jenny. "That bitch Bodgett could hardly wait to get to the phone. That's why she walked out, in case you didn't realize. She couldn't wait! I guarantee you she had Martin on the line in three minutes flat! The rotten, pretentious, *unethical* bitch!"

"I thought," said Grace, "she was very big on sisterhood."

"Exactly. Scorekeepers will try to make a *cause célèbre* out of it—can't you see it now? 'Doctor takes advantage of woman patient.' She'll get Martin disbarred, or whatever it's called."

"Oh, dear," said Naomi.

"How did Sam find out?" said Grace.

"I suppose he read my diary," said Jenny. "Sam and I have always kept journals," she explained to Deveraux, "ever since we were first married. It went without saying that neither of us would stoop to reading the other's most private thoughts."

"Didn't you ever read Sam's?" asked Grace.

"Well, once or twice I did," Jenny said demurely. "Of course I did. It's hard to resist, isn't it? But Sam's journal never had anything *important* in it. It was so . . . high-minded. All about his thoughts and theories . . . once when I read it I couldn't even imagine what he was talking about. I thought"—she colored and brought out her final words defiantly—"I thought he'd never bother with mine. I mean, it was so boring!"

"Until you met Martin?" said Grace.

"Right. Until I met Martin."

Grace offered to let Jenny stay with her, safe in the knowledge that her hospitality would be refused. What Naomi offered—respectability, a quiet corner in the bosom of her unruly but indisputably correct household—was precisely what Grace could not offer. If Sam should come looking for his wife and find her with the Weinstocks he would behave tolerably well, but let him loose in Grace's apartment and none of them would leave alive. Naomi was almost asleep on the floor of her living room; Grace took a cushion and placed it beneath her friend's head. Naomi was drooling slightly, from exhaustion, and Grace suggested that they ought to go. While Deveraux and Jenny carried on an awkward conversation about tranquilizers and sleeping pills, Grace went to the kitchen phone and called the hospital.

Mr. Bolovksy's condition was listed as fair. This, as she realized, meant nothing other than that he was still alive.

XV

"Oh, Gloria," Len moaned, "I love you so." He rolled off me like a frog off a lily pad, and that was that. It had been like this every night of our honeymoon, and I wanted to scream. Len had a big grin of contentment on his face, and me? I felt as if somebody had poured scalding water all over my body. I was so jittery and tense I knew I could never go to sleep.

"Honey," I said softly, running one hand over his chest and nibbling at his ear, "couldn't we try again?"

"For Pete's sake, Gloria, I'm not Superman!" Len's craggy features clouded over and he turned away from me. I couldn't have said anything worse. All during our honeymoon, whenever I tried to tell Len what would please me, he got sulky and withdrawn. "I'm a man, not a machine," he'd mutter. "Then maybe I'd be better off with a machine!" I taunted back. Of course I didn't mean it. I loved Len and wanted him, but I also wanted an orgasm. I'd read all the books, and I knew what I was missing.

It wasn't until we came back to Plainsville, though, that I remembered my wisecrack about a machine. My best friend Marge had come over to help me hang some curtains, and we were talking.

"Did you see what they've got displayed in Thurber's Drugstore, right in the window?" She was giggling. "Three guesses!"

"Don't keep me in suspense," I said. Marge was always like that—gossiping and telling secrets. I liked her, though. She was fun, and she wasn't ashamed to say what she thought about anything.

"Vibrators," she said. "Big as life." She shot me a look full of mischief. "Ever thought of trying one?"

Suddenly, my heart was pumping. "Why would I need a vibrator?" I asked, blushing. "I've got a brand-new husband."

Marge winked at me over the curtain rod. "Honey, half the women in town who buy 'em have husbands. That's just the point!"

I should have known better, but it was as if some little imp was leading me on. That night, in bed with Len, I wound my fingers in his curly hair and murmured, "Honey? Guess what they've got displayed in Thurber's Drugstore, right in the window?"

"Marcie! Are you all right?" The voice seemed to be coming from a long way away. I opened my eyes and saw Dell standing at the door of the bedroom. He was looking at the littered floor with disgust.

"What's going on here?" Dell began to wade through the piles of dirty laundry. "It looks like a hurricane hit while I was gone."

"Oh, honey," I pleaded, "don't be mad at me. I was going to do the laundry but I got to meditating and I just forgot."

Dell's smoky-blue eyes turned almost black with anger. "I've about had it, Marcie," he said tautly. "Every day I work from eight to six to keep up the payments on this house. All I look forward to is coming home to peace and quiet and what do I get?" He kicked a soiled pillowcase out of his way and advanced on me. "An unholy mess—that's what this house is. You're too busy meditating or playing with those stupid coins to do your share. You're selfish."

Dell was a Capricorn and I was a Scorpio. It wasn't always easy to make him see things my way. "Dell, try to understand," I pleaded. "I'm trying to improve myself so I can be a better person for you. It's all for you, honey, don't you see?"

"This is a heck of a way to prove it," Dell said grimly. "All that weird chanting and mooning around—the neighbors think you're crazy, did you know that? Sometimes I have to agree with them."

I ran to him and wound my arms around his neck, pressing my body close to his. "Dell, darling, give me a chance to know myself." I wriggled against him and felt his strong arms come around me, his warm lips crush down on mine . . . The messy room was fading away and all I knew was the warm, insistent pounding of my blood as Dell picked me up and carried me to our bed. My moon was in Venus and I knew our lovemaking would be even more ecstatic than usual.

"Marcie," Dell muttered roughly . . . "Don't try to change yourself. I love you the way you are . . ."

That did it. I rolled away from him, furious that he couldn't try to understand me. "Why are you so blind?" I screamed. "Why can't you—"

Dear [imaginary] daughter,

I regret to tell you that I may have been wrong in commending confessions magazines to you. A certain note of unbecoming levity has crept into their pages lately; a hint of contemptuous mirth which gives the show away. After all, if there is nobody left who—

It seemed to Grace that she had entered upon a new and not altogether pleasing phase of her life, but its meaning eluded her.

She was, for the first time, totally alone. Deveraux had gone to visit his family in Vermont, and she had refused his invitation to join him on the grounds that she had a seminar to teach; no sooner had he left than a custodial strike closed the university down until further notice. Mr. Ottway did not call or contact her in any way and she felt more dashed than she cared to admit. When she phoned Naomi to inquire after Jenny, Joe told her that Naomi needed total rest and was not to be disturbed in any way. This he said kindly, for Joe was always kind, but he would not elaborate in any way and Grace feared her friend was on the edge of some terrible despair none of them had seen. As for Jenny, Joe said she'd gone back to Sam. Edward sent a note explaining that he and Christine were planning a trip to the Canadian Arctic to buy sculpture. It was elliptically worded, though affectionate, and Grace thought she could detect a note of definite farewell. Although this was exactly what she had wanted she could not prevent herself from feelings of desertion.

Christine, too, sent a note. It was written in a small, round hand on pale blue notepaper and informed Grace that Edward would always be "there" if Grace should need him. Grace was not to feel an intruder if ever the day came when . . . etc., etc. It was signed: "Warmly, Christine Zulov." Grace had never known Christine's last name; at the sudden revelation she felt a surge of warmth toward Edward's brisk mistress. There was no further word from Fiona. Only Maurice had not left her, but he was as inaccessible to her as the others. All she could do was phone the hospital every day.

She spent her time vainly trying to read her magazines with the old interest, which was impossible, and taking long walks. She would realize with a start that it was late afternoon and she had not yet stirred from her bed. Then a panic would seize her. The magazines flew in all directions as she hurled back the covers and sprinted for her clothes. She dressed carelessly, but her fingers trembled as she buttoned a sweater or brushed her hair. Anyone watching might have mistaken this awkwardness for a certain eagerness to be out in the day before the light had waned, but she knew it was something more primitive. She felt, hopping in her impatience to clothe herself, that she was racing against an unseen rival. Once, thrusting her feet into boots and scrabbling in a drawer for a scarf, she looked up and caught her image in the mirror—she seemed a madwoman, at the very least a homeowner surrounded by flames, trying to rescue some precious possession before the fire claimed everything.

She walked in any direction her feet took her, without pleasure. Sometimes she headed up Broadway, or toward the river where the ancient train yards groaned and clanged with the coupling and uncoupling of freight cars, going nowhere. One afternoon she walked across the park and down Madison Avenue all the way to Murray Hill. She thought she saw Jules's eldest sister, Helen, emerging from a shop in the Fifties, but she could not be sure. So much time had passed—it might be any woman with dark hair and a vaguely predatory air. The woman halted and seemed to stare at Grace with more than ordinary interest, but she may have been looking past her, searching for a cab.

When Grace felt tired enough, or it had grown too cold for walking, she hailed a cab and went back home. Even her apartment building seem deserted. The pimps had gone south for the winter or remained indoors and her street corner was quiet, almost respectable. The old people, too, kept to their apartments during the cold months and frequently the lobby was empty and dim when Grace returned. Once she saw the tail of a Persian lamb coat just disappearing in the closing elevator doors and felt she had seen a ghost.

She bought greasy chicken and knishes from the Broadway shops where rotisseries never ceased to turn in the windows and carried them home to eat. She purchased liquor and cigarettes and confessions magazines and scurried home with her treasures, feeling like a bagwoman. The first thing she did when she had turned on all the lights in her apartment was call the hospital. When Maurice's condition had been listed as "fair" for three days in a row she permitted herself to hope he might recover, after all.

She thought often of his parting advice to her and it seemed a tribute to his wisdom that he was able in so few words to explain to her the failure of her life. The women in her love stories tried for little, calling it much, but they expected everything, else why their surprise when events did not fall together properly? She herself had expected nothing and tried for little—she had only to remedy the latter view to obey Mr. Bolovsky, but how to go about it? She would sit ruminating on the problem, refilling her glass and allowing grease stains to accumulate on the opened pages of *True Story* as she picked listlessly at her Merit Farms suppers.

Occasionally she was interrupted by the ringing of the phone, which she answered promptly in case it should be Mr. Ottway. Usually it was Deveraux, calling from some rural bar in the midst of Happy Hour, or one of the persistent men from her past. Her professor friend phoned to invite her to a party and the sound of his voice shocked her profoundly. How was it that people she never thought of from week to week could have the will to call? She told him she was busy and listened to him complain about his students for a quarter of an hour. "You know what your trouble is?" he asked toward the end of their conversation. "You think you'll last forever. What're you saving it for?"

"Very scholarly analysis," said Grace.

"Oh, well," he sighed, "give me a call when you're feeling insecure."

Another man called, late one evening, to ask her to dine with him sometime. His name was Paul. She could not recall having met him and tried without success to place him. At last she thought she remembered—he was a lawyer, a friend of Joe Weinstock's.

"How is Naomi?" she asked. "Have you heard?"

"Naomi who?"

And then she realized that Paul was Sam's friend, not Joe's, and marveled at her inability to connect events with names and voices. She told him she would be leaving town for an indefinite period.

Mr. Buonsuccesso called to suggest, timidly, that if the custodial strike continued they might hold the seminar in her apartment. "It means so much to all of us, Miss Peacock. I've talked to the others, and we all agree we don't want to miss another session. We need your (ha!) guidance." He was pleading, although his voice was as bluff and man-to-man as ever. She did not want to have them there; in fact, if he had proposed that the entire class come watch her in her bath it could not have offended her more deeply. If only she could not picture him so clearly at the other end! She thought he would be sitting, vast briefcase leaning against his knee, in his mother's kitchen, one leg propped on the door to keep the sounds of his large and quarrelsome family from entering their conversation. His prematurely heavy face would be wearing the *bon vivant* expression it assumed for their literary chats, an expression which seemed doubly sad to her because it remained, as if pasted on, even after he had been rebuffed. She acquiesced. She even detained him to ask if he had talked to Mr. Ottway. "I've never seen him outside of class," he said thoughtfully. "He pretty much keeps to himself."

Grace hung up and drafted a letter to the university resigning her post. She typed it neatly, then, and sealed it in an envelope, but she did not stamp it. Eventually she thrust it deep in a drawer of her desk and forgot about it. She drank a good deal of the Scotch she had bought and fell into sleep without difficulty.

The next day, seized with an uncharacteristic curiosity about her mail, she pulled an old coat on over her naked body and descended to the lobby. There was no mail of interest, only two bills and a circular promoting a new line of makeup. As she was scowling at the envelopes a woman swept off the elevator and came to join her at the letter boxes. She was a small woman of fifty years or so, who appeared bulky and commanding in her woolen suit; she had the sort of purposeful body which, terminating in frail ankles and wrists, appeared to have been borrowed for an occasion requiring great strength and energy. Her face was rather attractively seamed, as if she spent much of her time outdoors, but it was the eyes—piercing, brilliant, somehow familiar—that alerted Grace. The woman nodded briskly in her direction and bent to unlock the mailbox, withdraw its contents, and slam the small grill back in place with a breathtaking economy of motion. Grace was almost sure the letter box belonged to Mr. Bolovsky. She felt acutely her nakedness under the coat and was reminded of the time when she had thought salaciously of Maurice, fingering the contents of his medicine cabinet with erotic glee, nursing vivid images of his sexual organ as she sped down the stairs with his medicine pressed to her breasts. And now his daughter—it must be she—was standing in the lobby regarding her with covert alarm.

They rode up on the elevator together. The woman pushed the button for the eleventh floor as Grace had known she would. "Yours?" said the daughter of Sophie and Maurice, fingers hovering over the panel impatiently.

"Six," said Grace. "Are you visiting?"

"My father is in the hospital. I'm staying in his flat until"— she looked momentarily dispossessed —"until the end."

"Ah," said Grace. "Mr. Bolovsky?"

The woman nodded. "He won't let go," she said, as if Mr. Bolovsky were a bulldog who had fastened on the postman's trouser leg. "He just keeps hanging on."

"I can't say that I blame him," said Grace, "under the circumstances." The woman smiled thinly. The look on her face when the elevator cranked to a halt on Grace's floor was unmistakably one of relief.

She did not go out that afternoon. She unearthed an old photo album and sat for hours staring at the pictures. She thought there was something in their pattern which might clarify things for her, although she did not know what needed to come clear. The earliest pictures she had borrowed from Winifred Peacock long ago, taking them with her to college out of motives which puzzled her now as much as they had done at the time. Her mother had never asked for the pictures and they remained, stuck loosely in the margins of the book, only now beginning to fade.

Here was her father, dressed in a ludicrous suit with pleated pants, standing in their garden. The habitual sadness in his eyes was masked by the fact that he was squinting in the sun. Winifred, snapped on the same day, wore sunglasses and a white piqué dress. She was leaning against the family car, a dark Lincoln, and in its polished surface was the reflection of Charles Peacock, squatting some ten feet away, pressing his eye to the Leica's sighting device. Now Winifred again, toeing into sand at the lake shore and holding Grace's hand. Grace reached barely to her mother's thigh. Her hair was plastered inkily to the sides of her head, as if she had just come from the water, and she was scowling. This was all that remained of her early years; the album abruptly jumped ahead and there was Grace performing in plays at college. She looked urbane and wicked, or mysterious and suave, as the role demanded. There was only one picture of Grace at university in her natural role, that of herself, and this showed her with a group of fraternity boys and their dates. She looked plumper than she could ever remember having been, and her lips, black with paint, seemed enormous in a face that was a perfect blank, a moon of vapidity. She could remember the others in the photo as perfectly as if she saw them still, every day: Jan Rehnquist and Peter Loughlin and Roger Wilde and Mary Britten . . . she could recite the names without a moment's pause, yet she had not thought of them from that year to this day.

Jenny began to appear, in the early New York days. They had met in summer stock and some wag had photographed Grace and Jenny sitting back to back on the verandah of a theatre in Massachusetts, profiles lifted dramatically against a background of painted flats. She and Jenny had not changed much, to look at, and this seemed wrong. Grace scoured the pictures for some sign that more than a decade of living had sharpened their features, added something lovable or wise to the lift of the lips or the set of the eyebrows, but there was no discernible change.

She turned the page to find the sole surviving picture of Jules. He had ripped the few photos they had possessed in the heat of a terrible quarrel—what had it been about?—and now the only proof in Grace's album that he had lived was a page she had torn from one of his own magazines. In an effort to save on modeling fees, Jules and the other editors had often taken pictures of each other to illustrate their stories. Jules had posed for a full-page shot under the caption "Gals Who Go For Gangsters—What Are They Really Like?" and had been captured for all eternity in a slouch hat, a cigar clenched between his teeth. In an effort to appear more sinister he had raised one eyebrow at the camera; he looked perplexed rather than dangerous, and very young.

She leafed through the rest of the album, looking at numerous images of Edward, Edward and Grace, and Grace photographed in every conceivable activity by Edward. There were also several instamatic snapshots taken in Wiltshire outside Fiona's cottage, and a jumble of loose newspaper clippings belonging to no particular period. She studied them all, paying close attention to a review of the prize-winning short story she had written so long ago: "There is a curious blankness, a quality of *ennui* in the writing which, more than any other factor, conveys with precision and sorrow the spirit of alienation which afflicts America's younger writers." Grace remembered she had thought the story very upbeat, a sort of wry and affectionate comment on the aspirations of Midwesterners who came to New York. She had been more embarrassed than anyone knew by the heavy constructions laid upon her writing by the people who awarded the prize, and she had determined to quit while she was winning, to rest on her small laurel and abandon writing for good. She and Jules had quarreled about that, too.

"You realize what you're saying, Grace? You're telling me if you can do it then it isn't worth doing."

"If more people felt like that the world would be a far better place."

And so on.

When she had read every word of each newspaper clipping, she turned again to the pictures of Jules and of her father. They looked out across the years at her, trapped forever—Charles Peacock wearing the costume of a Father and Jules masquerading as a gangster, and nothing hinted at the fact that they had ceased to exist. No special mark or shadow distinguished them from the others in the album; Life Everlasting had been granted them through the miracle of photography. Grace wished she had a picture of Maurice.

She forgot about food that night and wakened, ravenous, at 3:00 in the morning. There was nothing in her cupboard, nothing to be done. She dug several old confessions magazines out from the secret hoard in her closet and reread some of her favorite stories. They were vintage stories, serious and dignified. No sly, snickering note intruded to degrade the heroine's splendid sin or mock the swiftness of her fall. Such was the majesty of the beautiful concluding paragraphs, so surely did they lead to redemption, that Grace no longer felt the pangs of hunger.

In the morning she called the hospital. Mr. Bolovsky's condition had changed at last. He was now, the voice told Grace, "critical."

She dressed carefully for her trip to the letter boxes, but Maurice's daughter did not appear. Grace walked to the greasy spoon where she and Jenny had talked and ate a runny omelette, cardboard toast. When she had paid the check she had three dollars left. Her check from the university was late this month and she had spent Edward's money. It occurred to her to feel ashamed that a woman of her years and experience should be in such a position, but she had never earned much money. For a time Charles Peacock's trust fund had taken care of her, then Jules, then Edward. They had seen to it, all of them, that she could act in plays, write stories, pursue careers which were not lucrative; they had allowed her to coast through the years of her young womanhood with an ease she hadn't even noticed at the time. She thought of the letter of resignation lying in her desk drawer and had to laugh at her own naïveté. She had no choice, really, but to remain at the university for as long as they would have her.

She envisioned years at the seminar table, a replaceable cast of Mr. Buonsuccessos and Mrs. Dorfmans and Alonzo Garcías turning eager faces toward her. Each would come convinced that he or she was special in some way, talented, and each would regard her with mute trust, expecting her to blow the warm life of "creativity" into them until they sprang as artists from the basement of the university into the world. A fluke had placed her in the leader's chair where she was required to encourage delusion. Only Mr. Ottway seemed to her destined for greatness, but she had had no hand in molding him.

She read again his imaginary dialogue with Leopardi, smiling at his reference to the "effective pains and false felicities" of life. She wished that he would come to her and convert Maurice's metaphysical advice to a practical lesson, but she had given up hope of hearing from him. She put the phone in a drawer and lay on her bed, face to the ceiling, watching the room grow darker. It seemed fantastic to her that she had feared her apartment that sleepless night at Edward's. She was quite safe here. Nothing could disturb her peace.

Dear [imaginary] daughter,

I think I have been advising you badly. Certainly I meant well, but my advice was incorrect. Or, rather, all advice is incorrect. It is quite impossible to teach anyone anything at all, as I'm sure you will realize as you grow older. I myself was never taught anything, which may account for my desire to instruct you so carefully.

I am cutting you loose. Live your life. Have a good time. Try for everything, expect nothing. Think of me sometimes; I am superstitious.

Your loving mother
etc., etc., etc.

"I am nothing if not direct," said Mr. Ottway, "and you look awful."

He eyed Grace soberly and she could see reflected in his face the degree of her wretchedness. What she felt, seeing him in her doorway, was joy, but her recent solitude had deprived her of the means of showing it.

"You haven't been doing drugs?"

"No." Grace touched her matted hair, drew the sash of her robe closer. She reached for the bottle of champagne he was holding, but he pushed past her, frowning with displeasure. "Let's just see what's happening here," he said. "I come here to celebrate and find a slattern instead of Dr. Peacock. How come?"

Grace shrugged, tried to smile.

"For one thing, you got your phone in the drawer again. For another, you haven't picked up your mail lately." He examined her beneath the unflattering light of the kitchen fixture. "You haven't washed for a while and I bet you haven't eaten, either."

"What do you have to celebrate?"

"First things first. I refuse to be seen in public with you, so we'll have to eat here." He propelled her up the hall to the bathroom. "You go get clean. I'll do the shopping." He paused, eyeing her with distaste. "Give me your keys," he said. "I'll likely be back before you've finished."

The simple ritual of bathing, washing her hair, took a long time because she was weak. She stood dizzily regarding her face in the steamy mirror for some minutes. She could hear Mr. Ottway whistling as he busied himself in the kitchen. She practiced smiling, stretching her lips until they no longer felt alien. When she thought she might emerge there was a new problem. She wanted something clean to wear. She opened the door a crack and called to him to bring something from her closet. He brought her a silver lamé jumpsuit she had bought once for a party and long since forgotten, thrusting it decorously through the door, eyes averted. Obediently, she put it on.

He was sitting cross-legged on her living-room floor when she joined him. He had taken a blanket and spread it over the carpet; on its surface reposed an enormous and eclectic array of foodstuffs from the local restaurants and shops. There were white containers of Chinese food, foil-wrapped ribs from Bill's Bar-B-Q, tostadas to go, hamburgers, corn on the cob, and grapes both white and purple.

"Pick and choose," said Mr. Ottway, rising gallantly to acknowledge her presence. "What you don't eat, I will." He opened the champagne and poured her a small amount. "Go easy on that," he warned, "you haven't eaten for a long time."

Grace sipped and coughed. "You look better," said Mr. Ottway. "Cheers."

"I saw the Morgan White show," said Grace. "Why didn't you tell me you were going to be on it?"

"I like a surprise," said Gilbert.

"When did you know? Was it the night you called me from that party?"

"Uh-uh. I was having a bit of fun at that party—told Briscoe and his old lady I was a reformed gang leader; a whole pack of lies."

"Why?"

He bit into a tostada and munched thoughtfully. "There's a lot you don't know about me," he said finally. "What do you suppose I was doing at that party? A lot of sociologists and like that, talking chin dribble on Central Park South? Where would I fit in?"

"I can't see you serving drinks in a white jacket," said Grace, "so you must have been invited."

"Correct. I told you that party was mainly people of color. Did I also tell you it was sociologists of color? Now—eat up, please, try a rib—there aren't but four or five black academic types in New York rich enough to live on Central Park South. One of them happens to be—just happens to be—my father." He looked at her over the rim of his glass, half-smiling and very pleased with himself. She could not even pretend that she was not astonished; her mouth hung open and she dropped a grape.

"You conned the whole class," she said. "All that talk about cold-water flats."

"Not true. I didn't lie. I never said I wasn't Dr. Horace Paintry's son. Anyway, I don't live with him. I happen to be *illegitimate.*" He beamed, proud of the title. "My mother, who raised me, is

Miss Marla Jean Ottway and she ain't never been married—doesn't believe in marriage. She has three other kids, all by different men. She's a legend in Baltimore."

"I should think so," said Grace.

"My natural daddy has just got to invite me places sometimes because he thinks—pay attention to this—I'm going to turn out to be something special. We pretend like I'm his nephew, or his protégé."

"You live alone uptown? There's no phone listed for you."

"Yes," said Gilbert, "I live alone, with the occasional company of lady friends. I prefer to live uptown. Dr. Paintry brought me here to have me educated. He would have preferred to send me to Yale, but I wanted to be in New York. All my mother's kids get educated—that's part of the bargain she makes."

"Is she beautiful?"

"Better believe it. Makes you look like a ghost, and she's got twenty years on you. Although I've always thought, understand, that you were a fine-looking woman."

"Was it your father who got sick and couldn't go on the show?"

"Naturally, except he didn't really get sick. He phoned up Morgan White and said"—Gilbert lowered his voice and spoke in measured, ponderous tones—" 'Mr. White, I think you might do worse than to ask my young friend Ottway to appear in my stead. He's had an unfortunate past, but he's a bright youth trying to recoup his losses . . .' "

Grace laughed, feeling the gears of her physical self begin to shift and tumble back to some remembered, simpler state. Her body was not able to accept much food and her hands trembled alarmingly, but the sound of her own laughter, frightening at first, was reassuring.

"Did he know what you were planning to do? All that stuff about gangs and violence? What about the Afro wig?"

"He left everything up to me. He trusts me. Anyway, if I'd disgraced myself, who's to connect us?"

Grace felt a pang of what she supposed might be envy. "You have a real family," she said softly. "How lucky you are."

Mr. Ottway quirked an eyebrow. "Hardly," he said. "There were times when I would have settled for a nice, fat mama at the stove and a no-good dad on welfare. I've been lonely, you know, but it's been good for me." He sounded shy.

"I liked what you said on the show," said Grace, "even if it was all lies."

"Lies? Girl, you don't know me yet. Everything I said was exactly what I meant, except for the facts."

"How do I know what you've just told me is true?"

"You don't. Just have to trust me, that's all."

"Why should I?"

"Because I got no stake in lying. I don't want to—pardon me, Dr. Peacock—get under your skirt. I don't need to learn writing from you, although I like your course. I don't reckon there's one thing you can offer me I can't do better for myself. I just like you. I'm your friend."

"You can't imagine wanting to get under my skirt?" Grace asked wistfully.

"Oh, vanity!" said Gilbert. "I don't seem to feel attracted that way to white women."

"You're young yet," said Grace.

"Amen."

They ate in silence for a time, and then Grace told him about her abduction. Gilbert seemed to think it hugely funny. "You mean," he shouted, "the whole time you watched that show you were a captive audience?" They discussed Sam's public branding of Jenny, which Gilbert had witnessed, and he said that Sam was a sadistic son of a bitch who never in his life had picked on someone his own size. "About Edward," he said thoughtfully, "he can't help meddling that way. People like him think they know what's best and go around strong-arming other folks for their own good. You may have noticed I'm a little like that myself."

"Tell me what you're celebrating," said Grace.

"Oh," Gilbert smiled modestly, "several things. I got an offer to write a book about youth gangs, and that Reverend Otto said he'd like to set up a series of lecture dates for me in Detroit. Also, director dude who saw the show invited me to try out for a play. I guess I'd have to wear my wig."

"It isn't fair," protested Grace. "You're only a child!"

"Life is short, Dr. Peacock, got to get moving."

"What do you want to be when you grow up?"

He threw a grape into the air and caught it in his open mouth with exquisite precision. "Haven't decided," he said. "What I want is lots of options. That's what you ought to want, too."

"Gilbert," said Grace. "Will you stay here with me for a few days? You could sleep here, or you could even have the bedroom."

"Can't do it. I have to go see my mama. If you were smart you'd wing on out to wherever you're from and visit for a while. Help that silly cousin of yours to have her baby; it'd be good for you."

"How did you know about Fiona?"

"She told me the night we all slept here. She woke up thirsty about dawn and tripped over me, and then we talked. Everybody tells me everything sooner or later. That's why I don't have a phone."

Grace pictured Fiona and Gilbert, deep in conversation while she and Edward and Deveraux slept on, unheeding. It had been her fate to be surprised and proven wrong at every turn lately. Things as she imagined them were not so; the elaborate devices she employed to keep the world at arm's length had served only to bring it, snuffling, to her door.

"I don't know why you've been treating yourself so bad this last week," said Gilbert, "and I don't want to know. Just don't go getting suicidal, because you'll get no sympathy from me."

"Give me one good reason why I should go home for a visit," said Grace. "You're not sentimental, Gilbert. I'm surprised at you."

"Documentary Dev told me you were always wanting to go to

the Midwest. That was while we were having coffee and you were pretending to be asleep."

Grace was silent. She could not, even now, bear to confess to Mr. Ottway the reasons which had motivated her. They seemed so remote. Her passion for True Romance, which had outlasted so much else, was quite suddenly over and done with. Her magazines were changing, moving away from her and from what she had found so exotic, so unapproachable. Sin and redemption had been banished, like Latin from the Catholic Mass, and everyone was made to feel comfortable. *Sic transit.* Only she and Mr. Ottway knew better. He had told the world—or all of it watching the anomie show on All Souls' Day—that his gentle ways did not exempt him from calamity. She took his hand and pressed it, hard.

"I would be very sorry if your life ended too soon," she said, "but not a bit surprised."

She felt lonely when he had gone. She stood motionless and checked herself for signs of the terrible sadness which had taken hold of her and found that it, too, was gone.

She dialed the hospital and was told that Mr. Bolovsky was no longer a patient there.

Then she dialed her mother. She did not use the hair dryer; after all, Fiona had scrupled most at the mechanics of her scheme. She waited patiently through the hums and bleeps which signified the making of a connection. Winifred Peacock answered on the second ring.

"Hello, Mother. It's Grace."

There was a stunned silence and then Mrs. Peacock cried: "Why, Grace! All the way from England!" There was a muffling sound at her end and Grace could hear her calling: "Fiona! It's Grace! She's calling all the way from England!"

"I can't talk long," said Grace hurriedly. "I just wanted to ask if I could come for a visit?"

"Why, of course, dear! What a lovely surprise!" Again the muffling. "Fiona—Grace is going to visit!"

Grace calculated when the university, if it ever reopened, would break for the Christmas vacation. "I thought I'd come around the middle of December," she said, "if that would be convenient."

"Are you all right, Grace? Is there anything wrong?"

"I'm fine," said Grace. "How's Fiona?"

"Oh, my," giggled Mrs. Peacock, "she's getting so big! I think the baby will be born early."

"I think we're losing the connection," shouted Grace.

"Not at this end, dear. It's so clear you sound as if you're calling from around the corner. Can you fly straight to Chicago?"

"I'll probably have to change planes in New York."

"Fiona's in your old room, Grace. We could switch around or you two could bunk in together. Whatever you like."

"I think they're going to cut me off. As long as you expect me, then—"

"Oh, we'll be expecting you, Grace. Won't it be fun?"

Grace assured her mother it would be fun and prepared to hang up. "One thing," said Mrs. Peacock quickly. "Could you possibly bring me some quail's eggs from Fortnum & Mason? Your father and I had some when we were in London once, and they were so *festive.*"

There must be a way. "Yes, Mother, I'll do that."

"I'll pay you back," said Mrs. Peacock anxiously.

"No need for that," said Grace. "It will be my treat."

The next day she took the elevator to the eleventh floor. The door to Mr. Bolovsky's apartment was propped open. A stack of crates and boxes stood in the corner, and the curtains had been taken from the windows. A dropcloth covered the floor and even as she watched a painter came into view, carrying a ladder. He saw her standing in the hall and shook his head. "The landlord's not showing it yet," he said. "Got to clean it up first."

Grace rode back downstairs, thinking of Maurice as he had instructed her to do. She walked to her bank and asked to see the manager about a small loan. He was one of the new sort, eager to appear informal and humane.

"Cheer up," he said. "It can't be that bad."

"My grandfather died," said Grace.

The banker looked surprised, as if the death of a grandfather had never, in his experience, brought forth tears. "That's a shame," he said kindly. "I suppose you were very close, you and your grandfather?"

"Yes," said Grace. "We were almost inseparable."